'Liz Trenow sews together the strands of past and present as delicately as the exquisite stitching on the quilt which forms the centrepiece of the story'
LUCINDA RILEY

'Extraordinary, fascinating . . .
deeply rooted in history'
MIDWEEK, BBC RADIO 4

'What a delicious read *The Silk Weaver* is. I was enchanted by this novel set in eighteenth-century Spitalfields; meticulously researched, richly detailed, the brilliantly structured story shimmered as the threads of silk wound through its pages. I devoured it in two days and was gripped from start to finish. The characters shine too and Anna is an absolute triumph. A fabulous book'
DINAH JEFFERIES

'Liz Trenow draws us in so that we inhabit her world, and it was a wrench to put the book down after the last beautifully written page'
GILL PAUL

'Totally fascinating . . . a book to savour'
KATE FURNI

THE SECRETS OF THE LAKE

Liz Trenow is a former journalist who spent fifteen years working for regional and national newspapers, and BBC radio and television news, before turning her hand to fiction. *The Secrets of the Lake* is her eighth novel. She lives in East Anglia with her artist husband, and they have two grown-up daughters and three beautiful grandchildren.

Find out more at **www.liztrenow.com**,
or join her on Facebook **@LizTrenow**
or Twitter **@LizTrenow**.

By Liz Trenow

The Last Telegram

The Forgotten Seamstress

The Poppy Factory

The Silk Weaver

In Love and War

The Dressmaker of Draper's Lane

Under a Wartime Sky

The Secrets of the Lake

LIZ TRENOW

The Secrets of the Lake

PAN BOOKS

First published 2021 by Pan Books
an imprint of Pan Macmillan
The Smithson, 6 Briset Street, London ECIM 5NR
EU representative: Macmillan Publishers Ireland Limited,
Mallard Lodge, Lansdowne Village, Dublin 4
Associated companies throughout the world
www.panmacmillan.com

ISBN 978-1-5290-3661-9

1 3 5 7 9 8 6 4 2

A CIP catalogue record for this book is available from the British Library.

Illustrations by Hemesh Alles

Typeset by Palimpsest Book Production Limited, Falkirk, Stirlingshire
Printed and bound by CPI Group (UK) Ltd, Croydon, CRO 4YY

Visit **www.panmacmillan.com** to read more about all our books
and to buy them. You will also find features, author interviews and
news of any author events, and you can sign up for e-newsletters
so that you're always first to hear about our new releases.

In memory of my mother and father,
who built the house on the lake.

How doth the little crocodile
Improve his shining tail,
And pour the waters of the Nile
On every golden scale!

How cheerfully he seems to grin
How neatly spreads his claws,
And welcomes little fishes in
With gently smiling jaws!

from *Alice's Adventures in Wonderland*
by Lewis Carroll

PART ONE:

SPRING 2019

I

That night she dreams of Jimmy: his almond eyes and chubby red cheeks, his lips curled into a smile as though permanently amused by life; a little boy scarcely touched by the cares of the world, who lived each day as it came, blithely unaware of his difference. A boy who loved ball games, the twinkling lights at Christmas, lemonade, biscuits, steak-and-kidney pudding and mashed potato with gravy. Who fell in love with anyone who showed even the smallest gesture of kindness; who wouldn't shake hands but preferred to hug people instead, even people he barely knew.

He's pestering her with endless questions, speaking with surprising fluency. Why does the sun come up in the same place each day? Why do they call those stars a 'plough'? What are we going to do today, Molly? What's for supper? She shouts at him to leave her in peace for just a few seconds, for pity's sake.

She feels his hot body in bed beside her, finds herself irritated by his snoring. She takes him back to his own room, only to find him returned again, entwined around her. And then . . . and then . . . she sees him floating, far

3

off on the other side of the lake. His eyes are open, his lips are smiling. Yet even from here she can tell he is dead.

She wakes with that familiar knot in her stomach. She knows it well, its weight, its position, its shape and even its colour as she imagines it: a deep charcoal-grey. But perhaps, now she's so old, it's actually turning into a physical tumour that has taken up permanent residence, that will grow and spread throughout her body. A cancer that will kill her in the end. Maybe that would be a blessing, she thinks. The last thing she wants is to linger on, being a nuisance to everyone.

Then she remembers why the knot has reappeared. The police are coming. Whatever can they want from her, after all these years? She recalls the hours of questioning, sitting on the sofa in her shorts with the woolly upholstery prickling her legs as the rain battered the vicarage windows, Pa pacing outside the door, the overwhelming feelings of guilt, the 'if only' loop going round and round in her head. The endless, futile prayers and that crushing sense of emptiness and helplessness.

All she can tell them now is what she told them then. She had, and still has, absolutely no idea what happened, or why. She toys with the idea of pretending she has dementia and can't remember anything. Except, of course, she can recall everything. Every moment, every sight, sound, smell, and all the players in the tragedy of that terrible summer: Kit, beautiful Kit, whose memory even now sends darts of electricity through her body; Jimmy's sweet innocence; her father's inconsolable sorrow and terrifying descent into madness.

She does not want to remember, does not want to go back. When journalists come to interview her they always ask: 'When did you first start writing children's stories?' or 'What was the title of your first book?' She always lies. All these years, all those dozens of stories later, after all the books that have made her famous and turned her into a household name, giving her the chance to meet children of all nationalities and cultures on book tours around the world, she has never even taken it out of its cardboard box. It is still stored in the darkest, furthest part of a deep bottom drawer: her very first book, the stories she wrote for Jimmy, the book that started it all. *The Ugly Dragon*.

But it seems she will now be forced to remember.

Yesterday – was it only yesterday? – she'd settled herself in her favourite chair, placed so that she can see anyone coming up the path to her front door from the lodge where the wardens live. She spends most of her daytime hours here these days, reading or dozing in the warmth of the sun, which, if it's shining, will reach her by ten in the morning and won't leave until mid-afternoon.

She'd just made her morning cuppa when she saw one of the wardens – Gillian, the nicer one – emerging from the office and starting up the wheelchair-friendly path towards the bungalows, looking more preoccupied than usual, stern even.

Dear God, Molly thought, hoping it wasn't bad news. Let it be a false alarm or, at worst, a minor alarm. The only other resident she knows personally is her right-hand neighbour, Fred, who used to enjoy a game of whist but cannot even remember his own name these days, poor old boy. But Gillian took the route leading to Molly's door. She knocked and let herself in.

'Cooee, Mrs Goddard. How are you feeling this morning?'

She pulled up a stool without waiting to be invited. 'May I join you?'

'Of course.' Any company was welcome these days.

'I need to tell you that the police telephoned me this morning. Nothing to be concerned about, I'm sure. Just routine enquiries, they called it.' Gillian leaned forward and took Molly's hand, warm and comforting. 'But you're not to worry, my dear.'

Hah! That phrase so perfectly calculated to cause instant panic. That's what they said when Jimmy went missing. Like the old joke: 'Start worrying, details to follow'. Only it wasn't a joke. Not funny at all. And they never got the details.

'They simply want a word with you,' Gillian went on. 'Something to do with a lake, they said. But I told them they'd have to wait until your daughter was here. I've given her a ring and she'll be over tomorrow morning. The police will come back then.'

A *lake*. The word shimmers in Molly's mind, like sunlight glittering on the surface when the water is disturbed by a gust of wind. A lake known as the Mere, its corners dark and hidden, surrounded by overgrown willows and dense billows of bramble bushes. The humps of the islands fringed with sedge and bulrush. When the weather was calm, the sky, clouds and trees were reflected in perfect reverse, creating a double image that she remembers as clearly as though it were yesterday and still believes to be one of the most beautiful sights in the world.

Even now, her eyes are dazzled by the brilliant yellow

of the marsh marigolds and her nose giddied by the sweet, medicinal scent of water mint. She can feel the smooth squelch of the grey-blue mud clinging between her toes, with its earthy, metallic odour. The air is filled with the sounds of small lives: the gentle cluck of a mother duck shepherding her flotilla of tiny ducklings, the sharp tick-tick of an alarmed coot, the distant call of cattle on the water meadows beyond. In the sky there is the squeal of swifts swooping low over the surface and, from time to time, the harsh, bossy squawks of geese as they circle before coming in to land, their webbed feet outstretched, like squadrons of small feathered aircraft.

Above all the noises of nature, if she listens carefully, she can hear the regular, unmistakeable thud of oars in rowlocks followed by the swish of the water as they pull forward. She leans over the side of the boat, trailing her fingers in the cool water. In the shallows are glimpses of a secret underwater world: grey shoals of minnows, tiny striped snails, worms, dragonfly nymphs and other murky creatures. In deeper water the lake grows black and mysterious, concealing all kinds of unknown terrors.

The memories are calling her, luring her back, but she resists them with all her might. At times they press into her head so ferociously that she is overwhelmed. Most of the time she manages to keep them at bay, but now, this very morning, the police are coming to ask her about a lake. She takes a deep breath, then another, trying to calm her thrumming nerves.

Bella arrives, flustered as usual. From where she lives on the other side of Colchester, the traffic is often unpredictable. The journey leaves her edgy and impatient, and she usually spends the first half-hour rushing about, clearing or cleaning, making the bed, taking an inventory of the fridge and the kitchen store-cupboard, wiping the worktops – busy, busy, busy – when all Molly wants is for her to sit down with a cup of tea to chat about life's joys and woes, about her troubled, troublesome clients and Lewis's latest sporting triumphs. She depends on her daughter to reconnect with the world outside.

Today is different. Bella takes off her coat, puts on the kettle, kisses her mother on the cheek and immediately draws up a chair. 'Whatever mischief have you been up to now, Mum?' she says, without preamble. 'What's all this about the police wanting to question you?'

Molly shakes her head. There's no point in trying to explain, when she doesn't even know what the police want to ask her. And she has already decided not to tell them much, so why alert Bella to the fact that she knows more?

'No idea, love. How would you like to make some tea?'

Half an hour later a car, garishly decorated in chequered dayglo yellow and blue, enters the gates and stops outside the lodge. Two people climb out, a girl who looks barely out of her teens, the man older, bearded. He hoicks up his trousers and the woman smooths her rather too-tight skirt as they glance around before approaching the warden's door and ringing the bell.

Soon enough they're following Gillian up to the bungalow, being invited inside and introduced to everyone. The room feels suddenly very small. At least they are not PC

Stubby and his mate, Weasel Face, Molly thinks. How could she forget them, with their sorry-sad expressions and the persistent grilling that made her feel as though it was all somehow her fault, when she could barely think straight for worry and lack of sleep?

Neither of these present-day coppers wears *Dixon of Dock Green* helmets and she can see no sign of truncheons or handcuffs, although they are garlanded with technology: phones, cameras, walkie-talkies. She supposes they're assuming that an eighty-four-year-old will go quietly, and is briefly diverted trying to picture the scene, should she choose to resist arrest. Imagine the scandal! What a treat it would be for all the other residents watching from their windows: an old woman being manhandled down the pathway by a burly copper.

Bella offers tea or coffee, the warden excuses herself and leaves. 'Let me know if you need anything,' she says. Finally they are all settled.

The beard does most of the talking. He's tall and awkward and rather poker-faced, while the girl smiles a lot. Whatever could a pretty young thing like her want with chasing criminals? Both perch themselves uncomfortably on the hard kitchen chairs that Bella has pulled up for them, and there's a smattering of introductory small talk.

'Apologies for inconveniencing you like this, Mrs Goddard. I hope you are feeling up to a little chat? Can you hear us all right?'

She feels like shouting, *For heaven's sake, stop patronising me. Just because I'm old doesn't mean I'm an idiot.* But she remembers, in time, that she has determined to present herself as a sweet and slightly dotty old lady.

'It's all right, my dears. I can hear you both perfectly well, thank you,' she says with as much grace as she can muster. 'But perhaps you can tell me to what we owe this unexpected pleasure.'

The man clears his throat, pulls a small notebook and pencil from his pocket. How charmingly low-tech, Molly thinks to herself, just like the bobbies who questioned her back then.

'Mrs Goddard.'

'That is my name, yes. Molly Goddard. Not "Mrs".'

Bella darts a look that says: *Don't be difficult, Mum. It'll only cause trouble.*

'Msss Goddard.' He holds on to the 's' for too long, so that it sounds like an angry fly.

'If you insist, Constable.' She has been single for so long – after that disastrous short-lived marriage – that she can barely remember a time when she was Mrs, but neither has she ever accepted being a Ms, or a Miss, and it irritates her when officials always insist. Her young readers know her as Molly Goddard. *Dear Molly*, they write in their wobbly, unformed hand as though they know her personally, and she considers it a great compliment.

He clears his throat again. 'We understand that for a short period from December 1949 to September 1950, your father, John Goddard, was the vicar of Wormley, in Suffolk?'

'That is correct. We lived in the vicarage, with my brother and a housekeeper. My mother had died the year before.'

'And we understand that in the late summer of 1950 your brother James—'

'Jimmy,' she interrupts.

'Your brother Jimmy disappeared.'

The lump in Molly's stomach moves higher, pressing on her lungs and making it difficult to breathe. 'Yes,' she whispers. 'Everyone gave up looking, and we never got any explanation.'

Bella puts a hand on her shoulder. 'Are you all right, Mum?'

'If this is too distressing, we can stop,' the policewoman says. 'We can come back another time, if you like?'

'No, let's carry on. I want to know why you are here, after all these years. Has anything happened? Have you found something?'

The girl takes up the story. 'Well, Ms Goddard, you might have read in the papers about the local water-company project to build a pipeline from the River Stour to reservoirs in Essex?'

Molly shakes her head. She never reads the newspapers these days. They're too full of politicians preening themselves.

The girl goes on: 'Unfortunately, an unpredicted consequence has been that local water levels have dropped, in particular at Wormley Mere. It has lost at least three-quarters of its water, and there are fears it might actually dry out completely before the work is finished.'

Molly finds this impossible to imagine. They always said the lake was bottomless.

'The residents are up in arms, of course, particularly the wildlife lot and the anglers who lease the lake these days. There's talk of lawsuits. The company is confident of correcting the problem.' She pauses, glancing sideways at her colleague before carrying on. 'Meanwhile, their contractors have reported some unusual findings.'

The lump has slipped even higher. It is now where Molly's heart should be, knocking at the inside of her ribs.

'These findings,' Bella asks gently. Her social-work training comes in handy for managing delicate conversations. 'What are they, exactly?'

The girl looks at the man again. He nods and she carries on. 'Well, erm, they appear to have found some bones.' She pauses for a second, and adds more quietly, '*Human* bones.'

Bella's hand slips into hers, squeezing it gently. Molly tries to breathe, slowly, in-out, in-out, like they teach you for childbirth.

The beard takes over. 'They've been sent to the lab for DNA testing. Are you aware of what this might mean, Ms Goddard?'

She tries to speak but nothing comes out. Her throat has closed.

'It might help you find out . . . ?' Bella says.

'That's right,' he says, gently. 'So, if you are willing, we'd like to take a sample from you, too, Ms Goddard, so that we can prove, one way or another . . .'

A sample? Molly's mind rebels. She hates needles.

'And what does that involve, exactly?' Bella asks.

He reaches into his bag and pulls out an envelope, which he opens to show two small plastic tubes containing long sticks with cotton buds on the end. 'It's very simple and quick. We just have to rub the inside of the cheek to get a few cells. It takes a couple of seconds, and doesn't hurt at all.'

Bella turns to her. 'Mum?'

'I don't mind,' Molly says. Not if it helps find out what happened to Jimmy, she thinks. Not knowing feels like a hollow ache that, in all these years, has never lessened. Perhaps to know might ease the pain, at last. She opens her mouth obediently.

When the procedure is over, he puts the cotton buds back into their tubes, seals the envelope, writes on it in biro and places it back in his bag.

'Well done, Mum,' Bella says. 'Will that be all, Officer?'

'There's just one more thing.' He reaches for his shoulder bag and takes out a slim sheaf of what look like colour photographs.

'No, I don't think it's a good idea . . .' Bella says, quickly.

'No, not to worry, Miss,' he says. 'This is something else.'

'Let me see them first, please.'

He flips through the prints until he reaches the one he wants, and shows it first to Bella. After a quick glance she passes it to her mother. At first Molly can't make it out; it looks like a tangled mess of mud and old branches, but then she sees, amid the browns and greys, a glimpse of something red. She manages to stifle a gasp.

'Have you any idea what this red material could be, Ms Goddard?'

She shrugs, trying to feign nonchalance. 'Could be anything, I suppose. Something blown in off the field, an old plastic fertiliser bag? Litter gets everywhere these days, doesn't it?'

But she knows immediately what it could be. She would recognise that particular shade of red anywhere: Jimmy's red mac, the one he was wearing when he disappeared. Or Kit's canvas boat, the one they christened *Robin* with a bottle of champagne.

Over the buzzing in her ears she can hear Bella saying,

'I think it might be time to give my mother a rest, if that is all?' Soon enough the police are on their feet, looming over her once more, saying their goodbyes, promising to be in touch as soon as they have any results – probably by the end of the week, depending on how busy the lab is – and thanking them for their time.

Molly wants to shout at them, *Oh, just shut up and go away, will you?* Instead she closes her eyes. In the blessed silence, once they are gone, Bella returns to her seat and takes her mother's hand.

'Do you want to talk about this, Mum?'

She shakes her head. 'Not now, love. Not now.'

❖

The next thing Molly knows is the knock of the evening carer bringing her supper. She must have been asleep here in her chair for several hours. The plate of sandwiches Bella made is still beside her, their edges already curling in the dry heat. The cup of tea is stone-cold.

For a moment she has forgotten what happened this afternoon and feels content. It's not a bad life for someone of my age, she tells herself. Eighty-five next March, for heaven's sake. However did she manage to hang on for so long? She's a bit creaky in the leg department and can no longer shop for herself, but she still has all her marbles, which counts for a lot.

Although she rarely sees them, there is comfort in knowing that all around her, in the other nineteen bunga-lows, there are people like herself. Not that they socialise much; most of them are too immobile, or too demented.

She doesn't feel lonely, though. She loves listening to audio books, and the best of the readers seem to become her friends so that, by the end, she's sorry to bid them goodbye.

Bella comes at the weekends, sometimes with Molly's grandson Lewis, who appears to have grown into a fully-fledged adult without notice. There are twice-daily visits from carers, and the warden drops by every evening. She counts herself fortunate.

This evening's carer enters with a waft of sweet fresh air. 'Hello, my dear,' she says breezily. 'You look as though you could do with a bite of something hot. How does shepherd's pie sound?'

Mention of shepherds reminds Molly of Eli and his hut. 'In them old days the shepherds'd drag it from field to field, so's the sheep could get the best grass,' he'd say, settling himself on the steps, clay pipe in hand. She'd never seen anyone else before or since smoking one of these, except in old photographs. 'Them old wheels 'on't turn no more but just here suit me fine, my little 'uns.' His eyes would twinkle as he took a long draw, exhaling clouds of aromatic smoke that he claimed kept away the midges. 'Cos from here I can keep an eye on that dratted dragon.'

And they would peer down through the trees to the bottom of the valley, to where the lake glimmered silently in the last of the daylight, half-longing and half-fearing what they might see.

2

All night she tosses and turns, dreaming vividly again, only this time her dreams are populated with red boats, black waters, white bones.

Waking with a start, Molly knows what she must do. She must go back to the village.

She has never returned, not once. Not since they took her father off in an ambulance, and the police gave up their search and she'd gone to live far away with an aunt she barely knew. Even though it is only an hour's drive, she has actively avoided the area as much as possible. It holds too many memories.

But after what the police have told them, she knows she can't bury the memories forever. Unless she sees the place for herself one more time before she dies, she will never rest easy. The prospect of the lake half-drained of its water feels terrifying but she feels compelled to witness it, just in case.

In case of what? She refuses to let her imagination wander any further. Not yet. Not till they get the results of the tests. But she must visit anyway, to honour the memory of Jimmy.

'Hello, love,' she chirps cheerfully when Bella answers. It's so quick to phone, now her grandson Lewis has added something he calls speed-dial. 'I want to ask a favour.'

'What time is it?' her daughter groans. 'Oh. For heaven's sake, Mum, it's six-thirty in the morning. *Sunday* morning.'

'Is it? I'm so sorry, darling. It's already light and the birds are singing their little hearts out. I thought it was at least nine. But while I've got you . . .'

'Go on.' She can hear Bella yawning.

'I need to go there, one last time. To Wormley. Can you take me? Today?'

'*Today?* It's Lewis's football, Mum.'

'Can't Andy take him?' Bella's ex is a fireman. Molly was sad when they split, because she now sees so little of him. They'd been together so long – since Bella's schooldays – that she'd come to think of him as a son.

'Possibly. Depends on his shifts. I'll have to ask.' A pause. 'You've never wanted to go back before, Mum.'

'Everything is different now,' she says.

❀❀❀

A few hours later Molly is being trundled down the path in her wheelchair, helped into her daughter's scruffy old car and trying to find a place for her feet in a footwell deep with the detritus of empty crisp packets and fizzy-drink cans.

The sun is shining and Bella seems to have recovered her good humour.

The traffic is light this Sunday morning, and they are soon skimming along the rolling switchback road through the county she has long considered her own. It is May, and the verges are laced with cow parsley, the hedgerows so white with blossom that they look like banks of snow. The long-forgotten memory of a sad poem she learned at school rises to the surface of her mind and she tells Bella about it: '*Lie long, high snowdrifts in the hedge, that will not shower on me.* It's a dying soldier longing to see his home country one more time.'

'That's a bit gloomy for a lovely spring day,' her daughter replies, accelerating past a tractor the size of a two-storey house. They make them enormous, these days, Molly thinks. Not like the little machines that trundled back and forth along the village street, past the vicarage, several times a day.

How curious she'd been, when they first arrived in Suffolk, to see all that agricultural machinery on the roads and in the fields. Having only ever known London, she was completely unaware of the rhythms of the seasons, the wild flowers that came and went with the passing months, or the focus of the community on growing livestock and cultivating the deep, fertile fields. She remembers being told about the harvest festival – the day when the village thanked the earth for its bounties and decorated the church with sheaves of real wheat and barley, piles of red apples and enormous green marrows. But she never got the chance to celebrate it.

Molly is so absorbed in her thoughts that almost before she has noticed, they have passed Sudbury. A gracious town, she recalls, with Georgian houses lining wide streets, a large church dominating the square, and the bronze statue of an artist flourishing his paintbrush and palette. She remembers going on a market day when, after the livestock sales were done, grizzled farmers would gather in the pub on the Market Hill, putting the world to rights. Around lunchtime they would be joined by their wives, who were laden with the spoils of a morning's haggling: the best cuts of meat, the greenest greens and whitest potatoes.

But they see none of this today, following a bypass punctuated with roundabouts, past unlovely industrial buildings in varied states of prosperity or decline. They make a short detour through a council estate, and soon enough they are on a road that seems to writhe like a snake as it follows the contours of the river.

Ah, the river, just a gentle meandering stream these days that has somehow, through the ages, carved out the wide valley along which they are now passing, a landscape that inspired great artists like Constable and Gainsborough, its floodplain creating lush pastures that fed the medieval wool trade and the prosperity that helped to build many of its mighty churches.

Now they are over the humpback bridge at Bures, past the pub on the corner, and The Pines looms ahead. It was such an iconic landmark in those days, that grove of ancient evergreens high on top of the hill, but the storm did for it that night and it has never recovered. Many of the trees have gone, and even those that remain look ragged and forlorn.

As the countryside becomes increasingly familiar and the stone weighs increasingly heavy in Molly's gut, her earlier resolve seems to leach away. Whatever is she thinking, going back there, she chides herself? But it's too late to change her mind now. The die is cast.

The road climbs through a deep cutting in the hillside, carved before the days of tarmac by centuries of countless carts and carriages. On either side, steep banks are covered in bluebells that, when they catch the sunshine, are of such an intense cobalt-blue that it almost hurts her eyes.

A painful memory punches through her consciousness: her father seated in a deckchair on the back porch of the vicarage, newspaper in hand, teacup close by, enjoying the spring sunshine. She sits down on the step beside him and they rest there for several minutes: a rare moment of calm and quiet time together, just the two of them. And then there's a shout, and Jimmy is running towards them across the lawn with tears streaming down his face, waving a bunch of wilted bluebells.

'What's up, Jim?' Pa asks.

'For . . . you . . . they . . .' His speech was never clear at the best of the times, but he found the word at last. 'Dead,' he shouts, tossing them violently to the ground before running into the house. They listen to his clumsy footsteps clomping through the hallway and up the stairs. Neither of them moves.

'Had I better go after him?'

'He'll be all right,' Molly murmurs, reluctant to break the spell.

'He picked them for me – I'd better go.' Pa heaves himself up from the deckchair. The moment is lost. How she'd hated her brother in that moment, ruining everything, as usual.

'Nearly there,' Bella says, slowing the car. 'Here's the turning.'

'How did you know?' Molly says, as they start down the narrow lane.

'I've been here before, Mum.'

'You've been *here*? Without *me*?'

'I wanted to see where you lived with Grandpa.'

'I didn't know you knew so much about it.'

'I don't, Mum. But remember that photo? The one they took when you first arrived?' Molly remembers it well: Miss Calver, editor of the *Village News*, produced a camera and made them stand outside the church.

'But I never knew about the lake,' Bella says.

'The Mere.'

'Mere, then. So where is it?'

'Past the church, down the hill.'

The church tower is visible before any other building, flintwork gleaming in the sunshine, and the sight of it makes Molly's heart contract. An unwelcome vision: her father high above them, standing precariously on the parapet, arms outstretched, shouting, 'Take me, God, I'm coming.'

She takes a few deep breaths, trying to calm her thoughts.

As they approach the church gate, the lane is almost blocked with cars parked carelessly on either side. 'Whatever's going on?' Bella asks, manoeuvring past.

'Sunday-morning service. Looks like there's still a healthy congregation. Let's go on down to the lake. We can come back afterwards.'

She is expecting to see the vicarage at any moment, but her view is obscured by a new wall of bright-red brick. Bella stops by gateposts topped with a pair of badly modelled concrete lions, comic-book renderings of those noble creatures. A slate sign with sharply laser-carved lettering reads: VICARAGE CLOSE.

'Oh my Lord,' Molly gasps, peering through the curlicues of wrought-iron gates. The old vicarage has gone, and in its place are four mock-Georgian executive-style houses set in perfectly manicured green lawns surrounded by newly planted box hedges. Like dolls' houses in a toy town, she thinks.

'The poor old place was looking a bit derelict last time I was here,' Bella says. 'But there was scaffolding up the chimney, so I assumed they were restoring it.'

After her initial surprise, Molly feels strangely unmoved. She never loved that vicarage, it never really felt like home. A plain four-square building of no great historical importance, cheaply constructed in the interwar period, its rooms were voluminous, the plumbing basic, the windows ill-fitting, with no insulation and certainly no central heating. The fireplaces were greedy for coal and far too small to keep the place warm in winter.

The best thing about it was the garden – those spreading acres on which these new houses now stand. It had seemed, to her young city-bound eyes, to stretch away to infinity, merging without fence or hedge into the woodland and fields beyond. This was her childhood, or a part of it at least. And now it is gone. 'Good riddance,' she mutters under her breath.

'Where now?' Bella asks.

'Down to the Mere. It's at the bottom of the hill.'

'You're sure about this, Mum?'

'Never been more sure,' she says, although her heart quails at the thought.

They pass the Old Crown pub, offering 'local ales and fresh cooked food', and agree to return for a sandwich later, before the drive home. The houses thin out as they leave the village, with the woods to their left, down to the bottom of the hill where the road levels onto the river's floodplain. The Tudor brick chimneys of Wormley Hall are just visible, peeping over the tops of the trees.

The first sign they see is hand-painted in uneven capital letters, nailed roughly onto an unsteady-looking post: *SAVE WORMLEY MERE*. Next is a larger official notice:

EASTERN WATER STOUR VALLEY PROJECT.
STRICTLY AUTHORISED VEHICLES ONLY.
DANGER, HEAVY PLANT TURNING.
NO ENTRY.

'Heavy plants don't sound too dangerous.' Molly's attempt at a joke is met with a sigh.

'So where is this lake, anyway?' Bella says, pulling up beside a gate leading to a rough farm track.

'Just over there. The only way by car is along this track.' Molly opens her window and the twittering song of invisible meadowlarks floods her ears from high above. She takes a deep breath, inhaling the smells of warm grass and spring blossom, with a hint of cow manure.

'That's that, then,' Bella says. 'There's no way I'm pushing your wheelchair along there. It's far too rough.' She gets out of the car, goes to the metal gate, gives it a push and rattles the chain fixing it to the gatepost. 'Anyway, it's locked,' she says, with a hint of triumph.

But something has become dislodged. The jaws of the

heavy padlock have parted, and the chain now hangs free. The gate starts to swing open of its own accord. As it gains momentum, Bella lurches forward to close it, but Molly shouts, 'Hold on, love. Now we can drive down.'

'"No entry," it says. Can't you read the sign?' Bella climbs back into the car.

'If we don't go now, I may never see it again,' Molly says. 'It's Sunday, love. No one is here to stop us.'

Bella rests her forehead on the steering wheel. 'That just about tops it. My eighty-four-year-old mother is telling me to break the law.'

'It's not the law, love, only a company notice. Please. It'll only take a few seconds.'

It is my last chance, she thinks. My last chance to . . . She cannot actually bring herself to say it, even to herself. But she knows her daughter too well: there is no point in pleading, so she sits quietly and waits.

After a few moments Bella sighs and starts the car, puts it into gear and cautiously drives through the now-open gateway and down the track. The gravel is surprisingly smooth and in no time at all the lake, or at least the area where it used to be, comes into view. But it is nothing like Molly remembers. Where water once glittered there is a deep, muddy crater, its edges churned into chaos by wheel tracks and footprints. Red-and-white plastic tape is strung from posts and trees, and more signs – ironic now: DEEP WATER, DANGER OF DROWNING. At the bottom of the crater is a puddle of tea-coloured water.

All around one end the trees have been felled and the boggy area where the stream used to feed into the lake, where the marsh marigolds bloomed every summer in such profusion, has been pulverised by the tracks of heavy vehicles. Two of them, a lurid orange, lurk in the far corner of the field like giant insects with their long arms folded, ready to pounce.

Molly puts her face in her hands. 'And to think that's where Jimmy's been, all these years.'

'We don't *know* that.'

'*I* know it. In my heart.' She hammers her chest with a fist. Molly accepts Bella's tissue and wipes her eyes.

In the end, everyone said Jimmy must have drowned, but no one had ever explained why his body was never found. At fifteen, she'd read enough crime stories to know that bodies always surfaced somewhere, possibly months later, unless they were weighted down, in which case it had obviously not been an accident. But who would do such a thing to a small, harmless boy? And even if he'd just got caught somewhere, in branches or tree roots, why had the police divers never discovered him?

'Let's go,' she says, suddenly. 'I've seen enough.'

Back up the hill, outside the church, the cars have mostly disappeared.

'Nearly time for lunch,' Bella says.

'Good idea. Shall we take a look inside first, now the service has finished?'

Bella pulls up the car. 'That path looks reasonable for your chair. Let's try it. Then lunch?'

'Then lunch.'

It is the smell of the church, rather than the sight of the

interior, that takes her back: old prayer books, furniture polish and dust, the cloying scent of lilies dying in their vases. She is immediately transported back to her teenage self, wriggling uncomfortably on the hard wooden choir stall, listening to Pa droning on about parish notices, jumble sales and whist drives, not to mention the endless readings from the Bible and, worst of all, his interminable sermons.

He would usually start promisingly, with a story about something that had happened to him or to an acquaintance, or something he'd read in a book or seen in the newspapers. But about five minutes in, with dreary inevitability, the topic would revert to the religious text. He would quote a passage from the Bible, or a psalm, and then he'd be off for the next twenty minutes, explaining what the passage meant and what we should learn from it.

'Can't you make your sermons a bit shorter?' she'd asked him once. 'Or even tell a joke or two?'

'Believe me, I would if I could get away with it,' was his answer. 'But if I try lopping off even five minutes, someone always complains they're not getting their money's worth. And I've come a cropper in the past, telling jokes. Believe me, some people have no sense of humour.'

Another time she asked him if he really believed – as he'd claimed in his sermon the previous day – that all human beings are essentially good.

He'd paused for a moment before replying, 'I think we're born good, sweetheart, but our lives shape us, and sometimes not always for the better.'

'Like Mr Blackman?'

He gave a curious hollow laugh. 'Yes, even someone like him was good, once upon a time.'

'I hate him,' she'd said. 'I hope he goes to hell.'

Pa's smile dissolved in an instant. 'Listen, Molly. The war changed everyone, and not always for the good. We all lost someone, or lived for weeks and months expecting to die ourselves at any moment, or were horribly injured. And most of us saw things no human being should ever be expected to witness.'

'But why should that make someone evil?'

He shook his head. 'Only God knows these things, darling. All I know is that the legacy of war is all around us, and we should give people the benefit of the doubt.'

'The other day I heard you calling him the devil incarnate.'

His face was severe now. 'Listen, you must never, ever repeat that, my darling. In my position, I have to be neutral in all things, as you know. If I lose the support of my congregation, I may as well pack up and go home now.'

'Home? Where?'

He'd laughed again, then. 'It's a manner of speaking, sweetheart. I mean, give up the parish and go somewhere else.'

'Don't you sometimes wish you *could* go somewhere else, to get away from Blackman?'

He sighed. 'Yes, I do. But there are many good souls here in this parish, and God tells me I must do my best to mediate, to make their lives easier. To restore harmony. And that, my love, is exactly what I am trying to do.'

He did his best, the poor man. But it broke him, in the end.

She's tried to prepare herself for it, but it still comes as a shock, all the same. At the head of the north aisle there is a kaleidoscope of bright colours in the window that was once filled with plain glazing.

'Can you wheel me over there, love?'

As they approach, Bella starts to laugh. 'Heavens, Mum, that's the funniest thing I've ever seen in a church window. A crocodile, eating a pair of legs? What on earth . . . ?'

The top half of the stained-glass design is traditional enough, a classic Arts and Crafts interpretation of a medieval knight and his lady. But at their feet is another knight, surely St George, slaying what is plainly not a dragon, but an enormous, green crocodile in the process of devouring a pair of legs that hang, comically, like strands of spaghetti from its fearful-looking teeth.

'A *crocodile*? Whatever's a crocodile to do with Wormley?'

It has everything to do with Wormley, Molly thinks to herself. Old Eli said the creature would bring evil and he was right enough, in a way, even though everyone mocked him for his prophecies. Poor Eli. So kind, so gentle, so lonely. So damaged by war and bereavement, like most people around that time. Except for Blackman, of course, who'd profited while others suffered.

Suddenly she feels terribly weary. Remembering is exhausting. What she would most like to do now is lie down with her cheek resting on the stone flags and stay there, until the cold seeps into her body with a heavy forgetfulness and she can slip away to join Father and Jimmy, wherever they are.

Bella's voice comes from somewhere far away. 'You look as though you could do with a bite to eat, Mum.' The window slips from view as Molly's chair is turned, and she is being wheeled back down the aisle towards the church door.

Later, when they are sipping soup of the day in the warm recesses of the pub, Bella says, 'Tell me about that window, Mum. Whatever is a crocodile doing in an English country church?'

Molly puts down her spoon. Where on earth to start?

PART TWO:

DECEMBER 1949

3

We arrived in the village in early December. The country-side was like a foreign land to me and Jimmy, you understand. Until then we'd only ever lived in the city.

He was ten, I was fourteen, and we were only just beginning to get used to life without Mum. I say 'getting used to' but we never really got used to it. The word 'cancer' had been whispered when the adults thought we were out of hearing, but we had sharp ears. Whatever it was that killed her took a long, long time. But even with all that warning, when the end came it was a hideous shock.

At first I simply couldn't believe it, nor could Jimmy. Someone had told him that Mum had gone to heaven and he sobbed every day because he didn't know his way there. How do you respond to that? To say that to go to her, he'd have to die as well? That Pa and me wouldn't be coming with him, not just yet? Or that we all have to die, sometime? There is no consolation. Death is final, and they are gone forever.

I wept too, of course, and got angry, stomping around the flat and cursing God with all the worst swear words I knew. But mostly I just felt numb. Everyday activities, like getting dressed and making toast, going to school and coming home, felt like wading through thick fog. For a long, long time I was sure I'd never properly feel anything ever again.

Pa dropped his bombshell barely nine months after that. Since returning from the war he'd been one of several curates at St Martin-in-the-Fields, the beautiful church on the corner of Trafalgar Square, right in the centre of London. I loved it for its great columns, the light from its tall windows, the cheerful sound of its bells and those enormous bronze lions in the square. And I always imagined it having once been in the centre of green pastures, for why else would it have been given that name?

Best of all, the curacy came with a two-bedroomed flat just twenty minutes' walk away, in the heart of what they call Bloomsbury, which is where, Mum told us, lots of famous writers and artists used to live before the First World War. There were still great gaps in the terraces, like broken teeth, where houses had been reduced to piles of rubble by German bombs. In fact, our own had cracks in the walls and the windows didn't fit very well, so that the rain came in at the corners and we had to hide the damp patches with strategically placed pieces of furniture. But we didn't mind. There were parks nearby, and Mum seemed happy enough. Until she got ill, that is.

Neither of them had ever talked about it to us, but I'd come to understand that Pa had had such a difficult time as an army chaplain that his nerves were shredded and he suffered terrible nightmares. So when he was demobbed, the church authorities offered him the curacy at St Martin's, because the work was not too demanding and there would be plenty of others around to support him. Now, so it seemed, they thought he had recovered enough to take on his own parish. We would be moving out to the country.

'It's a great honour,' he said, his face more cheerful than I'd seen it in a long time. 'I'm thrilled. We'll have a lovely big vicarage, and lots of countryside all around for you two to explore. It'll be a new start for all of us.'

It was so unexpected. We'd never lived in the country, except for a few brief months when we'd left London to avoid the Blitz. Moving to a new parish would mean leaving school, all of my friends and the people at St Martin's who'd been so kind when Mum was ill. It would be a complete upheaval of our lives.

'Couldn't they find you a parish in London?'

'I suppose if I waited . . .' He paused to think, pulling his left earlobe. 'But don't you think it'll do us all good to get out of the city for a while? The war's taken a toll on everyone, darling. Not just on the buildings, but in our hearts and minds. We're all a bit broken. What I hope is that living in the countryside for a while will heal us, help us grow stronger.'

What none of us knew, of course, was that the tentacles of war reached everywhere, even to the most tranquil, remote parts of the country. They may not have been bombed in the way that cities were, rationing may not have been so painful and you did not see so many people with disabilities and disfigurements, but the scars of war were there all the same, the trauma hidden deep in people's heads, as we were to discover all too soon.

But for the moment my concerns were about more

everyday matters. 'What about school? Will there be one for Jimmy, like here?' My brother loved the bright, sunny school ten minutes' walk away, where there were plenty of other children like himself. His speech had improved, he could even tie his own shoelaces now and eat his meals with a knife and fork.

'Don't worry, my darling, I've already checked. The village is only six miles from a large town called Colchester, where there's a special school for Jimmy and a girls' grammar for you, with an excellent reputation. You can both go by bus.'

'But who will look after us?' Even though everyone had rallied round during Mum's last few months, bringing food, doing the laundry, taking Jimmy to school and even cleaning our small flat, I'd found myself having to take on most of the domestic responsibilities, making sure that everything was planned for, everything covered. I could just about manage a small flat, with all the shops and friends nearby. However would I cope with a great big vicarage, without any familiar people around us?

'There's a housekeeper,' Pa said. 'A woman from the village, left over from the previous incumbent. I haven't met her yet, but everyone says she's a treasure. Her name is Mrs Diamond.'

'Hope she lives up to it. Being a diamond, that is,' I said, hating myself for sounding so grumpy.

Pa gave me a wan smile, clearly hoping to soften my resistance.

A sudden, worse thought. 'She's not going to actually live with us, is she?'

'Oh no, sweetheart. She's got her own home in the village and will come every day.'

Someone else to do the housework so that I could get on with my own life. Perhaps that would work out all right. I didn't want to leave London, but to console myself I wrote in my notebook:

Positive thoughts about moving:
1. *A housekeeper to look after us.*
2. *Jimmy would love the freedom of the countryside.*
3. *I might make new friends.*
4. *Pa could make friends with God again (very important).*

He was looking forward to making a new start, he said, so I hoped this meant he was planning a new start with God. Not that I believed in God any more. How could I, when He'd taken our mother away? You could pray all you liked, but now I had proof that no one was listening. Or, if they were listening, they didn't care. Even so, I went on pretending, so as not to upset Pa even more.

It was different for him, because believing in God was part of the job description for the clergy. During Mum's last days I'd heard him praying out loud: 'Oh God, why have you deserted me? Show yourself, I beg you. Hold my hand, help me through this trial.'

Pa hardly ever prayed out loud except when he was running church services, so hearing this made me shiver. But if he felt confident enough to get excited about becoming a proper vicar, then perhaps it was a good sign.

Wormley vicarage was cold, cavernous, unloved and filled with shabby, old-fashioned furniture. It was far too large for our little family. But by the time we'd packed up everything and driven the long, tedious journey from London I was so exhausted that I didn't really care.

Downstairs there were four main rooms: two at the front overlooked the village street and across to the church. One had obviously been used by the previous occupant as a study, and was dominated by a massive mahogany desk that looked more like a ship. On the desk sat an ancient Bakelite telephone and I was about to get excited at the prospect of using it, but Mrs D told us it wasn't connected, and somehow Pa never got round to that.

The back of the house was the sunny side, facing south over the garden and towards the woods. The kitchen had a linoleum floor, a solid-fuel range, shelves containing dusty kitchen implements and a large scrubbed-pine kitchen table. From here, a door led into a scullery with a deep square white sink and wooden draining racks and, beyond that, a useful lobby with dedicated spaces for boots and coats led out into the garden.

The dining room was the best of all, with sun pouring in through French windows into the garden, and two case-ment windows on either side. I suggested this would make a much brighter, warmer living room, but Pa wouldn't hear of it. 'I'm going to need that table for parish meetings and so on,' he said firmly.

The stairs turned at a half-landing, with a tall window overlooking the front path, useful for checking who might be coming to the door. My bedroom had twin beds, a chest with wonky drawers, a tall wardrobe and, best of all, a personal washbasin. In the wardrobe I found a box of old paperbacks, mostly trashy romances with titles like *Stolen Love* and *Together Again* and covers showing doe-eyed women in various states of dishevelment gazing longingly into the distance, hoping for their lover to return. Their spines were broken, their pages yellowing with age, but I took them out and arranged them along a shelf, like a proper library.

Then I sat at the small writing desk in front of the window and peered out through dusty panes at the green swathe of unkempt lawn and the bare black branches of the trees beyond.

At last I had my own private space, with a bolt on the door. This was where I planned to write, to imagine other people and other worlds; it was the start of my new life as a soon-to-be famous novelist and poet, so I imagined. My notebook and pens were laid out ready to go. All I needed now was the inspiration, and I felt sure my new life in the village would provide it.

***

Mrs Diamond lived up to her name, although it took all of us a couple of weeks to get used to the idea of someone else running the house. I was afraid she might look too much like Mum, but happily she could not have been more different: a tall, rangy woman of about fifty with dark, thinning hair tied back in a severe bun, and a serious expression that only occasionally cracked into a smile, all the more rewarding for its rarity.

She would arrive just after breakfast and whip like a

whirlwind throughout the house with her carpet cleaner, duster and polish, before settling into the kitchen to cook up a daily banquet of good, plain food. We had all become resigned to the continuing rationing of meat, butter and sugar. But out here in the country there were always a few 'little extras' to be had: eggs often, jars of honey, sometimes cheese and even the occasional whole chicken, delivered complete with head, legs and feathers. Happily, Mrs D knew exactly how to prepare it. We were all very grateful to be eating properly again.

She showed me how to riddle and refill the coke-fuelled Rayburn that provided the house with an unreliable and barely adequate supply of hot water. It had an array of hobs and ovens of different temperatures for cooking, although we never really got the hang of it and when she wasn't there we tended to use an ancient electric ring instead.

Each day she relaid the open fireplaces in Pa's study and the living room with careful pyramids of screwed-up newspaper and twigs or kindling, topped with a few lumps of coal. There was plenty of wood to be had in the countryside, but the fireplaces were only fit for burning the expensive coal that was delivered in sacks and emptied down a chute into a coalhole in the dark, cobwebby cellar. Being so unused to managing open fires, and Pa being too mean to stoke them up properly, we shivered through that winter, missing the gas fires that had kept our London flat so toasty warm. I'd never really appreciated the convenience of gas, until we didn't have it.

In addition to her duties at the vicarage, Mrs Diamond was a pillar of the church community and a mine of information about everything and everyone in the village. She organised the cleaning and flower rotas, and chivvied the volunteers who mowed the grass and weeded the graves and paths in the churchyard. Despite having lost a leg in the war, her husband, George, was still very active and always available to do odd jobs, she told us. And it was she who suggested that 'the Rev', as she called him, should hold a small sherry party after the morning service on Christmas Day.

'Nice for them to meet you personally,' she told him. 'Just a small glass does wonders, with orange squash for the children and the Temp'rance lot. And they won't linger long. They'll be hungry for their dinner.'

Thinking back, all the people who would come to matter to me, for better or worse, came to the vicarage that Christmas Day. Kit and his parents, the Blackmans, Robert, the Timpson twins, the redoubtable Miss Calver. Everyone except Eli.

4

Christmas in a vicarage is never much of a family time, which is just as well, because with only the three of us we didn't make much of a family. Any aunts or uncles or cousins were too far away, and Pa was too busy for us to travel back to London to be with friends. It was only our second Christmas without Mum, so it was probably a helpful distraction to have the house filled with guests.

Around thirty members of the congregation took up our invitation and came back for the promised glasses of sherry. I did my dutiful-daughter bit, taking people's coats, circulating with the heavy sherry decanter – 'Only an inch,' Mrs D had instructed me, 'or they'll never go home.' Jimmy passed around bowls of peanuts and potato crisps until he got bored and disappeared upstairs.

One face I hoped not to see on our doorstep was the man to whom I'd taken an immediate dislike at my father's first-ever service in the village a few Sundays before. It was such a minor thing, but it irritated me, and you get a sort of sixth sense about some people. It was Advent, and Pa had asked me to help Jimmy light the symbolic candles on the wreath. It was a responsible job, lighting the taper and making sure you didn't drip too much wax onto the white linen runner, and we practised the little ritual over and over, using sticks as pretend candles. They were to be lit in the same order each Sunday, so that by Christmas they would, in theory, have burned down by different amounts. By tradition, the special pink candle was left unlit until the third Sunday – Gaudete Sunday.

As we returned to our pew, a man whispered from the seat behind, 'You missed one.' I felt a pang of panic. Pa was standing in front of the wreath now, so I couldn't exactly see right away, but when he moved, it was clear that all the candles were burning perfectly. Apart, obviously, from the pink one. What an idiot, I thought. I learned later that the man was the church treasurer and a successful property developer. With his obvious business acumen, he would definitely be an asset, Pa said. You would have thought he'd have known about the pink candle.

But now here he was on our doorstep: a man in his middle years, about the same age as Pa or perhaps a little younger, well-fed and beaming, with an air of prosperity about him. You could tell, somehow, those people who hadn't suffered too much deprivation during the war years. Even though only of average height and build, he had a very powerful presence, with a thick thatch of dark hair growing low over his brow, which reminded me of the Neanderthal man illustration in our encyclopaedia. He was dressed to the nines in a three-piece suit with a red-and-blue paisley-patterned cravat.

'Miss Goddard, I presume.' He had a rather too-posh voice, the accent of someone who probably hadn't been to public school but wanted to convey the impression that he had. His handshake went on for longer than strictly necessary and was slightly sweaty, so that afterwards I felt a great urge to wipe my hand on my skirt. Something about him made my skin crawl even then, although I couldn't put my finger on it.

'I'm Henry Blackman, and this is my wife, Melissa.'

She was a glamorous woman with bright-red lipstick and a helmet of permed blonde hair immobilised with lacquer. 'Charmed, I'm sure,' she purred. 'May we call you Molly?'

I took their coats and offered a glass of sherry.

'So you are the young lady of the house? Welcome to Wormley. I'm sure you will all be very happy here. We're certainly delighted to have a new vicar. It's been too long since the last one left,' he said.

No one seemed keen to talk about the 'previous incumbent' – the phrase Pa used – but Mrs D told us that the poor man had gone slowly mad and started selling off the church silver. I'd found the tale utterly thrilling and even began to write a story about it. My first line was: *The goblet glittered in the firelight, luring him into its secrets.* I got stuck on whether or not 'its' should have an apostrophe, and never carried on.

'What are your favourite subjects at school, Miss Goddard?' Mrs Blackman asked. Despite the strangely fixed hairdo she seemed pleasant enough, so I decided to oblige, rather exaggerating my love of literature and history, particularly medieval myths and legends.

'Then we simply must get you an invitation to Wormley Hall,' her husband interrupted. 'It has such a splendid history: Queen Elizabeth stayed there at least a couple of times. We're such good friends of the Waddingtons, aren't we, my dear?' His eyes darted past me, scanning the room. 'In fact, I'm rather surprised they aren't here today.'

'That would be lovely,' I said, trying to edge away. He had a tendency to stand closer than felt entirely comfortable, and even the sherry fumes could not conceal the sourness of his breath.

'And where is that little brother of yours?'

'Probably upstairs. He's not fond of large gatherings.'

'Is there something . . .' He paused. 'Erm, not quite right with him?'

'He is perfectly well, thank you,' I snapped. Surely he knew it was rude to draw attention to people's differences?

He held up a hand. 'Oh dear. I seem to have struck a nerve.'

'Not at all, Mr Blackman,' I said. 'But if you will forgive me, I'd better carry on with my rounds.' Before turning on my heel, I whispered, 'And by the way, you'll have noticed that we don't light the pink candle till the week before Christmas.'

It was a petty little victory, barely worth a second's thought but, as we were to learn, Mr Blackman hated to be wrong-footed. And he could hold a grudge for years.

On the other side of the room, near the window, ladies in Sunday hats encircled Pa with upturned faces, apparently hanging on his every word. He must have said something amusing that made them chortle, and perhaps for the first time I saw my father as they did: a tall, slim man with dark-blond hair thinning only slightly at the crown, a broad smile, crinkly blue eyes and a strong chin. He was, I realised now, actually rather handsome for an old man of forty-something. Quite a catch. Hence the girlish giggles.

I was distracted by the arrival of the Waddingtons: mother, father and son. I'd seen the boy in church and couldn't help glancing in his direction slightly more often than necessary. He was about the same age as me or perhaps a year or two older and, while not classically handsome, he was quite striking, with high cheekbones, a ruddy, healthy complexion and an expressive face that seemed to switch from sulk to smile in an instant.

'Good morning, I'm Captain Waddington,' the father said. 'This is my wife, Janey, and my son, Christopher.' The captain had the demeanour of an Air Force hero; the mous-tache clipped within an inch of its life, the upright bearing and his precise manner of speaking were impressive, even terrifying, and I would later come to understand how diffi-cult it must have been for Kit to have such a father, or for Mrs Waddington to have such a husband. She was pretty, with a sweet, apologetic smile, but paper-pale, and looked as though she might blow away in the slightest breeze.

'Call me Kit. Everyone else does, except my father,' the boy said, with that teasing grin I would come to know so well. Dark hair flopped over his face, except when he flicked it back, which was often. I longed to have more time to talk to him, but almost immediately after that more people arrived and I was called away on coats duty.

Later, I saw Kit chatting to some older ladies who seemed utterly charmed, hanging on his every word, mesmerised by the way he spoke with such animation, his hands flying to illustrate every point, his face mobile and expressive, his eyes wide and alert. As the party drew to a close I saw him join a group of younger people, the Timpson twins and another boy of the same sort of age, who had been introduced as Robert. They were sharing a joke and seemed to be having so much fun that now, for perhaps the first time since arriving in the village, I began to think living here wouldn't be so bad after all.

Just as other people were beginning to drift away home, Miss Calver appeared, late as always. She must have been in her seventies but seemed ageless; a small, wiry person, bursting with energy, oblivious to the niceties of fashion or what they used to call 'polite society'. I never saw her in a dress or skirt. Trousers and a well-worn tweed jacket were her preferred garb for all occasions, and this one was no exception, although she did remove the denim cap as she entered the doorway, folding it in two and stuffing it into one of her plentiful pockets.

Mrs D had already told us about Miss Calver. Apparently she'd enjoyed a distinguished career as a newspaper journalist, even having reported from the field hospitals in France during the First World War. What she didn't tell us, but was common knowledge around the village, was that Miss Calver sought to drown her wartime horrors in a glass of whisky, or three. Despite this, she bustled about the village with the air of someone always late for a deadline, and drove her little Austin Seven along the country lanes at such a lick that people had to leap into ditches to avoid being run over.

'Your father tells me you're a writer,' she said, downing her glass of sherry in a single sip and taking another from my tray without a hint of hesitation.

I stuttered something about liking to write stories.

'You must keep it up – keep it up, my girl,' she said, downing the second glass before taking out a cigarillo and lighting it with a large tin-metal lighter. 'That's the only way to get better at writing.'

I was about to ask about her experiences in journalism when Pa appeared and whisked her away. He'd already told me he wanted to buttonhole her about becoming editor of the parish newsletter, which he was determined to revive. I'd already offered to help with it, and the prospect of getting to know Miss Calver better made the thought even more appealing.

When they came to leave, Mrs Waddington took my hand. Her hold was so limp it was like tangling with a piece of wet seaweed. 'It was charming to meet you, my dear Molly,' she said. 'You simply must come to the Hall and we can tell you all about its history – won't we, Kit?' She turned to her son, beside her. 'You can take her on the lake, perhaps? Show her the islands?'

A lake? With islands? It sounded so impossibly like *Swallows and Amazons* that my imagination took hold in an instant. Could it really be true? 'That sounds wonderful,' I managed to gasp.

'It would be my pleasure,' Kit said. It was such a quaint, old-fashioned phrase, and as he said it he dipped his head in a very slight bow, as though he was in a period play. A curious character, I thought, unlike any boy I'd ever met before.

Afterwards, as we were washing up, I asked Mrs D about the Waddingtons. 'What do they do, to live in such a grand house?'

'Inherited money, of course.' She tapped the side of her

nose, confidentially. 'Her brother was heir to the estate but he died in the war so it came to her and, ever since that, her husband's been lording it about like he owns the place. Not that he's here much – spends most of his time in London, they say. Stockbroker or something.'

'They're friendly with the Blackmans, aren't they?' I'd seen the two couples chatting animatedly towards the end of the party.

'Thick as thieves, that Jane Waddington and Melissa Blackman.' Mrs D might be a mine of intriguing snippets of information, but she rarely elaborated.

'It's all clear, Jimmy, you can come out now. Lunch is on the table,' I shouted up the stairs.

'That went very well, don't you think?' Pa said. 'You were wonderful, my darling. The perfect hostess.'

'And your sermon was better than usual.'

'You think so?' His face brightened. Sermons were a persistent source of anxiety for him, and writing them seemed to take forever.

'Put it this way, I listened most of the time.'

He laughed. 'I couldn't do this without you, my sweetheart. But it's not going to be easy.'

'What do you mean? They all thought you were charming – certainly the ladies. They were hanging on your every word.'

He shook his head. 'The bishop warned me that you get a honeymoon period for the first few weeks or months, when everyone is kind and all seems smooth and easy. But I sense undercurrents in this village. I get the feeling it's not all going to be plain sailing.'

I wanted to ask him what he meant. What undercurrents?

And how did he know, after such a short time? But my stomach was rumbling and Jimmy was banging his spoon impatiently on the table, so this was not the time.

***

Starting at a new school is never easy. Pa and I had been to visit shortly after our arrival. The girls' grammar sat in wide acres of playing fields in the leafiest part of the town, and the headmistress, although severe-looking and rather brusque, turned out to be quite pleasant after all.

'The dog collar always helps,' Pa whispered as we waited for her. She certainly seemed to relish addressing him as 'Reverend' as she showed us around the school. We were invited for coffee in her study, during which she asked about what I'd been doing in mathematics, English and science at my previous school, as well as a few easy general-knowledge questions. She seemed pleased with my responses.

'Well, Molly, I am delighted to welcome you to the school,' she said, reaching into a drawer. 'Here's a list of our uniform requirements and where you can buy them. And here is our school calendar. We look forward to seeing you at the start of the spring term.'

Naturally I was nervous on my first day, but it turned out so much easier than I'd feared. The bus stop was on the main road at the top of our street and, as Jimmy and I walked up there that first day, I heard a voice from behind. 'Molly Goddard? Are you going for the bus?'

It was the Timpson twins, a pair of indistinguishable sisters about a year younger than me, whom I'd met briefly at the Christmas Day party.

We waited for them to catch up.

'What school are you going to?' asked Jane, or was it Juliet?

'The Girls' High. It's my first day.'

'We go there too. We're in the upper fourth. What about you?'

'Lower fifth.'

'Ooh, that's when it gets serious, isn't it? Lots of home-work.'

'I expect I'll find out.'

They chattered non-stop on the bus and the short walk to the school about the various rules, the foibles of different teachers – strict, kind, mean, inspiring, dull – the cleanest toilets, the most generous dinner ladies and the best buys at the school tuck shop. By the time we got there the place felt almost familiar.

We met again at the end of the day. 'How did it go?' Jane/Juliet asked.

'Brilliant.' It had been easy enough to get my bearings, the girls in my class were friendly, I hadn't been late for a single lesson and had earned praise from the hockey teacher for my passing skills. A good day, all round. Hopefully it wasn't some kind of honeymoon period, like the one Pa talked about.

On the homeward bus I learned more about the twins. I knew that their mother ran the church choir, because she'd been pestering me to join it ever since that very first service. Besides the twins, the choir consisted of six older women and a couple of men.

'You should come,' they chorused. 'It'd be fun.' I protested that I couldn't read music but they insisted it was only a matter of learning the tunes, and I promised to think about it. Before arriving in Wormley I had no idea that girls could sing in a church choir. At St Martin's they had a proper choir, all men, who sang in four-part harmony with choir-boys and male altos.

The twins lived in one of the thatched cottages further down the street from the vicarage, while their father, who was something rather important in the Civil Service, had a flat in London and came home at weekends. The twins' mother was friendly with Jane Waddington and Melissa Blackman, and Melissa gave them lifts in her red sports car to the life classes they attended. Life classes? I didn't like to ask.

'Did you talk to Kit Waddington?' Jane – or was it Juliet? – asked. 'He was at your party on Christmas Day. Isn't he dishy?'

'Yes, we said a few words,' I said, trying to sound casual, even though I'd thought about him almost every day. 'Have they really got a lake? With islands?'

'Ooh, yes. Get yourself invited if you can. It's amazing.'

'But I haven't seen him since,' I said.

'He's away at some posh boarding school,' they replied. 'But he'll be back at Easter, if not for half-term.' A pause and then, 'Oooh, you're blushing, Molly Goddard. You fancy him, don't you?' The twins giggled.

'I barely know him, for heaven's sake,' I said, my cheeks growing hotter.

5

Jimmy and I adapted slowly to country life. The weather that January and February was so cold and wet that, when we weren't at school, we spent much of our time indoors, helping Mrs D or, in my case, doing homework and trying to write my stories, most of which I tore up in despair. Jimmy was often bored.

'Keep an eye on your brother for me,' Pa would say, dashing out of the door, late as usual. That phrase again: *Keep an eye on Jimmy.* I'd come to dread it.

I missed Mum every day, so much that it actually hurt, a physical pain inside my chest like the stitch you get after running too far. How different it would have been if she'd been here. We would have sorted out the house, baked together, mended old clothes and sewn new ones. Or we'd have taken long walks together, the three of us, learning all about the new sights of the countryside, the wild flowers just starting to bloom in frothy white blossom like bridal veils in the hedgerows, the trees tinged with green as they burst into leaf and the birds that were already chorusing noisily from dawn to dusk.

Now she'd gone and left me to look after Jimmy on my own. It wasn't that I didn't love him – perhaps I loved him too much – but he was a big responsibility and I really wasn't ready for that.

My brother was born right in the middle of the war and, even from his early days, it was clear that he was different from other babies, although no one explained anything at the time. He had funny eyes and a flat head, found it difficult to suckle and cried a lot.

When his call-up papers arrived, Pa felt he could not, in all conscience, stay at home when so many of his congregation were fighting. He was appointed army chaplain, and it was left to me and Mum to look after Jimmy, who seemed to be taking his time about everything: smiling, rolling over, crawling, taking solid food. It felt as though he would be a helpless baby forever. He also suffered permanent colds and coughs, which Mum put down to the poor London air. During one particularly difficult period I overheard Pa saying, 'Perhaps he would be better off in a home, my darling?' and my mother shouting back, 'If you ever dare to say that again, I'll . . .' I never heard what she would do, because after that, I heard muffled weeping and Pa apologising: 'I'm so sorry, my darling, so sorry.'

Throughout all this – moving out of London to stay with Auntie Mary in Buckinghamshire, moving back once the Blitz was over, the loss of our house to a V-1 rocket, and having to live in temporary accommodation with another family – I never felt adrift with Mum by my side. Scared of the bombs, yes, and desperately worried about Pa's safety. But even when I'd had to move school twice in one year, or when bomb damage made it impossible to get there, Mum insisted on continuing my lessons at home, and I never once imagined that everything would not work out fine, in the end.

Jimmy was five when the war ended, and I was ten. Even though he had no physical scars, Pa was like a stranger when he came home. Loud noises made him jumpy, and he snapped at Jimmy when he cried. Mum was worried about him, I could tell. He smiled and joked sometimes just as before, but often looked as though he was only partly with us and would wander off for long, unexplained walks, sometimes into the night, or to the church to pray. At least that's what he claimed, although I couldn't imagine anyone being able to kneel for so many hours at a time.

Then came the terrible day when Mum eventually admitted that she was really feeling quite poorly. 'It's a bit more than the flu this time, my darlings,' she said, in a mastery of understatement. After several weeks in hospital she returned as thin and white as a ghost, with all the usual sense of energy and fun knocked out of her. Throughout those gruellingly painful last months, Pa came to rely on me more and more. Slowly, over that time, he began to confide in me and, although I hated the reasons why, at last it felt as though I was doing something useful.

'It's you and me against the world now, darling,' he would say when he kissed me goodnight. Somehow, through all the fear and sadness, I'd felt sure we would survive.

Those first few months in the village, Pa was so caught up with trying to make a good impression in his first proper parish that I'm sure he never noticed how lonely I was.

Although school was going well and I'd made several friends in my class, we all lived too far from each other to meet up at weekends and during holidays. I'd seen no sign of Kit or Robert since Christmas. Most of the children who lived in the village itself were pre-school or junior-school age, so the Timpson twins – Jane and Juliet – were my only friends in Wormley, and when my fifteenth birthday came around Mrs D suggested I invite them to the vicarage for tea. She made delicious fish-paste sandwiches and a carrot cake with real sugar frosting, and Pa joined us too. They gave me a book about butterflies so it was not a bad birthday, after all.

I met the twins each day on the school bus and we sang together in the church choir on Sundays, with a rehearsal every Thursday evening. But they were such a self-contained unit; they didn't need anyone else. Watching the way they understood each other without speaking and finished each other's sentences, the way they sometimes held hands walking down the lane, I found myself aching with envy.

Filled with adolescent turmoil, thinking of myself as nearly adult, but actually feeling as lost and confused as a child, I devoured the paperback romances from cover to cover. Although we'd only met once, briefly, Kit always appeared as the hero and I as the love-struck heroine who 'softly rested her cheek against his shoulder, breathing in the scent of his warm skin'.

Lately, in an attempt to cheer myself up, I'd been listing the good things about living in the countryside. At the moment the good list wasn't winning:

Good	*Not good*
Pa happier	Miles from anywhere
School fine	Bus only every two hours
Mrs D nice	Having to look after Jimmy
Twins friendly	Missing my London friends
Kit Waddington	Nothing to do
interesting	Missing Mum more. Not sure why.
	Weather miserable
	House freezing

What I struggled with most was the way people in the village looked at my brother: as if he was some kind of non-person – like a creature in a zoo. When we went to the little shop and post office I would encourage Jimmy to do the asking, and the paying. It was part of educating him towards independence, which was what Ma had always been keen to promote. But the lady in the shop never answered him, and always looked at me instead, so that he got sidelined and ignored, which I know he found frustrating, although Jimmy would never have been able to express it like that.

I suppose we'd become so used to him that we never saw his difference. Pa told me that when Jimmy was born, the hospital authorities suggested that he should be put into a special home, because children like him would never learn the skills for everyday life. But Ma had absolutely refused to let them take him away, and she'd been proved so right: he could walk and talk (sort of) and feed and dress himself reasonably well. He loved company, and his family, and his friends at school.

In London, where everyone is so varied, it didn't seem

to matter so much. But in Wormley they'd never seen anyone like Jimmy before, and although people were polite – how could they be otherwise, when he was the vicar's son? – and no one said anything overtly, you could tell by the sideways glances that they were suspicious, even perhaps afraid. I felt like shouting at them, 'For heaven's sake, be friendly. He's just a little boy with feelings like everyone else.' But, of course, I never did.

So when he came rushing back from the churchyard one afternoon, buzzing with enthusiasm and an air of someone about to impart thrilling news, I couldn't help getting a little bit excited.

'There's a . . . a . . .'

'Spit it out,' I said impatiently.

'Drag . . . dragger. Dragon,' he finished, with a triumphant grin.

A dragon. Just some silly little-boy thing. My excitement evaporated in an instant.

'Where's the dragon, Jim?' Pa asked kindly.

'In the M . . . m . . . Mere.'

'What's a mere?' I asked.

'It's a marsh, or a lake,' Pa said.

'The Waddingtons' lake, do you think?' I said, perking up. The idea of the lake with the islands had fired my imagination. And if there was any chance I might see Kit again . . .

'Down the . . . lay . . . lane.'

'Have you seen it?'

He shook his head.

'Then how do you know it's a dragon?'

'Old man said.'

'Which old man, Jimmy?'

'In the graveyard.'

'Ah, that'll be Eli.'

'He's a bit of a mystery, isn't he?' I asked. 'He comes to all the services, but he always sits at the back and disappears before the rest of us come out.'

'We pay him to dig the graves and tend the churchyard, but I don't know much more than that,' Pa said. 'He was a Chapel man, he told me, till they closed it down. He was the last one left in the congregation. They say he lives in a shepherd's hut somewhere in the woods, though I've never been there. But dragons, Jimmy? I'd take that with a very large pinch of salt, if you ask me.'

I didn't care about the old man or the dragon, except that they provided the perfect excuse to discover for ourselves where this lake was, and perhaps get a glimpse of Wormley Hall. And even Kit.

The following day dawned bright and crisp, for a change. 'Where are you two off to?' Mrs Diamond said, as we were pulling on our boots.

'Going for a walk,' I said cheerfully.

'Find dragon,' Jimmy added.

She frowned. 'You've not been talking to old Eli, have you?'

Jimmy nodded, his cheeks reddening. I put my arm round him, trying to reassure him that there was no shame in what he'd said.

'Well, don't you go bothering that old boy. He's not all

there, if you get my meaning,' she said, tapping the side of her head. 'And he can have a fearsome temper on him.' She clanged the empty soup tureen into the butler's sink so roughly that it made us both jump. 'You wouldn't want people to think the vicar's children believe in a load of heathen nonsense, would you? It's a touchy topic around these parts.'

Whatever did she mean by 'heathen nonsense'? Of course we didn't *actually* believe in dragons.

'We're only going to the woods,' I said.

'Then mind you're back for lunch. Twelve sharp. I've made soup.'

❦

Whoever suggested that the Suffolk landscape is flat had never been to this valley. The path through the woods led steeply downwards until at last we could begin to see glimpses of sunlit fields and the red-brick chimneys of Wormley Hall.

The slope flattened out now, and between the trees we could just about make out water shimmering in the sunlight: we were getting close. The footpath swerved and we were stopped in our tracks by a high wire fence decorated every few yards with notices declaring 'PRIVATE, NO TRESPASSING'.

But the path continued to our right, and five minutes further on we came to a point where the bushes thinned out to give our first unhindered view of the lake. It was so much larger than I'd imagined: a wide, clear expanse of water, uninterrupted save for two or three small grassy islands planted with willow trees. Wormley Hall was out of sight, hidden behind trees to the left.

In most places the banks were overhung with brambles, but quite close to us was a gentle sloped shoreline populated with bulrushes and luxuriant, almost exotic-looking growths of brilliant yellow flowers, like giant buttercups.

The lake glittered invitingly, ripples reflecting the sky like a scatter of diamonds. How wonderful it would be to sit on that bank, I thought, splashing your face or even soaking your feet in the cool, clear water. The fence here looked neglected: posts had fallen or wire netting had rusted into holes. It was so tempting: it would be quite possible to get through.

A moorhen came into view, swimming in its jerky manner and making loud ticks of alarm. We soon saw why. A skein of at least thirty geese appeared in the sky, squawking to each other as they circled twice, before plunging downwards and landing on the water with their pink webbed feet held out as brakes. They regrouped, shaking their wings, extending their necks and honking comically, as though congratulating themselves on a successful flight.

Jimmy laughed, pointing.

'They're geese. Like we used to see in Hyde Park, remember? Noisy, aren't they?'

The birds swam to the bank and hauled themselves out, settling down to preen themselves or idly crop the short grass, and all was peaceful again.

Soon after that the sun went behind a cloud, the breeze dropped and the surface of the water stilled and darkened. Without sunshine, the lake was transformed into a shadowy, mysterious place, full of potential danger. A chill went down my spine. It was easy to imagine how people had come to believe that fearsome creatures might be hiding in its bottomless depths.

'Where dragon?' he said, pouting.

'Perhaps they're all hiding today, Jim-boy.' I put an arm round his shoulder, as much to reassure myself as him. 'We'll come back another time, shall we?'

It was that very afternoon, returning home from the lake, that we saw Pa wandering at the far corner of the cemetery. Jim was about to run across to him, but something odd about Pa's behaviour made me hold him back.

He was pacing back and forth between the ancient gravestones with his head down and muttering to himself, although we were too far away to hear what he was saying. From time to time he would stop and look up to the sky with wide eyes, like a wolf howling at the moon. For the second time that morning I was filled with an indefinable sense of dread.

Jimmy shifted uneasily by my side. 'Wass he doing, Moll?'

'I don't know, my darling.' I took his hand and pulled him away. 'We'd better go, though. We're late for lunch.'

Pa didn't turn up for the meal. Mrs D said she'd kept a plate for him in the larder, because he'd had to rush out for an urgent meeting with Mr Blackman.

As Blackman was the church treasurer, I assumed it must have been about money. Pa had already talked about the multiple problems the church faced: the wobbly flagstones along the aisle that threatened to trip worshippers every Sunday; the hole in the vestry roof that let in the rain; and the slit in the leather bellows that had now grown so large that the organ could no longer be played. Without accompaniment it became harder for the choir to pull the congregation along with them, so that our hymns were often slow and ragged, and painfully out of tune.

'What about?' I asked.

'Not my place to know,' was all Mrs D would say. 'Now, get on with your food and stop asking silly questions.'

6

As Easter approached, a change came over the countryside and, although I kept a sharp eye out, we saw no repeat of Pa behaving strangely, so I began to feel a little more cheerful.

After weeks of rain and wind the weather settled and warmed. A gentle breeze carried the scent of blossom everywhere, bringing with it a new sense of optimism. It was difficult to worry or be miserable when every bird in the hedgerows seemed determined to out-sing its neighbours, and the churchyard was filled first with snowdrops and brilliant yellow aconites, followed by creamy primroses, cowslips and the white flowers of wild garlic that Mrs D brought in to flavour soups.

A few weeks later, the bluebells arrived.

Jimmy and I took the footpath into the woods and had walked only a couple of hundred yards when we topped a rise and found ourselves looking down into a wide glade on a south-facing slope. Both of us gaped: the woodland floor was a carpet of vivid, almost dazzling blue, striped with rays of sunshine, transforming it into an enchanted grove. The sound of birdsong was almost deafening.

'Wha . . . what? Look,' Jimmy stuttered, pointing.

'Bluebells.' I'd no idea they could look like this. 'Can you smell them too?'

He rushed forward and began to pick the blooms. I pulled him back. 'They don't last if you pick them. Better to enjoy the sight of them growing in the ground. Let's go on.'

The path led downwards through the sea of blue. Jimmy skipped ahead, and seeing him so happy lifted my heart. My eye was caught by a robin waiting on a low branch, probably hoping that our footsteps would turn up a juicy worm.

Its red breast glinted in a ray of sunshine. I was entranced. The only birds I'd ever been this close to before were the pigeons in Trafalgar Square, which were always so greedy and aggressive. This little fellow looked as though he was actually welcoming me to this beautiful wood, his home territory. It tilted its head and observed me with a single black eye, as though about to engage me in conversation.

'Hello, my friend,' I said quietly, but my voice alarmed him and he flew off. When I looked up, Jimmy was already far ahead, way down the slope. As I quickened my step he turned a corner and went out of sight.

'C'mon, Jimmy, we're not playing hide-and-seek today,' I called, but there was no response. 'I know you're not far away, so stop being a clot. Come back.'

It was darker here, and cooler; tall pines blocked out the sun and their shadows felt unfriendly. I realised that we had never penetrated so deep into the woodland before. It was unfamiliar, even slightly sinister. I shouted Jimmy's name over and over again but my voice just echoed back, as though the trees were mocking me.

'Jimmy, *please*. Where are you? Come back, for heaven's sake. You're frightening me.'

Minutes passed. I began to run. At another fork in the path I stopped and listened until my ears ached. My brother was rarely quiet, often panting or muttering to himself, and so clumsy that surely I'd be able to hear the thud of his footsteps or the crack of twigs under his feet? But there was nothing – only the creaking of the trees and the song of distant birds.

How could he have disappeared so completely in just a few minutes? My heart was thudding as I tried desperately to decide what to do. Go forward, or back to where I'd last seen him? Surely he couldn't have got lost in such a short time?

In London there were always people to help. Mum had bought Jimmy an identity tag, which he used to wear on a leather lace round his neck, just in case. Now, I cursed myself for not being able to remember whether he was still using it, realising with a rising sense of panic that we had never got round to updating the address.

Would he be able to find his way home? How far did these woods stretch? Where did they end? I had absolutely no idea what dangers the countryside might hold.

And then I heard it: so soft as to be almost inaudible, but unmistakeably a man's deep voice. 'Hello, laddie. What're you doing down here?'

I began to run in the direction of the voice, barely noticing how the branches scratched my arms and brambles tore at my bare legs. I stopped and listened some more, then called, 'Jimmy, Jimmy?'

The man's voice again: 'Over 'ere, dearie.'

At last I emerged into a clearing and there, in front of a dilapidated wooden hut, was Jimmy. As he turned round and smiled, I almost cried with relief.

The hut was set high off the ground on iron wheels, with a stable door and an arched roof that projected forward over a raised porch reached by wooden steps, at the top of which stood Eli, with a beaming smile. Beside him, a camel-coloured mongrel with rough, scraggy fur snarled and bared a mouthful of sharp teeth, as though it might cheerfully tear me from limb from limb, given half a chance.

'Quiet, Sarge,' Eli commanded, and the dog slunk back into the shadow of the hut. 'Take no notice of 'im, 'e's a real softie once he git ta know you.' He spoke in that soft Suffolk accent I was slowly learning to interpret. 'This little lady summat to do with you, laddie?'

'He's my brother.'

The dog raised its head and gazed at me with yellow eyes, still growling quietly.

'You're that new vicar's kiddies, ain't ya? What're your names, my friends?'

'I'm Molly, and this is Jimmy.'

'And I'm Eli,' the man said. 'Short for Elijah the prophet, though if I could tell the future, we'd all be rich.' He chuckled with a deep bronchitic rattle. 'My folks was strict Chapel,' he added, as though that explained everything. 'Anyways, you is most welcome to my 'umble abode on this fine day. Can I get you summat? A cuppa perhaps? I've just made a fresh brew. Maybe I could find a biscuit too.'

As he disappeared into the darkness of the shed, the dog growled again, more menacingly this time. 'Thank you, Mr

Eli, but we ought to be on our way,' I said, grabbing Jimmy's arm. 'C'mon, we should go.'

But the word 'biscuit' had worked its magic on my brother. He pulled free, climbed the steps and sat down firmly on the bench. When Eli re-emerged, Jimmy accepted a mug of tea and immediately began to sip it, giving little grunts of pleasure.

'Go on, try it. It's sweetened with honey,' Eli said, holding a mug out to me, using his other hand to steady his tremor.

The mug didn't look that clean, but good manners wouldn't allow me to refuse and I took a tentative sip. It was delicious: sweet and aromatic, nothing like the bitter brown liquid Mrs D brewed at home.

I began to relax, a little. Here in the woods I saw Eli the gravedigger through new eyes. The old brown tweed topcoat, tied at the waist with string, blended perfectly with the colours of the woodland. The long white beard seemed to give him an air of wisdom. Given a red suit, he might have passed for a scruffy Father Christmas.

He returned inside and came back with a tin that turned out to contain flapjacks. 'Little treat for me visitors,' he said, offering them to us.

It had been a long time since breakfast, and hunger overcame any qualms.

'Here, ease your legs, lassie,' he said, producing a curious-looking footrest. 'Thass an old milking stool. Them three legs is designed for rough ground. Gew on, try it.'

He and Jimmy sat on the bench while I squatted on the surprisingly comfortable little seat, and for a few moments the three of us munched on our flapjacks, listening to the birds. The dog rested his chin on his paws and went back to sleep. I sipped my tea, wondering what Eli did with himself when not tidying the churchyard or digging graves – an infrequent demand in such a small village. He never socialised with the other members of the congregation after church. It must have been a lonely existence, living in the woods, but he seemed happy enough. Perhaps he liked the solitude.

'Pa says you help keep the graveyard tidy and dig the graves sometimes,' I said, to make conversation.

He shrugged. 'It keep me busy, even if me old bones sometimes feel ready for the grave 'emselves. Your father's a good soul. He give me regular money – not like that other fella, who only paid when some'un died.'

He puffed some more on his pipe. I followed his eyes as he glanced round his little glade. Here the trees grew more sparsely and shafts of sunlight glimmered through the early green foliage, patterning the carpet of last year's fallen leaves on the woodland floor, which was dotted with bluebells and the purple spikes of what I'd later learn were wood orchids.

'And where's you two off to this fine day?' he said.

'See dra . . . dragon,' Jimmy said. That hadn't been part of my plan, and Jimmy hadn't mentioned dragons for a few weeks, but seeing Eli must have reminded him.

The old man began to laugh with a wheeze that caught in his throat and became a full-blown coughing fit. I remembered what Mrs D had said about him having been gassed in the First World War. At last he caught his breath and wiped his eyes.

'There's more to this laddie than meets the eye,' he said,

ruffling my brother's hair. Normally Jimmy would have hated it, but somehow with Eli he didn't mind. 'He remembers what I told 'im weeks ago. In the churchyard, wasn't it, laddie?'

'It's only a fairy story,' I said quickly.

Eli chuckled again. 'You's right, Missy. Some people say I oughta keep them stories to meself. But there don't seem no harm in 'em.' He adjusted his old felt hat and packed his pipe again. 'Course, it weren't no proper dragon, anyroads.'

'Then what was it?' I was intrigued, despite myself.

Eli put his mug down and carefully rested his long clay pipe beside it. 'Well, it gew a bit like this,' he began, adjusting his hat.

Jimmy gazed up at him, open-mouthed in expectation.

'They say that long, long ago, back in what they call the Middle Ages, someone give the king a present what he'd brought back from Africa. Everyone thought it were a dragon, cos they'd never seen a crocodile 'afore. He kep' it in the Tower of London and fed it plenty, till it grow bigger and bigger.'

Eli held his palms wider and wider apart until he could reach no further, and Jimmy's eyes threatened to pop out of his head.

'Eventually that old beast got strong enough to break out of its cage and escape into the River Thames.'

He filled the pipe, struck a match on the sole of his boot and held it to the bowl, took a deep draw and exhaled, resting back against the wall of the hut.

'That poor old king was sorry to lose his pet and offered rewards, but nothing was seen of the creature for months, until some'un saw it just down there.' He pointed down the hill. 'Reckoned it swam down the Thames, along the coast and up our little ole river. Believe that and you'll believe anything, but that's how the story gew.'

We were both entranced. Eli was a gifted storyteller.

'Anyroad, it soon started terrifyin' the village folk and they tried to kill it, of course, but their arrows jus' bounced off its tough old hide. Somehow rumour spread that it could only be pacified by feeding it humans. It seemed to like young girls specially . . .'

He paused for effect. By now I had goosebumps.

'Eventually a knight come along and offered to slay the dragon – or crocodile, whichever way you want it. Some claim he was successful and the villagers was eternally grateful. But others say the creature was only injured and crawled into the Mere for safety, and it's been there ever since.'

'Has anyone ever claimed to have seen it, in recent times?'

'Not that I knows of, anyroads. But they do say that if it is ever disturbed, it'll bring evil to the village.' He tapped his pipe against the sole of his boot so fiercely I feared he might snap it. 'Not that there ain't already plenty of that, round these parts.'

'And has it been disturbed?'

'Someone said they saw bubblin' in the water the day afore them bombs.'

'Bombs? In Wormley?'

'In 1940, it was. They reckon the bomber was jess tryin' ta find his way back to Germany and decided to drop his payload to lighten the plane. Two of 'em fell beside the church and blew out the stained glass – thass why them winders is just plain these days. Personally I like 'em – brings a bit of sunlight inta the place.'

'Heavens. Was anyone hurt, Mr Eli?'

His voice dropped to a near-whisper. 'It destroyed me cottage, and me wife along with it. She died there and then.'

'How dreadful. I'm so sorry.' I fell into shocked silence.

'Thass all right, lassie. Yous get used to these things. We bin 'ere in the woods ever since. Ten years now. Still, we get along all right, don't we, Sarge?' he said, leaning down to stroke the dog's head. 'Despite what they say.'

I was about to ask him what 'they' said, when Jimmy jumped in: 'Water bubbling?'

Eli grinned. 'You do like that ole story, little fella,' he said. 'Like a limpet, you is. Well, I'll explain. The old dragon lives deep down under the water, farther than anyone can measure, cos the lake's supposed to be bottomless. Anyways, they says it's jess biding time and, if it's disturbed, it'll come up again to punish us.'

Jimmy's eyes were as wide as saucers.

'It's only a fairy story, Jim,' I said quickly.

'Course it is, laddie,' Eli added. 'That's just a bit of ole folklore, boy.'

Eli's storytelling inspired me. That evening I took out my large notebook and began to write it down, exactly as he'd told it. But somehow, on the page, without his Suffolk accent and inflections, without the trees and the birds all around us, it felt flat and dull. I tore it up and started again.

Two hours later, I had tried various different ways of telling the story – attempting to reproduce Eli's dialect, writing it in the first person, and reimagining it as a children's story – and the waste-paper basket was filling fast. And then it came to me: I would write it as a story for Jimmy, starring himself. *The Ugly Dragon* was born.

THE UGLY DRAGON
by Molly Goddard

Chapter 1: Jimmy meets the dragon

Once upon a time there was a young boy named Jimmy, who was longing to meet a dragon. When he learned that there might be one hiding in a nearby lake he pestered his sister to go with him, because he knew he was not allowed to go on his own.

Each time they visited he would call out: 'Are you there, dragon? Come and see us.'

Nothing appeared. But they returned day after day until, one hot afternoon, the still surface of the water seemed to ripple and a strange-looking head appeared. It was greenish-black with two big eyes on either side of its forehead, and a very, very long snout topped with two large nostrils. Its mouth was filled with hundreds of sharp white teeth and seemed set in a permanent grin.

Jimmy was a very brave boy and did not run away. He just said: 'Hello, Mr Dragon.'

'Miss, actually,' she said. 'But you weren't to know. Can I join you?'

She hauled herself out of the water and settled down beside him. It was a scary sight: she was six foot long and reminded him very much of a picture in one of his storybooks. She had short, sturdy legs, lumpy spines all down her back and a long tapering tail. But somehow Jimmy did not feel afraid.

He told her what his friend Eli had said about the dragon in the lake. 'But you look more like a crocodile to me.'

To his surprise, her eyes filled with huge tears, the size of marbles.

'Sorry, I didn't mean to upset you,' he said.

She shook her head, flinging the tears away, and clattering her teeth alarmingly. 'It's been like this ever since they took me from my river in Africa. They told the king that I was a dragon, and at first he was very proud of me, showing me off to all his courtiers. But when I overheard them laughing, saying, "What an ugly dragon," it made me sad.

'After a while the king decided that he didn't want an ugly dragon that people laughed at, so he threw me out of the palace. I managed to find a river and swam and swam till I found this place. It's quiet here, and no one bothers me.'

'So why are you so sad?'

'I don't want to be ugly. I just want to be normal, like any other dragon.'

7

On the last day of the spring term we finished early and Dinah, one of the girls from my maths class, said they were going to a coffee bar to meet boys from the local grammar school. Why didn't I join them? she suggested. The others were all friends and, although they acknowledged me perfectly politely, soon resumed their conversations: the boys talking about the chances of success for Colchester United the following weekend; the girls gossiping about other girls, homework and clothes. But I didn't mind too much; I was happy to sit and listen – until one of the boys, Frank, who seemed a little older than the rest, with a wispy ginger growth on his chin and upper lip, turned to me.

'So where have you popped up from, Molly?'

'I live in Wormley. My father's the new vicar.'

'How come we haven't seen you around before now?'

'We only moved here just before Christmas.'

'Where did you live before?'

All these questions. Was he really interested or was he simply being kind?

'London,' I said.

'Wow.' He seemed impressed. 'Did you stay there all through the war, with the bombs and everything? We had a few dropped around here, but nothing like you got in London.'

'Actually we moved out to stay with an aunt when my dad went off to France, but we came back after the war.'

'It must be quite a shock, moving to a sleepy little place like Wormley.' He addressed another boy across the table. 'Hey, Bingley, isn't that where your friend lives?'

'Where?'

'Wormley.'

'Yes, Kit Waddington. Why?'

They had my full attention now.

'Molly lives there too. Her dad's the vicar.'

'Have you met Kit yet?'

'Only briefly, at Christmas. They live in the big house. Aren't they rather grand?'

'His pa does something fancy in the City and is rich as Croesus, but it's his ma who inherited the place, apparently. Kit's quite a character. Knew him at prep school. Brilliant at sport and public speaking, not massively well-endowed in the brains department. Bit bonkers – never could rely on him. Didn't pass the eleven-plus into the grammar, so they sent him off to a posh boarding school.'

Dinah nudged me with her elbow and whispered, 'Made a hit there, Molly.'

'Whatever do you mean?'

She tilted her head towards Frank, sitting two away, and raised her eyebrow. 'With Frank. Can't you tell?'

'Tell what?'

'Oh, you are such an innocent. He fancies you like crazy, you dolt.'

The truth was, I had not the slightest interest in Frank. My head was filled with thoughts of Kit. So it seemed as though fate was on my side when, at breakfast the following day, Pa was flicking through the pile of brown envelopes – bills – with a series of quiet sighs, until he pulled out a different-shaped letter in heavy cream bond.

'Whatever can this be?' He slit open the top with a knife and pulled out a single sheet of paper, putting on his half-glasses to read. 'Heavens. It's from the Waddingtons. They've invited us for tea.'

'Us – you mean all of us?' I immediately felt nervous and excited, all at once. 'Jimmy too? Will it be just our family, do you think, or other people too?'

'I have no idea, my darling. We'll just have to wait and see.'

Most of that morning was spent trying on and discarding various items of clothing and despairing of finding anything suitable that was smart enough, yet not too formal, or too warm or too chilly for the changeable spring weather. Finally I hit on a compromise: a skirt on which Mrs D had already worked her charms, reshaping it into a more modern pencil design and lowering the hem, paired with a blouse that had once been Mum's and wasn't too tight across the chest. Then I spent ages in front of the mirror examining my face, and made a disastrous attempt at shaping my eyebrows with Mother's old tweezers. They ended up looking even more wonky than before.

Mrs D caught me trying to straighten my hair with the clothes iron.

'Heavens, girl, whatever are you doing?'

I slammed down the iron, feeling foolish. 'Trying to get

rid of my curls.' The picture on the cover of one of my romance novels showed a glamorous woman with long, wavy hair falling over her shoulders.

'You'll do that soon enough if you scorch them to a frazzle, dearie,' she said. 'And what's wrong with them lovely curls?'

'They're childish,' I said, feeling even sillier.

Mrs D put down her bucket with a kindly sigh and went out into the scullery. She returned with her basket and took out a magazine, then sat at the kitchen table turning the pages until she reached the photograph of a beautiful woman with short, dark curly hair.

'Jean Simmons. One of our most successful actresses – a huge hit in Hollywood these days. Would you say she looks childish?'

'No, but my hair doesn't look anything like hers.'

She examined me, tilting my head with a finger. 'True, but it wouldn't take too much. Have you got any kirby grips?'

Within quarter of an hour my hair was dampened and coiled into sections pinned flat to my head. Now all we had to do was wait until it dried. Mrs D didn't actually explain why forcing it into curls would make it less curly, but she was right, as she so often was. A couple of hours later she took out the hairpins and gently brushed and stroked my hair into what were now gentle waves rather than tight curls. It looked so much more sophisticated, and even distracted attention from the wonky eyebrows.

Wormley Hall was possibly the prettiest house in the whole world, but it hid its charms behind a long winding driveway with tall hedges. Although I had already glimpsed its tall brick chimneys peeping over the tops of the trees, nothing prepared me for what came into view as we walked round the last bend of the drive.

'It's a moat, Pa!' I almost shouted. 'With water in it and everything.'

Jimmy rushed ahead and I chased after him, as best I could in my tight skirt. A family of ducks scattered, rising into the air with a noisy chorus of alarm calls. 'Nothing like advertising our arrival,' Pa said.

Most people think beauty lies in symmetry. At least that's what women's magazines say about faces. But Wormley Hall disproves the point. It is all higgledy-piggledy, with extra bits added on over the centuries: a porch here, a double-stacked chimney there, a couple of dormer windows in that roofline, a single-storey outhouse to the side.

If you stopped to count the windows – I'm guessing about thirty, just on the side we approached from – you might begin to comprehend the size of the place. But all the little additions seem to conceal its real scale, and even though it is large, the house doesn't look overly grand or self-important, in the way of some mansions. It just appears friendly and inviting. The red brick has aged and mellowed over the years, and that afternoon it glowed in the sun with such warmth and character that it seemed to emit an inner beauty of its own.

I was so overwhelmed by the wonder of the place that there was barely any time to get nervous, but after Pa pulled the long cast-iron bell-pull and we waited, listening to the reverberations inside the hallway, my confidence seemed to slip away. Whatever would I say to Kit? What did people talk about over tea? What was the correct way of holding a teacup and saucer?

I'd seen Mrs Waddington at the party and occasionally in church, but she wasn't the sort of woman who made an instant impact. In fact, my first impressions had been that she might waft away in the wind, for she was as slim as a willow branch and just as delicate. Or she might simply dissolve into the background because, with her pale skin, white-blonde hair and a wardrobe consisting of soft pastel shades of grey and cream, she appeared to have no colour of her own.

'Come in – come in, my dears,' she said in her light, wispy voice and ushered us through the dark hallway into a bright living room. The sun poured in through tall windows overlooking an expanse of perfectly trimmed green lawns and beds of flowering shrubs, displayed against the darker green of the woods beyond.

Crisply pruned box hedges created intricate geometric shapes in what looked like a low maze, lined with gravel paths that enclosed beds of red roses and purple lavender – a knot garden, she called it. Beyond that, a perfectly trimmed lawn of the purest green led to the edge of the moat where a pair of swans stood, serenely preening themselves. It was a picture of perfect harmony.

Jimmy said it first. 'Pretty,' he whispered, tapping the window with his fingers and leaving sweaty marks on the pane.

Mrs Waddington turned to Pa. 'What a sweet boy you have, Vicar. And look at you, Molly, growing up fast. Now, let me call the others, so we can have tea. We'll take a stroll in the garden afterwards, if you like.'

When Mr Waddington walked into the room everyone automatically pulled their shoulders back, even Jimmy, like troops standing to attention.

'Where's that wretched boy?' he barked, as though it was his wife's fault their son had not yet appeared.

She flinched a little and went to the door, calling, 'Our guests are here, Kit.'

When Kit finally sloped in, I felt a certain sympathy with his father's impatience. He greeted Pa with a casual and rather cursory handshake, before slumping into the chair next to me with his long legs stretched out, brushing back that lock of dark hair, a slightly grumpy expression on his face. 'What's for tea, Ma?'

'Sit up straight, for heaven's sake, Christopher,' his father snapped.

Kit glared at him as Mrs Waddington chattered on about the weather and other inconsequential matters, trying to ease the frosty atmosphere.

A maid in crisply starched black and white uniform arrived with the tea trolley and there was much fussing over passing cups and saucers, sugar and tongs, plates and napkins, along with a plate of elegant white-bread sandwiches cut into tiny triangles and containing either cucumber or fish-paste. There was cake to follow, with a choice of chocolate or lemon – clearly they suffered from no scarcity of eggs and butter in this house.

As Pa and Mr Waddington started a conversation about St Martin-in-the-Fields, Kit turned to me. 'And how are you this fine day, Miss Molly Goddard?' That old-fashioned way of talking disarmed me, along with his manner: cheeky and a little insolent, but at the same time luring you in, as though he might be about to tell you the most delicious secret. He had a languorous kind of confidence about him that was both intriguing and disconcerting in equal measure.

'I am well, thank you.' My head whirled, trying to find another topic of conversation, but I could come up with nothing. 'I suppose you are back from school for the holidays now?'

He sighed. 'Afraid so. There's not a lot to do here in Wormley, is there? Don't you find it rather dull?'

What should I say? Should I admit that it was lonely and boring, and I longed to go back to the city? 'I'm growing used to it. It felt odd at first, being in the country after London.'

'I've always wanted to live in London. My father has a flat near Hyde Park, where he stays during the week and some of the weekends. I'd prefer to be there, to be honest, even though we don't really get on too well most of the time. But they won't let me, cos he's out all day and they think I'll get up to mischief. Which, of course, I most certainly would, given half a chance. What about you?' Blue eyes met mine, searching and challenging.

'I suppose so . . .' I was stumped. It had never really crossed my mind to 'get up to mischief' in London; I'd been too young, I supposed, and anyway was never given the chance. Meeting school friends in a coffee bar in Colchester was the current extent of my excitements.

'You go to the Girls' High, I suppose?'

'Yup.'

'Thought so. You seem the brainy type.' Was that code

for 'boring'? It was hard to tell. 'I failed the eleven-plus, so they shipped me off to boarding school,' he went on. 'Actually I didn't mind. It was more fun than being stuck here.'

In the pause I could hear Mrs Waddington explaining to Pa how it had come as something of a surprise when she'd inherited the Hall, after her elder brother – a pilot in the war – was shot down and her father died of a heart attack a few months later.

'Which is why we are so keen to create some kind of memorial for him, aren't we, darling?' She looked across to her husband for confirmation. 'And we were wondering whether the church authorities might consider a new stained-glass window – you know, to replace one of those blown out in the war?'

So this was why we had been invited to tea, with the elegant sandwiches and the beautifully decorated cakes. I watched Pa's face working, as he sought the right response.

'That sounds like a splendid idea,' he said. 'Although, of course, the church has a number of rather pressing demands on its finances at present, as I'm sure you're aware.'

'Oh no,' she said, more earnestly now. 'We wouldn't ask the church to pay for it. We are offering to foot all the bills: design, creation, installation. My friend Melissa has already offered to do the design for us, and I'm sure she'll come up with something delightful.'

'Mrs Blackman?'

'She's a very talented artist, you know. It would be our memorial to my beloved brother, David.' Her voice wavered to a whisper.

After a second, in his best clerical consolation voice (I swear they teach it at vicar college), Pa said, 'We are so sorry for your loss, Mrs Waddington. And this is such a generous offer. I am sure we should be able to ease the way forward with the diocese to make it come to fruition. Leave it with me.' She looked at him like an adoring angel at Christ's crib, as though she might simply collapse into his arms. In the uneasy silence that fell over the room, Kit glanced at me and raised an eyebrow in such a comical way I nearly giggled.

All this while Jimmy had been sitting quietly beside me on the sofa. He'd been on his very best behaviour, drinking his barley water and eating his sandwiches in a remarkably civilised way. Sometimes he did this awful gobbling, stuffing food into his mouth as fast as possible and then chewing with his mouth open. But that day he was perfect, and I loved him for it.

As Mr Waddington embarked on an account of the former inhabitants of the house, which included several rogues and near-royalty, I watched Kit out of the corner of my eye. For all his casual air and the veneer of confidence, I began to sense that, inside, he was actually rather ill at ease. He could barely sit still for a few seconds before shifting his pose, putting down his plate and then picking it up again, reaching for more food before it was offered, finishing his tea and immediately holding his cup out for more. What was making him so edgy, I wondered? Surely we were not too scary: two children and a vicar? Or was there something else going on?

Kit's gaze flicked disconcertingly between us: to his father and Pa, then to his mother and back, then to Jimmy, then me. I caught his eye and he smiled confidentially, as though we were conspirators in some obscure game. I still could not decide whether I liked him or not. At times he came across as plain arrogant; at others he was funny, and even sensitive. I was fascinated, all the same. Kit intrigued and unsettled me, all at once. It affected Jimmy, too. He began to wriggle, upsetting his plate and the remains of his sponge cake onto the floor and spilling some of his lemon barley water.

'Oh, for heaven's sake,' I heard Mr Waddington mutter. 'Get the maid, will you, Christopher.'

Kit unravelled himself, stood up and disappeared.

Mrs Waddington padded the spill ineffectually with her napkin. 'Never mind, my dear. It's an old carpet and doesn't matter at all. Anyway, isn't it time for a walk in the garden? Time to wear off some of that energy, young Jimmy? There are swans on the moat – we can take some bread to feed them.'

Jimmy pushed past me to her side and took her hand, which is the sort of thing that breaks my heart. He falls in love so easily with anyone who takes notice of him, and then has to learn the hard truth that their affections are only temporary.

We were walking through the knot garden, and Mrs Waddington was telling us how it had been laid out in an ancient Celtic pattern like the original Tudor versions, and I suppose none of us noticed that Jimmy was missing until we heard him shouting from the far side of the lawn.

'Look at me!'

He had somehow managed to climb a high pillar at the edge of the moat and was teetering dangerously on the top, embracing the outstretched wings of a large stone swan with one arm and waving excitedly with the other.

Kit was the first to react, leaping over the box hedges like an Olympic hurdler and sprinting across the lawn at impressive speed. He climbed a low wall and reached up for Jimmy, calling to him to turn and come down backwards, the way he'd climbed up. The rest of us were rooted to the spot, watching the drama unfold.

After that, everything seemed to happen in slow motion. Jimmy turned to look at Kit, but at the same time he let go of the stone swan and lost his balance, wobbling for a second before starting to topple. Kit stepped forward on the wall and managed to catch him, but couldn't keep his own balance, and the pair of them tumbled down together, with Jimmy on top and Kit below, breaking his fall.

By the time we reached them, Jimmy was already on his feet, looking a bit dazed but apparently unharmed. Pa grabbed him by the arm, rather roughly, shouting, 'For goodness' sake. Whatever did you think you were doing? You're a big boy now and should know better than to run off like that.'

Jimmy burst into tears.

Kit was still sprawled on the ground, his face a funny shade of grey. His mother kneeled beside him, lifting him up tenderly into a sitting position.

'Oh, my darling, are you hurt?'

'A bit . . . strange.' His head slumped to one side, and there was blood all over his white shirt and his mother's sleeve.

'Call for a doctor,' his mother cried.

'Don't fuss, dear,' Mr Waddington snapped. 'He's only bumped his head.'

Kit came round soon enough. His father helped him

onto his feet and then half-walked, half-carried him back to the house, where he collapsed into a chair. We stood back, feeling rather helpless as Mrs Waddington appeared with a first-aid box. Her husband elbowed her out of the way and began to investigate Kit's injuries. He must have cracked his head on something hard and sharp, because they found, concealed under his hair, a rather large wound still oozing blood.

'We need to control this bleeding. Lint-compress, quick sharp.' Mrs Waddington produced a white pad that he held to the wound. 'He'll need stitches. Ring the doctor. Say it's urgent,' he commanded, and she scuttled away.

Pa whispered, 'Time to make ourselves scarce, I think.'

We offered profuse apologies and thanks, and let ourselves out. We walked home in silence, wrapped in our own thoughts. Jimmy was sulking because Pa had ticked him off, and my own footsteps were heavy with guilt. The accident would never have happened had I not allowed Jimmy to wander away like that. Kit had been a hero all right, saving Jimmy's fall, and it could have been so much worse. But now he would probably never want anything more to do with us.

※

That evening I read Jimmy my dragon story. He loved it and wanted more, but I had to admit that was as far as I'd got. I was heading for my room, fully intending to write the next chapter straight away, when I heard a crash in the kitchen, followed by a muttered oath, and went running downstairs to find Pa on his hands and knees, trying to sweep up shards of glass out of a puddle of brown liquid. The room smelled like a public house.

'What on earth? Are you all right? Mind you don't cut yourself.'

I fetched an old newspaper from the scullery and, between us, we managed to clear up the mess, wrapping the glass carefully before putting it into the dustbin, just as I'd seen Mum do long ago.

'Thank you, my darling,' he said, rinsing his hands under the tap. 'I was only trying to find a bottle opener and I dropped the damn thing.' As he reached for a tea towel, I noticed his hands were trembling.

'Are you all right, Pa?' I asked. 'You look a bit shaken up.'

'I'll be fine as soon as I get a beer inside me,' he said.

I went to the pantry, but the shelf was empty. 'None left – sorry. Will this do instead?' I said, bringing out a half-empty bottle of sherry. Pa had never been a big drinker, but he did like a tipple from time to time.

'That'll do perfectly.' He poured a large glassful and swigged it back in a single gulp. 'That's better.'

'What's up?'

He demurred for a few moments, trying to put me off. 'Nothing you need to trouble yourself with, my darling.'

'I'm already troubled by what I see,' I said.

'It's this church-window plan,' he said. 'The Waddingtons say they'll pay for everything, but honestly, it's hardly a priority, when the roof is leaking and the loose slabs in the aisle are a veritable death-trap. But I'm being steamrollered, I'm afraid. The wives have already been talking to each other, before I've even had a chance to take the idea to the diocese.' He poured himself another glassful. 'And, frankly, I could do without that, what with everything else.'

'Everything else?'

'It's the church finances, my darling. Not to put too fine a point on it, they're a complete mess. It's worse than I expected.'

'Hasn't Mr Blackman been sorting them out?'

'He's trying to. But it seems the previous incumbent got in a terrible muddle. A substantial sum appears to have gone missing.' He rubbed his temples, looking worn and weary.

'Where's it gone?'

'If I knew that there wouldn't be a problem, would there?' he snapped.

I knew so little about the world of money. We'd never had much, but always enough for the basics of life and so, apart from feeling mildly envious about the luxuries that other girls seemed to prize – large houses, ponies, new clothes, tennis lessons – it never troubled me much. But I knew, from court reports in newspapers, how easily people could get into trouble over money: debts, bankruptcies, lost inheritances, theft. *Theft*. The word left a metallic taste in the mouth. But who would steal from a church?

8

I passed an anxious night worrying about Kit and hoping he had not been too badly hurt, as well as wondering what excuse I could invent to make contact again without being seen as a bother. Then I had a brainwave: we would write a thank-you letter to the family and deliver it by hand, with a bunch of roses from the garden.

As Jimmy and I passed through the gates, a first-floor casement flew open and Kit's head appeared, swathed in a large white bandage.

'Hey there, you two,' he shouted. 'You're a sight for sore eyes. The parents are both out, but the doc said I've got concussion and must take it easy for a few days. I'll come down.'

Despite the bandage and the blue-black shadow on his forehead, he still resembled a Greek god, almost too beautiful to be among us ordinary mortals. Was I already falling in love? No, not yet. That would come later.

'These are for you and your parents,' I said. Jimmy thrust forward the roses and I handed Kit the letter. 'We wanted to thank you for saving him.' I nudged my brother. 'Go on,

Jimmy. What I told you.' I'd been coaching him all the way down the hill.

'Sorry, and thank you,' he said, clear as anything.

'I hope your head is mending?'

'It's fine,' Kit said. 'I woke up with a bit of a headache, but I'll be right as rain. I won't have to wear this thing after tomorrow, and the stitches will come out in a week. Honestly, I don't know why everyone made such a fuss.'

'You were covered in blood. It was very dramatic.'

'Yeah. The shirt's a goner anyway.'

There was a slightly uneasy pause, and I tried to think of something interesting to say. Reluctantly, after a moment, I said, 'Well, we'd better be going.'

Kit glanced up the drive behind me. 'Won't you come in for a bit? I'm under house arrest and as bored as a badger. You won't believe how pleased I am to have visitors. No one else is at home. My father has gone back to London, and Mother is at one of her endless classes – painting or knitting or keeping fit, whatever it is today – and she's given Elsie the day off. It'd cheer me up no end.'

He led us into the kitchen, a room four times the size of our own, with an old-fashioned flagstone floor, a wide table in the centre and a long range – the grown-up version of our old Rayburn – along one side. The worktop and shelves were arrayed with the latest varieties of kitchen equipment, crockery and utensils.

'What shall we have? Lemonade, tea, hot chocolate?' Kit said, opening doors and cupboards randomly, clearly unfamiliar with the kitchen layout. 'Cook made some biscuits the other day, I think.'

'Have you got a vase for these roses?' I asked. 'They could probably do with a drink.'

'Of course, of course . . .' he muttered, pulling open more cupboards. 'Will this do?' He brought out an enormous earthenware jug, far too large for the purpose.

'That'll be fine, for the moment,' I said. 'Where's the sink?'

'Oh, it's out here,' he said. 'Let me. This thing weighs a ton.'

At last we were all settled, sitting at the kitchen table with glasses of lemonade and a plate of delicious raisin biscuits.

'Tell you what,' Kit said, his face brightening now, 'how's about a bit of adventure?' He turned to Jimmy. 'You'd enjoy a bit of fun too, wouldn't you? No climbing walls this time, promise?'

Jimmy nodded, his mouth full of biscuit.

'Should you?' I pointed to the bandage. 'Aren't you supposed to be taking it easy?'

'I'm perfectly fine,' he said. 'And I'll go mad if I have to stay indoors a moment longer. Come on, let's go.'

He led us through the garden, crossing the moat on a narrow footbridge and down a path that led along the bank of the lake for a hundred yards or so, until we reached the wooden structure overhanging the water on stilts that I'd spied from the other side.

'This,' he announced, pulling a key from his back pocket, 'is the boathouse.'

He unlocked the door and pushed it open with some difficulty, inviting us into a dark, dank-smelling space. After my eyes became accustomed to the gloom I realised that the floor of the shed was actually water, with just a narrow walkway all round. Floating, secured with a rope, was a small wooden boat, complete with oars.

'Let me introduce you to the good ship *Mary Jane*,' Kit said. 'Or, as we sometimes call her, *The Jolly Roger*. C'mon then,' he went on, leaping down into the boat.

My brother's hand crept into mine, and I squeezed it to reassure him.

'Where are we going?' I could see no exit to the boat-house, except for the door we'd entered through.

'Wait and see,' he said, helping Jimmy down into the boat first, then me. 'Sit still and don't stand up unless I tell you.'

He unhitched the rope and pushed the boat away towards the front of the hut. It was only then that I noticed the double doors. He slipped two bolts, hooked back the doors and eased the boat out into the open water. There was not a breath of wind; even the finest fronds of the willows were motionless and the lake lay totally still, reflecting the trees in a perfect mirror-image. Only the ripples spreading out from the gentle movement of our boat disturbed the picture.

The first and last time I'd been boating was in a small paddleboat on the Serpentine, with Mum and Jimmy, the summer before she became too unwell for such expeditions. Memories flooded back: the colourful boats, the excited calls of children across the water, the lake glistening like diamonds in the sunshine, the towers of tall buildings shining beyond the trees of Hyde Park. Remembering it made me feel sad and glad, all at once.

'You okay, Molly?'

'Yes, I'm just happy, that's all,' I said. 'It's so beautiful here.'

'Being out on the lake always makes me happy, too.' Kit pulled out the oars and fitted them into the rowlocks, and with a few swift movements we began to glide out towards the middle of the lake.

My brother was sitting perfectly still by my side, his little fingers gripping the edge of the seat.

'How're you doing, Jim-lad?' Kit asked.

'It's fun, eh?' I nudged Jimmy gently. 'We're going out on the water like we did in Hyde Park. With Mum.' There was no chance that he'd recall it; he must have been only five at the time. But I wanted him to remember our mother and the happy times we'd had with her.

'Why didn't your mum come to tea yesterday?' Kit asked.

It was always a difficult one, this, but I usually found it best to answer directly. 'She died a couple of years ago,' I said. 'From cancer.'

'Oh, I'm so sorry. How horrible.' He frowned, concentrating on his rowing for a few moments. 'You must miss her loads.'

'We do. Every day.'

'We all need cheering up, then. I'm going to show you my favourite places.'

There were four islands in the lake. None of them was much to get excited about, just irregularly shaped mounds of land no more than twenty or thirty feet long, covered in grass and shrubby willows, with no distinguishing features. But each island had a name and a little piece of history, and as we passed each one, Kit told us how generations of his mother's family had enjoyed themselves there.

We reached The Retreat first, a flat island quite close to

the shore and nearest the Hall. A narrow boarded walkway led from a small landing stage to a summer house that had seen better days. 'It was built by my grandmother,' Kit said. 'Apparently she couldn't bear being cooped up in the house with the children and used to escape to her island to write her poetry.'

I imagined myself sitting there, notebook in hand, writing my novel. 'Do you still have any of them?' I asked. 'Her poems, I mean.'

'Dunno, to be honest. She's still with us, though. Lives in the Dower House, but doesn't go out these days. Not since my uncle died.'

Rabbit Island, so called because in the past children had kept their pet rabbits there, was the smallest – simply a round hump of land rising a few feet above the water. Even so, the willows had dug their roots deep into what soil they could find and towered high, out of all proportion to the size of the island.

'Mum and her brother thought their precious pets were safe there,' Kit explained. 'But one day the rabbits disappeared and no one knew what had taken them. They thought perhaps a hawk, or a cunning fox that had learned to swim. It was a tragedy. No one's kept rabbits there ever since.'

Pirate's Lair was the largest island of all, a conical hillock with steep sides, away from the main body of the water. Long ago someone had cut away part of the sloping side and built a wooden landing stage, which was now derelict, although it was still possible to make out a signboard roughly painted with a skull and crossbones.

'We used to play here every summer with my cousins,

when I came to stay with Grandma,' Kit said. 'We had a lot of fun.'

'Don't they come any more?'

'Too many sad memories for them after my uncle died, I suppose.' He sounded wistful. Was he actually a bit lonely here in the big house, with his boarding-school friends scattered far and wide for the holidays?

Finally we rowed across to a long, low island called The Crocodile because it had a flat 'snout' end, a hump towards the middle and a tapering 'tail' end.

'Has it got anything to do with the legend?' I asked. 'Old Eli says if the creature is disturbed, it will bring evil to the village.' I laughed, to show I didn't believe it either.

'That old dragon story,' Kit scoffed. 'We don't take any notice.'

'Where . . . dragon?' Jimmy, who had been as good as gold for a full half-hour, began to wriggle in his seat. I put a restraining arm round his shoulder, which he instantly shrugged off.

'He's obsessed with the idea,' I explained.

'It's just the shape of the island, Jim-boy,' Kit said. 'There aren't any real ones. It's only a fairy story.'

I loved the way Kit talked to him: not condescending like so many people, but as you would to a younger brother. Jimmy seemed to accept the explanation and settled down again.

'I used to pretend I was Captain Hook – you know, the pirate from *Peter Pan*. The one with the parrot and the hook for a hand?' Kit went on.

'The one who was chasing the crocodile and could hear him coming, because it had a clock in its stomach?'

'That's the one.'

'I loved that story. But I was always Peter Pan, of course.'

'It's no fun being the goody,' Kit said. 'Although Peter's a strange one, isn't he? I always liked him too. Who would you be, Jimmy?'

Jimmy thought for a moment and then, suddenly and very loudly, he said, 'The parrot!'

Kit began making squawky parrot noises and flapping his elbows like wings, which Jimmy quickly copied and I joined in. Soon we were all laughing so much that Kit had to stop rowing to wipe his eyes. It was wonderful to see my brother so happy, and being included in the joke for once.

Kit took up the oars again. 'Want a go, Molly?'

'I don't know how.'

He laughed. 'You said you'd been on the Serpentine.'

'That was a pedal boat, not a rowing boat. I've never rowed in my life.'

'Then now's the time to learn. Come here, next to me.' He patted the bench beside him. 'You can start with one oar first.'

I moved, keeping my weight low and trying not to make the boat rock too much. Kit showed me how to hold the oar, and the motion you needed to dip the blade into the water, pulling the handle upwards towards you, then down away from you so that it swung back through the air into the right position for the next stroke. I found it impossible at first, and several times ended up 'catching a crab', as he called it – missing the water entirely and nearly falling backwards into the boat. But slowly the rhythm came, and he rowed too, at my speed, counting out loud so that we coordinated our strokes and stopped going round in circles, beginning to move forward in the water. It was an exhilarating feeling.

After a few moments of this, Kit said I was ready to row on my own. He handed me his oar and moved to the small seat in the front of the boat, kneeling behind me with his arms reaching round and holding mine, moving them. 'Pull up and towards you, remember, then down and away.' I tried to follow his directions, but the feel of his breath on my neck and the warmth of his chest on my back were too distracting.

'Come on, Molly, concentrate. You did it before. Just relax and let me help you.'

After a few moments I began to get the rhythm again, and after a while realised that Kit's hands had let go. I was rowing, on my own. We meandered a bit, of course, and I caught a very large crab, which had me falling backwards into his arms, but he set me upright again, and at last I managed to keep in a straight line and gain some speed.

'You've got it, well done. Keep going,' he shouted.

Jimmy laughed and clapped his hands with glee. Then, quite unexpectedly, he stood up, reaching forward, trying to catch the oars and causing the boat to rock alarmingly.

'Me now . . . ?'

'Sit down, Jimmy,' I shouted. 'You'll have us all in the water.'

From behind Kit said calmly, 'Let him have a go, if he wants to.'

'Are you sure?'

'Of course. He's perfectly strong enough. It's just a matter of getting the hang of it. Change places carefully, and I'll show him how.'

I handed over the oars reluctantly, certain we were heading for disaster. What Kit didn't know was that when he couldn't manage something, Jimmy would get frustrated, throw things and walk away. If he threw away the oars, we would be stranded in the middle of the lake.

But my fears proved unfounded. In fact, he seemed to get the knack faster than I'd managed, and before long Jimmy was rowing on his own in a straight line and gaining speed, an enormous grin splitting his face from ear to ear, his face red with the effort.

'Steady now,' Kit said, leaning forward to guide the oars. 'Right hand down, old boy, or we'll end up in the brambles.'

Just then there were voices from the direction of the Hall – hidden behind the long bank of willows and tall grasses – and we heard his mother calling, 'Cooeee. Christopher? Where are you?'

'Bloody hell,' Kit said. 'My mother's back earlier than she said. I'm going to cop it now.'

Selfishly, I thought of myself. Would they blame me for causing yet more trouble, only a day after the accident?

Kit leaned forward and took the oars from Jimmy. 'Move to the back, laddie – careful now. I'm going to row you to the bank, is that okay? You can walk home from there through the woods.' He pulled away with such power that the boat quickly picked up speed. 'Don't want you copping it too, do we? Wouldn't be fair, after me leading you on.'

We reached the bank in a few short minutes. 'Thank you for a lovely afternoon,' I said as we clambered out.

'It was my pleasure, Miss Molly,' he replied, smiling. 'You saved me from terminal boredom. Let's do it again sometime. Now, if you could give me a shove off, I'd better get back, before the old lady goes mental. Wish me luck.'

❧❦❧

That evening, I took out my diary and revisited my list of 'good' and 'not good' things about Wormley:

Good	Not good
Kit! Kit! Kit!	*Pa worried about money*
The lake, especially	*Still miles from anywhere*
The Retreat	*Not much else to do*
Learning to row	*Having to look after Jimmy*
Jimmy happy/learning	*Bus only every two hours*
to row	*Missing my London friends*
Mrs D nice (the best)	
Eli and his stories	
Wild flowers and robins!	

For the first time, the 'good' column was longer than the 'not good' column and I felt happier than at any time since arriving in Wormley. I took out my notebook and wrote the next chapter.

THE UGLY DRAGON
by Molly Goddard

Chapter 2: The importance of forgiving yourself

Jimmy was feeling sad. A few days ago he'd been playing and fell from a wall, hurting someone else on his way down. His father was angry and told him off.

To cheer him up, Jimmy's sister Molly suggested that now the weather was improving they should return to the lake to see whether they could find the dragon again. They decided to take something to eat, in case they got hungry.

They spent the morning baking and, after lunch, walked down through the woods to the lake. Just as before, the dragon appeared as if by magic out of the still, dark waters of the lake, with only a small ripple on the surface before her long green snout popped out of the water.

'Hello, dragon. How do you always know we are here?'

'I can hear your voices,' she said, hauling herself onto the bank. 'Sounds travel quite well through water. And my ears are very sensitive.'

'I can't see any ears,' Molly said.

'They're inside,' she said, rather mysteriously. She tilted her

head and flared her nostrils, peering at Jimmy. 'Can I smell something nice in that bag, by the way?'

'Rock buns,' Jimmy said, 'for our picnic.'

'Yum, yum. I'm very hungry,' the dragon said, her voice more like a growl.

Jimmy pouted. 'They're not meant for dragons.'

'That's silly,' she said. 'Of course they are.'

'I'm not silly,' Jimmy snapped.

'What's got into you today, my young friend?'

Molly explained that Jimmy was still smarting from something their father had said to him. 'But Pa is in a funny mood at the moment,' she added. 'He's got big things on his mind.'

'Ten to one he'll already have completely forgotten why he was cross with you,' the dragon said, munching on a bun. 'Mmm, these are delicious. Most people forgive and forget very easily,' she added.

'But I was being silly,' Jimmy suddenly shouted. 'And it was my fault Kit got hurt.'

'Aha,' the dragon said. 'I see what the problem is. Everyone else has forgiven you, but you haven't managed to forgive yourself. That's the hardest part.'

Jimmy looked confused.

'No long-lasting harm was done, was it?' she asked.

He shook his head.

'And your father hasn't mentioned it since?'

He shook it again.

'And what have you learned?'

'Not to climb on walls,' Jimmy muttered, at last.

'So, now you can forgive yourself. We all do silly things from time to time. You're a lovely, kind boy, Jimmy, and don't you forget it. Now cheer up and pass me another one of those delicious rock buns.'

9

After that I couldn't stop thinking about Kit, the dark hair flopping in his eyes, his laughter, his sense of mischief. When you were with him everything felt tinged with excitement, always on the brink of danger. He made me realise, perhaps for the first time, how tame and dull my own life was, how filled with anxiety about what people, especially the grown-ups – Pa, Mrs D and the others – would think of me.

Being with Kit was intoxicating. Was this what love felt like?

I read the romance novels over and over again. They were mildly risqué and Pa would definitely have disapproved, but while I knew they were silly and unrealistic, it was fun to fantasise, for once. They suited my mood perfectly: filled with passion and longing and heartache, with women who seemed destined always to fall for the wrong kind of men, whose hearts 'beat like fluttering wings', whose 'glorious golden locks tossed in the breeze' and whose breasts 'heaved like billowing waves'.

In my version Kit was always in the starring role, as I

felt the warmth of his chest against my back, the way he held his hands over mine as he taught me to row, and I yearned to feel that again, to have more of him, more and more.

But the Easter holidays were over, so I was unlikely to see him again for at least six weeks, possibly longer. If only I'd suggested that we should write, but of course our parting had been too hurried. I decided to take the initiative:

Dear Kit,

Just a note to thank you for such a lovely day on the lake. I really enjoyed seeing all the islands, and Jimmy won't stop talking about how he's now an expert at rowing – although I try to explain that he mustn't tell Pa or Mrs D, in case you get into trouble.

I expect you are off back to school again now, but it would be lovely to hear from you if you ever feel like writing.

Yours,

Molly

I addressed the envelope to *Kit Waddington, c/o Wormley Hall*, and wrote 'PLEASE FORWARD' in capital letters at the top, hoping it might somehow reach him. And then I waited.

Every other Saturday morning Jimmy and I went to the church with Mrs Diamond and her rota of other ladies to help prepare for Sunday services. They were a kind lot, and this was the one place, I'd discovered, where Jimmy could be sure of being fully accepted. He was allowed to help with the sweeping and dusting, and they put him in charge of retrieving the prayer books from their cupboard and stacking them on the table by the door in piles of ten – the most he could count up to – ready to hand out as the congregation arrived the following day. It made him feel useful and important.

It wasn't expected of us, but it was what Mum always used to do. 'Those volunteers give their time so cheerfully, and with such love and dedication,' she'd say when she returned home from her weekly stint, dark hair glistening with cobwebs. 'They're the true heart of the church, to be honest, and the least I can do is turn up once in a while and lend a hand. It boosts morale no end, and does wonders for your father's reputation.'

That Saturday I was in the vestry, ironing the cotton surplices that we wore in the church choir. The ladies had learned to trust me, and it became my regular job. I found it quite satisfying, seeing that row of beautifully starched and ironed surplices hanging up at the end of the morning, ready for us to wear the following day.

I'd come to enjoy the weekly ritual of dressing up, filing into our places in the choir stalls and singing as lustily as possible. I knew all the tunes already, of course, which was just as well, because the rows of what looked like black tadpoles leaping about on the staves meant nothing to me. But that didn't seem to matter, because we didn't sing any fancy anthems like the choir at St Martin's. Here, our main purpose was to support the congregation through the hymns.

'We need to give worshippers the courage to praise the Lord with their singing,' Mrs Timpson would say at our rehearsals, urging us to sing out. Certainly, without us, the hymns would have been a feeble affair, several beats behind the organ and at least a tone flat.

As I ironed, I listened to the ladies' conversations – they were always enlightening. By the end of a session I would have caught up with the news of so-and-so's recovery from an operation for unexplained 'women's troubles', and the fate of another beleaguered soul whose husband apparently disappeared for days at a time. 'He's home again,' they'd say, shaking their heads. 'Though why she do take him back every time's a mystery, for sure.'

That day, over the chatter of the other volunteers, I heard the familiar squeak of the church-door hinges and assumed it was another volunteer arriving, until that familiar voice boomed out.

'Good morning, ladies. Hope you don't mind if we come in to take a gander at this church window? We won't get in the way of your work, I promise.'

Hidden from the visitors, the ladies with me in the vestry left off their mending and lifted their heads to listen.

'That'll be that nice Mr Blackman, I'll be bound,' one of them whispered.

'Ain't his wife a beauty?' said the other. 'The new one, I mean.'

'*New* wife?' I asked. 'What happened to the old one?'

'No one knows exactly. Swapped for a younger version, they say. All happened afore they come here.'

'How long have they been here then?'

'Ooh, just a few years – six or seven mebbe?'

'They do good things for the village, them two. Old Joe works for 'im, as well as Mrs Tebbutt, you know.'

'There's bin talk about them up at the big house paying for a new stained glass.'

'Mrs Blackman's an artist,' was the reply. 'She's offered to design it.'

'Well, ain't that a nice thing to do?'

The sour smell of scorched cotton reached my nostrils. I jerked up the iron, but it was too late. The cover of the ironing board was stained with a pale-brown mark. I sent up a small prayer of thanks that it was not the surplice itself that I'd ruined.

❦

The plan for the new window moved quickly. Pa was keen to spread the good news in the first-ever edition of the revived parish newsletter, grandly titled *The Wormley Village News*. The copy was all written, he said, but Miss Calver needed help with the printing, so I gladly offered, so long as Mrs D could look after Jimmy for the morning.

Miss Calver – I knew from Mrs D that her first name was Violet, but she never invited me to use it and insisted on calling me 'Miss Goddard' – lived alone in a tiny end-of-terrace cottage towards the top part of the village. She ushered me into a small room over-filled with furniture, every surface overflowing with books and papers, and without a further word of small talk, began to explain our task for the morning. As a first edition, it was to be a modest affair: a single sheet of paper, double-sided and folded in two. We were to print three hundred copies, one for each house in the village. It would be reproduced on the hulking metal contraption lurking in the corner of the room, which she called a 'Gestetner'.

The content included the list of services, the volunteer rota for cleaning and flowers, and the very brief column of 'Hatches, Matches and Dispatches' of which, since our arrival, there had been no weddings, two deaths and only a single birth. 'We're a declining breed,' she commented drily.

There was a short letter from Pa, saying how pleased he was to have been chosen to be the vicar of such a beautiful village and thanking everyone for making him and his family so welcome. And on the back page was this:

NEW STAINED GLASS FOR CHURCH WINDOW

Some residents will recall the terrible night when a German bomber dropped its load onto our village, killing two residents, destroying four homes and blowing out the windows of several others, including the beautiful medieval stained glass in the east transept of All Saints Church.

Now, through the generosity of Mr and Mrs Waddington of Wormley Hall, the stained glass will be replaced in the East Window. It will be dedicated to the memory of those who lost their lives in two world wars, and a memorial plaque will honour Captain David Burrows, Mrs Waddington's brother, who died in 1944 while fighting to liberate Italy.

We are especially fortunate that local resident Mrs

Melissa Blackman, a gifted artist, has offered her services
to design the glass, free of charge.

Miss Calver had already typed the content onto two
fragile-looking waxed stencil sheets. One of these was
attached to a drum pressed onto an inky pad, against which
we would have to rotate three hundred sheets of paper
twice, once for each side. Then we would have to fold them.

'What do you think about this stained-glass plan, Miss
Calver?' I asked, panting slightly with the effort of winding
the heavy handle as the slightly smudged sheets flicked out
into a slowly growing pile.

'It's not my job to have an opinion,' she said, with a wry
smile. 'Our job is to report, as truthfully as possible. First
law of journalism, young lady.' She refilled her whisky glass
and took a long slug. 'But if you want my personal view,
I wouldn't trust anything that man is involved in.'

'Mr Blackman?'

'"The Blackness", they call him.'

I looked up at her. 'Crikey, that bad?'

She lit a cigarillo. 'Tell your father to take care around
that man,' she said, batting away clouds of smoke with her
spare hand.

'But he's the church treasurer . . .'

'Indeed.' The word hung in the room, weighted with
meaning.

'And is that a problem?'

'Let's just say we go back a long way. But I like your
enquiring spirit, Miss Goddard,' she said, laughing now.
'Come on, girl, no slacking. You'll never get those copies
through if you slow down. Let's get this job done, shall we?'

After we'd finished, she made me a cup of tea and poured herself another glass of whisky. 'Shall we sit outside? It's a lovely day, for a change.'

The house might have been in need of a lick of paint, but her garden was immaculate: filled with colourful spring bulbs, with a large patch dedicated to vegetables and a small orchard of fruit trees covered in lacy blossom. In the shelter of the outhouse was an ancient bench, where we both sat in the unaccustomed warmth of the sunshine.

'Your father says you'd like to be a writer, Molly,' she said, lighting another cigarillo.

'Oh, it's nothing,' I said, feeling my cheeks colouring.

'It's the best age to begin,' she said.

'Why? When did you start, Miss Calver?'

'About your age. I sent articles to my local newspaper under a boy's name. John Calver's "Stories from the school gate",' she said dreamily. 'Dear John did quite well for a while.'

'What happened then?'

'They twigged that I was a sixteen-year-old girl and told my parents. And that put a stop to that. But I'd got the bug by then, and after college I went back and badgered them till they let me make coffee and type up copy. Later I got to be their first-ever woman war correspondent. Best days of my life, Molly. So keep up the writing, my dear. And if you ever want someone to read your stuff, I'd be happy to help.'

I thanked her for her kindness, but knew that was many months away, even years. I was nowhere near being ready to show anyone my dragon story – except for Jimmy, of course.

That weekend Jimmy and me delivered the newsletter, walking the streets and pathways of the village, reaching hidden-away cottages you'd hardly know were there, and steeling ourselves to open letter boxes behind which barked fierce dogs. We even went down to the Hall and I plucked up the courage to ring the bell, hoping for a chance to ask whether they had been able to forward my letter to Kit. It had been three weeks now, and I'd received no answer. But the bell rang hollowly inside and no one came to the door, not even a maid, so I had to post the *Village News* through their letter box.

Why hadn't Kit replied to my letter? Had he even received it? Perhaps he was just a terrible correspondent. Most boys were, Dinah tried to reassure me when, in desperation, I finally confided in her. Or perhaps he really didn't care and had forgotten all about me? The thought was almost too painful to bear. I took refuge in reading yet more romance novels, weeping in sympathy with the heroines as they nursed their sorrows. *He'd broken her heart and walked out of her life without so much as a flicker of remorse in those haunting eyes.*

The next day we arrived home from completing the newsletter deliveries to find Pa at the dining-room table.

'Come and take a look at this,' he called.

We hastened in. Covering nearly the whole table was a large sheet of paper held down with books at either corner. It took a few moments to realise that we were looking at the reverse side of two strips of wallpaper pasted together to create a canvas more than a yard wide and treble that in length. A complex drawing covered the whole of the paper, coloured in with water paint.

The design was divided lengthwise into what I now saw represented the two panes of a church window, separated by a stone pillar – the 'mullion' was what Pa called it. On either side of it were portraits of two knights, a man and a woman, both in full medieval suits of armour. She was holding a shield decorated with the red cross of the English flag. He had a sword in one hand, and in the other a set of scales that appeared to be balancing an effigy of Christ on the cross against what looked like a proper fire-throwing dragon.

'Is he weighing Christianity against heathen legend?'

'Who knows?' Pa said with a shrug. 'Let's have a look at the rest.'

When he unrolled the lower end of the scroll, Jimmy shouted, 'Croc . . . croc.'

Sure enough, at the feet of the two knights was an extraordinary scene. In the background a castle stood on a hill; to the right a lady kneeled with her arms beseechingly outstretched and, on the left-hand side, a knight was mounted on a rearing white horse. He was holding a very long stick striped like a barber's pole and seemed to be attempting to poke out the eye of a vast, bright-green and very vicious-looking crocodile, with a malevolent eye and rows of pointy teeth – nothing like the friendly dragon character I'd imagined for my story. Dangling from its lips were two thin, pale legs, apparently still alive and waving, even though the rest of the body had been fully consumed.

It was a scene so graphic that it was almost comical, and I actually laughed. 'That's a bit gory, isn't it?'

'Melissa Blackman says the crocodile – or should we call it a dragon? – terrorised the villages of St Mary's and

Wormley for years and years, until they persuaded a knight to come and kill it.'

'What do *you* think, Pa?'

He pondered for a moment. 'I'm not entirely sure, my darling. We'll have to run the design past the diocese first, in any case.' He rolled up the scrolls of paper, put them to the side of his desk and gave a deep sigh. 'To be honest, I could do without another ruddy problem right now.'

10

In May and June the evenings grew longer and the trees and hedgerows bloomed even more abundantly. To Jimmy and me, used only to whatever nature the city could provide – plane trees, wild buddleia blooming on bomb sites and neat planting in the parks – the sight was astonishing. White borders of delicate cow parsley laced every verge, and with the help of the colour illustrations in Mrs Diamond's *Wild Flowers of the British Isles* I could soon tell the difference between dandelions, daisies, primroses and cowslips. The country names stirred my imagination, each one so descriptive and evocative: cranesbill, loosestrife, meadowsweet, foxglove, stitchwort and willow herb.

Jimmy was never happier than when we were out in the woods and fields, exploring new routes and discovering wonderful, secret places. One Saturday we took a picnic up to the copse of Scots pines that topped the hill overlooking the valley. Local folk knew it simply as The Pines. It consisted, back then, of just a dozen or more ancient trees, but in their position at the very pinnacle of the hill they could be seen for miles around.

'Go to see Eli now?' Jimmy said, as I packed up the picnic.

'We can check whether he's at home. I don't see any smoke,' I said.

We took the path downwards to the junction, then followed the whitewashed stones. There was no one there, the hut was locked. But a few seconds later we heard whistling.

Sarge appeared first, his tail wagging like a flag in a stiff breeze. He didn't bark any more. We were old friends now. His master followed close behind, and Jimmy ran forward to greet him. If he'd had a tail, he would have been wagging it as furiously as Sarge.

'Well, well, well, who do have we here?' the old man said, grinning widely as he ruffled Jimmy's hair. 'Thass a sight for sore eyes. I'm right ready for a brew and a biscuit. How's about you?' He went to the side of the hut and reached under the arch of the wheel, pulling out a key. 'Come on, laddie. Let's get that ole kettle on.'

He showed Jimmy how to lay the fire in the black pot-bellied stove that sat on four legs near the doorway, its chimney reaching up through the ceiling. First he screwed up coils of newspaper – 'not too tight or it won't catch' – then topped it with twigs of fine kindling, carefully stored in an alcove to make sure they were good and dry. On top of this careful construction he placed a small log.

Then he reached up to the shelf and took down a large box of Swan Vestas. 'Now come the magic,' he said, lighting the newspaper coils at each side before closing the door. 'We'll let that draw for a minute or two, then we can add a big 'un when it get going.' Jimmy watched, fascinated, as the fire caught and the flames flickered red behind the fan-shaped vent in the stove door.

While they were lighting the stove I took a moment to glance round the rest of the hut. An arched ceiling made the single room appear larger than I'd expected. At the far end, curtains of old army blankets were drawn back to reveal a bed with drawers beneath. A cupboard and shelves held a few cooking utensils – wooden spoons, blackened saucepans and a battered frying pan. There was no sink, but a large metal milk churn stood by the door, filled with water. It was a shock to realise that Eli had to haul every pint that he needed either from the stream or from a tap in the village. A kettle rested on the hob.

I hadn't considered that Eli would be much of a reader, but a quick glance at the bookshelf proved that his interests were varied: a few Agatha Christie mysteries, *Pride and Prejudice*, *A Christmas Carol*, a book of collected English poetry, a small encyclopaedia and *The Countryman's Book of Birds*. Propping them up at one end was a pile of *London Illustrated News* magazines and, at the other, a box-file marked 'Land'.

'That 'on't take long now.' Eli showed Jimmy how to fill the kettle with water from the churn using a large soup ladle, placing it back on the hob. It sizzled immediately and began to hum. Before long we were sitting outside, enjoying mugs of scalding hot honey-sweetened tea, with Eli teaching us how to distinguish different birds from the cacophony of song in the woods that day.

The chiffchaff was the easiest, because the song simply consisted of repeating its name over and over again. Robins, blackbirds and wrens were more tuneful, but to my ear they all sounded much the same. The cuckoo, on the other hand, was unmistakeable.

'Me heart allus lifts when I hears the first one each spring,' Eli said. 'It tells me I've survived another winter.'

'Don't they sing in the winter?'

'Happen they do, but not here,' he said. 'They only stick around a few months, then they fly south, like the swallows. To Africa, so folk believe. They's naughty creatures, though, laying in the nests of littler birds and pushin' out them fledglings. But their song do cheer me up, all the same. Brings good luck, but only if you hears it with your right ear.'

That made me laugh. 'How can you tell which ear you're hearing it with?'

He ignored my question, cocking his head and concentrating hard. 'Ah. Now here's a new 'un. Listen to them whistles and clucks.' He listened some more. 'Is a barley bird,' he declared triumphantly. 'First of the year. You're mighty honoured, my little friends.'

'Barley bird?'

'Cos it come with the first heads of the barley. Most call it a nightingale. Listen.' Now I could hear it, a series of ticks and gurgles followed by a few rising liquid phrases, not really a song in the proper sense.

'I thought they only sang at night.'

'Thass only cos most birds stop arter dusk, so at night you hear just the nightingale. Best sound in the world, when the woods is silent.'

He sat back, closing his eyes, to concentrate. I tried it too, and it was remarkable how much clearer the sounds became. When I opened them again I watched Eli, his face peaceful, pipe resting in his hands. Even the deepest wrinkles seemed to flatten out and he appeared younger, the most contented man in the world.

'You love it here, don't you, Eli?' I said.

'Who wouldn't, with an orchestra like that on me doorstep every day?'

'What about the winters? Don't you get cold?'

'There's plenty of wood for me little stove and we gets by well enough, doesn't we, Sarge?' he said, rubbing the dog's scraggy neck. It groaned appreciatively. 'Well, we woodda, if they'd ruddy well let us be.'

Something in his tone alarmed me. 'Who's *they*, Mr Eli?'

He shook his head. 'Ach, you don't want to know. Besides, he says if I talks about it, that'll be the worse for me.'

'Who says that? Is someone threatening you?'

'Not exactly. But they wants us off of this land.'

'But why? I don't understand.'

He offered no explanation. But even though the sun was still shining and the sky perfectly blue, the peaceful mood of the woodland had disappeared.

'Look, Mr Eli, I know Pa thinks highly of your work in the churchyard. And I'm sure he'd come to your aid, if you need it. You only have to ask.'

'Thank you, my dearies,' he said, simply. 'Come see me again, won't you?'

* * *

'Hello, we're back,' I called. 'Anyone home?'

Mrs D's face appeared round the kitchen door, finger to her lips. 'Your father's in a meeting with Mr Blackman. Says they mustn't be disturbed.'

My heart sank. I took a book into the garden, hoping for a few moments of peace, but after about five minutes Jimmy came outside, pestering me, so I gave up the idea of revising and suggested we did some weeding. Mr D did his best with the garden, mowing the lawn every few weeks and cutting back the more unruly shrubs, but his artificial leg made it hard for him to kneel, for reaching into the flower beds. Earlier that week I'd found Pa walking around the garden, pulling ineffectually at the weeds strangling the rose bushes.

So, taking a trug and a couple of pairs of gardening gloves from the greenhouse, I showed Jimmy how to identify and pull out the bindweed, and how to avoid getting pricked by the roses. He loved to feel useful and proved to be surprisingly careful in his task.

We'd been at work only a few moments when I heard the latch of the dining-room window and saw Pa's hand pushing open the casement a few yards away. Then, as clearly as though we were in the same room, I heard him say, '. . . and are you telling me that this money has just disappeared into thin air?'

We should have moved to another part of the garden, but the longer I dithered, the more difficult it became. Henry Blackman seemed to emphasise every syllable with a series of vocal hammer blows: 'The church has three bank accounts: current, revenue and capital. The previous incumbent and I were signatories to the current and revenue accounts, but because of a mix-up at the bank, they failed to change the signatories for the capital account. I have only recently been able to gain access to one of them to check out how much is in it.'

'And . . . ?'

'And it's empty.'

'*Empty?*'

'As I said, empty.'

'How much was supposed to be in it?'

'Five thousand pounds. Or thereabouts.'

I nearly dropped my trowel. *Five thousand pounds.* Enough to buy several houses.

After a moment of silence, I heard Pa again: 'Well, there has to be a rational explanation. We need to go to the bank together to sort it out.'

'Of course,' Blackman said. 'But I need to add that, should we not be able to resolve this issue, Vicar, the church will be in dire financial straits. It will be very difficult to get the diocese to help us at the moment, with so many damaged churches needing restoration. And with a small population, raising funds is a very tall order.'

'You don't need to tell me that, Henry.'

'But I think I know a way to solve it.'

'I'm all ears.'

'My proposal is that we should consider selling some of our land.'

In the silence that followed, I imagined Pa tugging at his earlobe. 'We don't have any land, do we?' he said. 'Save that small piece of woodland behind the church. That can't be worth much.'

'That is where you are wrong, Vicar. I've been advised that land could raise several thousand pounds. But not with an illegal tenant in place. You are aware, are you not, of the illegal encampment in the woods?'

'I haven't seen any tents down there,' Pa said.

'Not tents. But an old shepherd's hut appears to be continuously occupied, and with no lease, which is entirely irregular and contrary to village by-laws.'

A shepherd's hut? He was talking about Eli's hut. My heart began to thud, crashing inside my ribs.

'How do you know that it is continuously occupied?' Pa asked.

'Because I have been keeping notes,' was Blackman's reply. 'If you want to check, they are all here in my file, dated and signed.'

The longer I listened, the more angry I became. Had he really been lurking in the woods, spying on the old man and his every move? Eli had gone to live in the hut when his house was bombed and his wife was killed, for heaven's sake. He was an old man, and he loved it there. But something else was also becoming very clear. Mr Blackman was clever, he knew his way around property law and he clearly hated to be challenged.

'Look here,' Pa said, more firmly now. 'I'm all in favour of making things regular. And I'm certainly in favour of sorting out our finances. But we need to be mindful and humane in the way we do it. Surely we must follow Christian principles? Hounding people out of their homes is not the way to do it.'

'Just one last thing, Vicar.' Blackman's voice went so low that I had to strain to hear it. 'I recommend that this matter should remain confidential between you and me. It would not do for people to start suspecting any irregularities, so early in your incumbency. Are you agreed?'

Irregularities. So early in your incumbency. In these few

short phrases, Blackman had made his meaning perfectly clear: Do as I suggest, or you will get the blame.

My father was being blackmailed.

❦

Later, when I knocked on the door of his study, Pa managed a weary smile. 'Hello, sweetheart. How was your picnic?'

'Fine, thanks. Jimmy and I have been doing some gardening.'

'Good, good,' he said, distractedly shuffling papers.

'I've got a confession to make,' I said.

'Spit it out, sweetheart.'

I told him what I'd overheard through the window.

He frowned. 'This was a confidential matter, Molly. You shouldn't have been listening. It is none of your business.'

'Has five thousand pounds really gone missing?'

He looked up sharply. 'So the bank says. But I'm sure there's been a mistake, somewhere. Don't worry, my love, we'll sort it out soon enough.'

'By selling the woodland? And kicking out Eli? That's so unfair. He's not doing anything wrong living there. His house was bombed in the war, you know, and his wife was killed.'

Pa nodded. 'Bad business really, poor old fellow.'

'You won't evict him, will you?'

'Not if I can help it. I won't support the sale of the land. But I can safely say that my honeymoon period is well and truly over.'

'Mr Blackman's trying to blackmail you, isn't he?'

He looked genuinely surprised. 'I wouldn't use that word, exactly . . .'

'But that is what he meant: suggesting that your conversation should be confidential, for now.'

Pa's shoulders seemed to slump and he sank back into his chair. 'I suppose you're right, my dearest. I suppose you're right,' he murmured again.

'I'm so sorry, Pa. Please let me know if there is anything I can do.'

His hand on mine was warm and reassuring, but his eyes were full of confusion and worry. 'Thank you, dearest. I appreciate that. I remain confident that a visit to the bank will sort out the problem of the missing money. But there are other battles to be fought in this village, and I'm not at all certain of winning. Right now I think I'll go over to the church, to pray for guidance.'

I truly hoped that his God would step up to the mark this time and show Pa the way out of this horrible mess.

Using the excuse of returning the few undelivered newsletters, I checked that Mrs D could keep an eye on Jimmy and went up the street to see Miss Calver.

'My dear, what's happened? Has there been an emergency?' She was not one for small talk.

'What do you know about Eli Chadwick and his hut, Miss Calver?'

'How long have you got?'

'As long as you have the time for.'

'Then you'd better come in.'

Once settled with her whisky glass and a lit cigarillo, she asked, 'So, Miss Goddard, what do *you* know about Mr Chadwick?'

'I know he's one of the few people in the village who's shown any kindness to my brother,' I began.

'And . . .'

'And we've been to his hut and we can see how much he likes it.'

'And . . .'

'And I've heard that some people want to get him off the land, because it belongs to the church. There's a proposal to sell it, to fill the hole in the church's finances.'

'Some people?'

I was beginning to understand how she was employing her interview skills and decided to try turning the tables. 'I think you know who, Miss Calver.'

She gave a loud guffaw. 'Very good, Miss Goddard. You will go far.' She sucked on her cigarillo. 'I do indeed. Could it be the person we spoke about a few days ago?'

Even though I barely knew her I felt, instinctively, that I could trust her. 'Apparently Eli's hut is on church land and he hasn't got a lease.'

'Go on.'

'I haven't got any more to tell you,' I said. 'But I'd love to know why Blackman seems to have it in for Eli.'

'Goes back quite a few years,' she said. 'I'll not trouble you with the details, save to say they've had their differences in the past, these two men. Eli knows more about Mr Blackman and his dealings with the previous incumbent than he's ever divulged – of that I am sure. Which is probably why Blackman fears him. But as I said before, and as

I learned to my cost a couple of years ago, the Blackness is not a man to be trifled with.'

'To *your* cost?' I was shocked. She'd had her differences with him, too?

She shook her head. 'Don't press me, Miss Goddard. Water under the bridge and all that.'

'But is there anything we can do to help Eli?'

She emptied her glass. 'My advice would be to watch and wait. Tell your pa to be very careful, if possible. And come back to me if you hear any more, won't you?'

When I got back to the house Mrs D had gone home, and a note said that Jimmy was with Pa at the church. But when I got there, I found Pa in the vestry, looking through some old ledgers.

'Have you seen Jimmy?' I said.

He stood up unsteadily, his breath sickly with the sweet smell of communion wine.

'For heaven's sake, Pa. He's supposed to be with you.'

'He was here a moment ago,' he said, his voice slurred.

'What are you doing with those old account books?'

'Trying to work out . . . to make sense . . .'

'Come on, let's get you home,' I said, taking his arm. 'You need to eat some supper and get a good night's sleep.'

Soon afterwards Jimmy arrived back, beaming from ear to ear, clasping a bunch of daisies. 'Love you,' he said, presenting them to me with a little bow. I tried to smile, and arranged them in an eggcup as the centrepiece for our supper. How could I feel cross with my brother when it was Pa who'd been the irresponsible one, who had failed to take care of him?

Once they had both gone to bed I sat out in the garden for a while, listening to the evening bird chorus, which I usually loved. But even that could not soothe the worries churning in my head. Through all that had happened to us, Pa had always been the single strong and reliable person in my life. If he weakened or cracked, where would that leave Jimmy and me?

Nothing happened at once, of course; it never does. It's only when you look back on it – weeks or even months later – that you realise it was the start of the horrible things that followed.

It was a village of just a few hundred people, and everyone knew everyone else. What we innocent new arrivals hadn't yet discovered was that, in some people's minds at least, knowing someone does not mean you owe them any loyalty, or even kindness. Some people have other priorities, although heaven knows it's sometimes almost impossible to work out what they are, and why.

What we had also failed to understand is that in a small community it is almost impossible to stay neutral. You have to take sides and, as in medieval times, when the leaders of your side fall out of favour, you are bound to fall with them.

THE UGLY DRAGON
by Molly Goddard

Chapter 3: Not everything is always as it seems

This time it was the dragon's turn to look sad. Her scales seemed droopy, her tail flopped to the ground and she was barely showing her teeth at all.

Jimmy opened up the bag of flapjacks that he had with him and she cheered up a little.

'Who'd have thought dragons would like flapjacks?' he said, as they munched.

She didn't reply.

'There's still something wrong, isn't there?' he asked. 'You can talk to me, you know?'

She shivered her scales and said nothing.

'You really cheered me up, last time we met. Talking helps.'

At last she began: 'The thing is, Jimmy, I feel like a fraud. I hoped to grow up into a proper dragon, but it's been hundreds of years now and I still haven't got any wings, I can't blow fire and I'm afraid of knights and swords.'

'You're still quite scary, though,' he said. 'All those teeth.'

'You're very kind. But you must have noticed that I'm green,

my legs are short and I've got knobbly skin instead of scales. It's no wonder they called me ugly. But if I'm not a proper dragon, what on earth am I?'

Next day Jimmy and his sister went back to the lake, with his copy of his storybook about Peter Pan. He opened the page they'd marked and showed it to the dragon.

'What on earth is that?' she asked.

'It's a crocodile,' he said. 'It's green, has short legs, knobbly skin and lots of teeth. But it hasn't got any wings. And it doesn't breathe fire.'

'Heavens, it's just like me,' she said, crawling forward to the edge of the lake and tipping her head sideways to peer at her reflection in the water. 'So you think I could be a crocodile – not a dragon after all?' By now she was smiling with all her teeth.

'I think it's a definite possibility. And if it's true, then you are definitely the most beautiful crocodile I've ever met,' he said. 'Isn't that better than being an ugly dragon?'

'Much better,' she said, nudging him affectionately with her snout.

II

It was the last day of the summer term and anyone observing our weepy farewells would have believed us to be parting forever, not for just a few weeks.

On the bus home, even with Jimmy at my side, I found myself feeling bereft and empty, staring at the unending stretches of countryside going past. There was still no news from Kit, and I was tired of reading trashy romances. There were only so many happy endings I could take, when there didn't seem to be any prospect of one for me. To hell with Kit! He didn't deserve me anyway, that's what Dinah said. 'There's plenty of fish in the sea,' she said breezily. Except that in terms of boyfriend choice, Wormley was more of a puddle than an ocean.

And now six long weeks of summer holidays yawned ahead, with nothing to do except look after Jimmy and try to make sure he didn't wander off or get into trouble. Pa seemed increasingly distracted and was often away at meetings, or at the church. I tried to suggest he should come for walks with me and Jimmy, now that the better weather had arrived, but he put on that falsely jolly smile and said he was sure we'd enjoy ourselves better without a boring old adult coming along. I watched for any further evidence of him drinking too much, but either it was under control or he'd got better at hiding it.

That first week of the holidays Mrs D kept us busy, helping make cakes for the church fete. They needed dozens of sponges, loaf cakes, fairy cakes, scones and biscuits. 'My stall raises more money than most of the others, and it's the most popular; we usually sell out within minutes,' she said with a glow of modest pride, taking another batch of raisin scones from the oven.

'Is this fluffy enough?' I asked, stopping to stretch my back after what felt like hours of creaming an enormous bowl of butter and sugar. Jimmy had been set to work on a smaller task, but had given up after only a few minutes and gone into the garden. My arm ached and my head throbbed, but I wasn't allowed to complain, because Pa told us Mrs D had been going without her own personal rations for months to hoard enough sugar, flour and butter to make these cakes. 'Such a generous woman,' he said. 'The money we raise from the fete is direly needed, and it's the least we can do to support her.'

The day of the fete dawned dry; not exactly sunny, but at least no rain was forecast. At least that was what Mr Diamond had predicted, based on the long strand of brown seaweed that hung in the porch of his cottage, and which always appeared to be uncannily accurate.

Jimmy and I helped carry fifteen Victoria sponge cakes, ten ginger and ten honey loaf cakes, nearly fifty iced fairy cakes and as many raisin scones across to the playing field, laying them out on one of the trestle tables from the village hall, covered with a tablecloth of Mrs D's pristine white bed sheet.

The crowds arrived – more people than I'd ever imagined, and certainly more than any I'd ever seen in church. I glanced round anxiously, looking for the Waddingtons, hoping against hope that Kit might come and we could meet again in a casual kind of way, resuming our friendship, but there was no sign of him.

Soon enough it was eleven o'clock. Pa stood precariously on a chair to declare the fete officially open, and within seconds our stall was thronged with eager customers. Just as Mrs D had warned, it was cleared in a matter of twenty minutes, save for a few slightly wonky scones and a fairy cake with Jimmy's fingerprint in the icing.

'Now off you go, you two, and enjoy the fete. You've earned a bit of fun,' Mrs D said, reaching into the cash belt tied round her waist and pressing two sixpenny pieces into my hand. 'That's for the both of you, mind. Have a go on some of them stalls.'

Jimmy dragged me towards a table stall stacked with bottles. 'Orange juice . . .' he said, with an expectant grin. It was only when we got closer that I noticed the stall was manned by Melissa Blackman. Just as we approached, her husband appeared and my heart sank. I had no desire to face the man I'd come to think of as Eli's enemy number one, but Jimmy was determined.

'Hello, laddie,' Mr Blackman said, with a smile that seemed to have been pasted on at the last minute. 'And Miss Molly. What a pleasure.'

'Can we buy two bottles of orange pop, please?' I asked in my politest voice.

'Well, my dear, the drinks are not for sale, I'm afraid. It's a kind of tombola, you see. You have to buy a tuppenny ticket and see it if matches the number on a bottle.'

'And if it doesn't match?'

'Then I'm afraid you get nothing. It's like a lucky dip, if you like,' he explained, enunciating over-carefully. I hated it when people patronised my brother. Jimmy didn't understand, of course, and insisted on buying a tuppenny ticket, which to my astonishment turned out to match one of the bottles, except that it was a bottle of home-made beer.

'Could we swap it for orange?' I asked.

'Sorry, the rules are that you can only take the bottle that matches your ticket.'

I considered asking him to show me the book of rules – which he had no doubt written in triplicate – but thought better of it. He was already holding out the beer bottle. 'Your father will enjoy it,' he said. He certainly would, I thought to myself, if I let him near it. Which I wouldn't.

Jimmy took the bottle, clasping it to his chest like a prized possession. 'Drink it now?'

'No, Jimmy, it's beer. Alcohol. Not suitable for children. Let's go and find you some orange juice instead,' I whispered, taking his hand.

'No, *now*. Thirsty,' he said, his feet planted firmly on the ground and his face crumpled. He was building up to a proper tantrum. '*My* drink,' he shouted.

'I said we'll get you something else. Look, over there.' I pointed to the refreshments tent.

'No. Won't.' He stamped his foot and tossed the beer bottle to the ground, the cork blew out and brown fizzy liquid sprayed out all over the grass. Good riddance, I thought. At least I wouldn't have to hide it from Pa. A gang of boys nearby turned to watch and started giggling.

'You okay?' asked one. 'Anything wrong?'

'No, there's *nothing* wrong,' I snapped back, the flush rising on my cheeks.

It was only once the boys moved on that I realised the one who'd spoken – and I'd snapped at – was Robert, Kit's friend.

Jimmy's mood could switch from night to day in a second; he was suddenly all sweet and sorry. 'Orange juice now?'

We were sitting outside the refreshment tent, sipping home-made lemonade, when there was a loud bellow of laughter from a nearby stall. It was those same boys again: Robert and three others all around the same age, who'd been at our Christmas party. They were crowded around a curious contraption: a diagonal drainpipe fixed to a frame. Accompanied by much joshing and hilarity, they took it in turns to smash the end of the pipe with a rounders bat. After watching enviously for a few moments, I decided to swallow my pride and, when we'd finished our drinks, took Jimmy over to join them.

'Hello again,' Robert said. 'You're the vicar's daughter, aren't you?'

'Yes, I'm Molly Goddard. You're Robert?'

'Robert Parsons, at your service.' He gave a mock salute.

'Sorry for snapping just now. I thought you were making fun of my brother.'

He looked at his feet, suddenly awkward.

The stallholder was George Diamond. 'Any good at "Catch the Rat", Jimmy?'

'What do you have to do?' I asked.

'Tuppence for six tries, Miss Molly,' he said, holding up an old sock stuffed with something heavy. 'I drop this into the top of the pipe and you have to hit it when it comes out the other end. Like catching a rat in a drainpipe. If you catch it, you get a lollipop or a sherbet dip.'

It looked easy enough, but after several attempts I began to understand what all the laughter had been about. It was the most infuriating game in the world. I tried every tactic: smashing the bat just as soon as the rat had disappeared; waiting two seconds before whacking it; and hammering the frame constantly. The boys encouraged me, cheering and booing, and somehow my failure hardly mattered. I hadn't laughed so much in weeks.

'Me now?' Jimmy tugged at my sleeve, desperate to have a go.

'Of course.' I handed George another tuppence.

Jimmy held the bat over his shoulder and leaned in to peer up the pipe.

'Stand back a bit, laddie,' Mr D said. 'Okay, that's right. Now, are you ready?'

He missed the first two 'rats' but then, with his face set in grim determination, whacked the third as hard as he could and, to everyone's astonishment, caught it fair and square. He continued whacking the stuffed sock until Mr Diamond stopped him. 'That's properly dead now, young man, and you've won two lollipops, one for you and one for your sister. Or would you prefer sherbet?'

As we turned to leave, Robert came to my side. 'Are you around for the rest of the holidays?'

'I'm always around,' I said. 'Vicars don't really get holidays.'

The other boys were calling him. 'Sorry, I've got to go. But let's meet up sometime.'

'That'd be nice,' I said to his departing back.

At least someone liked me.

Jimmy and I stayed late at the fete, helping to fold up the trestle tables and trundle them on wheelbarrows back to the village hall, then picking up every scrap of litter off the grass. By the time we left, the sports ground had been returned to a pristine swathe of green, as though the fete had never taken place.

'Had a nice time, Jim?' I asked, as we walked the short distance home.

'Yup.' He skipped ahead, trying to chase our shadows, made twice the length in the low sun. The air was still warm, growing thicker as it always appears to towards sunset after a hot day, and I felt as happy as I'd ever been since our move to the village. Kit hadn't turned up, which was disappointing, but I'd been helpful all day and Mrs D was full of praise. Jimmy had been well behaved, on the whole. And Pa had seemed relaxed and cheerful – I'd spied him smiling as he chatted to groups of parishioners. Best of all, I'd made a new friend. Perhaps things were taking a turn for the better.

Several days later I was upstairs at my dressing table, trying out different hairstyles, when the doorbell rang. There was nothing unusual in that, the vicarage was full of comings and goings – parishioners seeking moral or religious guidance, church staff needing practical advice, others arriving for meetings.

It was usually possible to tell who it was, even before opening the door: parishioners gave a single discreet knock that could easily be missed; church colleagues knocked jauntily, sometimes a rhythmic tap-tappy-tap-tap; important diocesan people gave a confidently firm double knock. The likes of Blackman and his cronies leaned on the bell and brayed importantly on the porch as they waited.

This one was different: three short, gentle rings, like the start of a piece of classical music. 'Get that, someone, please,' I heard Pa shouting from his study, followed by Jimmy's footsteps clomping to the front door.

Then I heard Mrs D. 'Can I help you, young man?'

'Er . . . I've come to see Molly.' It was Robert. 'Are you free to take a walk?'

I turned to Mrs D. 'Is that okay? Do you mind keeping an eye on Jimmy, for an hour or so?'

Mrs D sighed but she was smiling too, so I knew it was all right. 'If your father agrees, it's fine with me. Just for a while, though, Missy. I'm off home to give Mr Diamond his lunch at half twelve.'

It was still only ten o'clock. 'You'll hardly notice I'm gone,' I said, with an ever-so-grateful smile.

My feet wanted to skip, only that would have seemed terribly childish. But my heart was dancing inside. It was a beautiful summer's day with barely a cloud in the sky. The roses in the cottage gardens were a glorious kaleidoscope of colour and the birdsong was almost deafening. And I was with a boy. A nice boy. To hell with Kit Waddington.

I glanced sideways at Robert as we walked. He was taller than I remembered, with mousy-coloured hair cut quite short, rather traditional-looking. He wore a plain cotton shirt with rolled-up sleeves, nothing showy, and khaki shorts showing off long tanned legs with blond hairs that glistened in the sunshine. To be perfectly honest, his face was pretty ordinary except when he smiled, which was quite often. It was a good smile, sweet and straightforward, the sort of smile you could trust. It made me happy.

'Where are we off to?'

'I thought we might go for a paddle.'

I couldn't think of anything nicer on a hot day like this. 'In the river?'

'Thought we might go to the lake.'

'The lake? It's private, isn't it? Belongs to the Waddingtons.'

'They're fine with us going there.' I smiled to myself. If Kit saw me with Robert, it might make him jealous. It was a common enough ploy used by romance heroines. *It was only when he saw how much he'd lost that he realised how much he had needed her.*

I hadn't approached the lake from this route before. At the bottom of the lane was a cart track that led across a field and into the lower end of the woods, where we emerged onto a broad stretch of close-cropped grass that sloped gently towards the water with a foot-wide strip of gravelly sand at the margins. The edges were punctuated with little outcrops of a spiky-leaved plant – sedge; I looked it up in one of Pa's books afterwards. And on every upright spike clung a long, thin insect. As we approached, they flew upwards in a cloud of astonishing iridescent blue.

'Wow,' I sighed.

'They're damsel flies,' Rob said. 'Pretty, eh?'

'Magical.' We fell into silence, looking around. The lake

was deserted and as still as a mirror, reflecting a cloudless sky in a sheet of blue, unbroken apart from the shadows of the trees in the furthest, darkest corner. It was like being in paradise.

'I'm up for a paddle.' Rob was sitting on a small rock close to the edge of the water and pulling off his sandals. 'You coming?'

'Of course I'm coming.'

The gravel was sharp on the soft soles of my feet, but the chilly water around my ankles felt delicious. We must have crushed a minty-type of plant as we waded in, because the smell reminded me of peppermint humbugs. The lake was so clear that we could see our toes, and tiny long-legged insects darted around on the surface of the water.

Rob was striding ahead now.

'Come on, Molly. It's perfectly safe.'

I waded cautiously towards him, he took my hand and we stood in silence, watching the circles of ripples spreading away from our legs across the surface of the lake, creating ever-changing patterns from the distorted reflections of the sky and the trees. For a few moments I felt flooded with peace. But it wasn't to last.

From the woods behind came a volley of shouts and wolf-whistles. Rob dropped my hand suddenly, as though I'd burned him.

'Oh, hell. It's the others.'

'The others?' Kit, perhaps?

'The lads. Remember? From the fete?'

I remembered all right. The three boys who'd stared at Jimmy when he'd thrown down the beer bottle. The ones who'd smirked when George Diamond had offered Jimmy a go at 'Catch the Rat', and who had been silenced by his success.

Rob was already wading back to the beach, abandoning me with my skirt tucked into my knickers and muddy water up to my knees. I followed him, scowling with resentment.

Ashley, Brian and Peter. Strange the things you remember after all these years, when I can't even recall the name of someone I met yesterday. Ashley was tall and fair, like Rob. Brian was short, spotty and ginger-haired. Peter was dark, thickset and serious-looking. They acknowledged me with shy smiles.

'What've you done with that funny little brother of yours today?' That was Brian. The chippy one, I remembered now. And rude.

'His name's Jimmy,' I retorted. 'He's at home with my dad.'

In the company of his friends, Rob appeared younger and sillier. We sat in the sun and Peter produced a bottle of lemonade, which he passed round.

'Bloody hell, it's hot,' Brian said suddenly. 'Anyone for a swim?'

It felt like a dare. The other boys hesitated, checking his expression. Was he teasing? It didn't seem so. He swiftly shed his shoes and socks; now he hauled off his T-shirt to reveal an acre of pale skin dotted with acne scars.

'Steady on,' Rob said. 'Spare Molly's blushes, won't you?'

But Brian was not to be deflected. He was in his shorts now, his skinny chest bared defiantly.

'We can cool off paddling, can't we?' Ashley said.

'Don't be a wimp,' Brian said. 'C'mon. Last one in's a sissy.'

Masculine pride was at stake, and there was no holding them back now.

'Are you coming?' Rob asked me, as he stripped to his shorts.

'No, thanks.'

I retreated to the shade of a small willow copse to the side of the grassy area and sat on a log, watching them belly-flopping into the water with bellows of shock, then starting to horse around, racing with splashy strokes, swimming underwater to grab one another's legs, trying to duck each other.

By now I was feeling deeply awkward. Paddling with Robert was nice, and being at the lake on our own, quietly, had somehow been magical. The arrival of the boys ruined all that. Their careless noise seemed to desecrate this beautiful, peaceful place. Had they forgotten that the lake was supposed to be private property?

The more I thought about it, the more uncomfortable I felt, and the more I wanted to get away. I tried to attract Rob's attention, but he was having too much fun to notice. Just as I was about to leave I heard a shout: 'Hey! You lot. What's going on? Don't you know it's private property?'

I hid behind a tree, expecting at any time to see a burly gamekeeper wielding a shotgun. Or, worse, Mr Waddington. But no, a tall, slim and dark-haired boy was striding towards the piles of shoes, socks and shirts hastily strewn across the grass. It was Kit.

'Waddington!' Rob shouted. 'Where the hell have you been all these months?'

'Oh, here and there,' Kit called back. 'Now, lads, how do you like your clothes? A bit wet, or just sopping?' He gathered up the piles of clothing and ran to the edge of the lake, dropping them one by one into the water.

'You bastard!' Rob said, rushing to tackle him, so that they both fell into the shallows, laughing wildly. Socks and shirts floated all around them, like small coloured islands. I lingered in my hiding place, watching, unable to take my eyes off Kit as they played in the water. He had a sporty body: his legs muscular and tanned, and his chest so much broader than any of the others'. Robert seemed spindly, childish by comparison. Kit was well on his way to becoming a man, while the others were still only boys.

I couldn't help laughing at their playfulness. How enviable it was to be so free of care and responsibility. I tried to imagine my friends from school doing the same, but failed. They would all be too conscious of their hairstyles, their new clothes, their *dignity*. Not for the first time I wished I'd been born a boy. And that I wasn't the daughter of a vicar.

The distant sound of church bells chimed twelve; half an hour before I had to be back at the vicarage. The boys were coming out of the water now, gathering up their wet things, wringing them out and hanging them over willow branches to dry.

Rob looked round. 'Molly, Molly,' he shouted. 'Where are you?' A pause, then, 'You can come out now.'

'She must have gone home,' one of the others said.

'Molly Goddard, you mean?' Kit asked.

'His new girlfriend,' someone explained.

'Not *girl*friend,' Rob said quickly. Even from this distance, I could see him blushing. 'She was here a minute ago.'

'I know her. Rather pretty, isn't she?'

My heart flipped. Kit thought I was pretty.

And yet he hadn't answered my letter. He must have been home from boarding school for well over a week and hadn't bothered to get in touch, or come to see me. What did he really think of me? How could I find out what was going on in his mind?

12

It hadn't rained for weeks and according to Mrs D the farmers were becoming fretful, concerned that the heads of their corn might fail to fill out in time for harvest. I was learning that every kind of weather felt like a threat to their crops: too cold and the seed might not germinate; too wet and it might rot; too windy and the crop might be flattened; too dry and it might not grow or swell. In all the months we lived in the village I never once heard a farmer declaring that the weather was 'perfect'.

My freckles merged into blobs across my nose and cheeks, resisting daily applications of lemon juice that made me smell like a citrus pudding. Poor Mrs Diamond huffed and puffed as she dusted and swept, complaining that it was altogether the wrong weather for housework.

'Why don't you leave it until it cools down?' I suggested.

'Whatever would the Reverend say if we let standards slip?' she grumbled. 'Cleanliness is next to godliness, my mother would say, and she never let me forget it.' I felt sure Pa would barely notice if the house wasn't cleaned for a year, and I doubted that God – even if He existed –

would care about the odd speck of dust, but I held my tongue.

Jimmy and I were sitting on a shady bench in the church-yard, trying to find some air, when Eli ambled up.

'Mind if I joins you?' he asked, sitting down anyway with a groan. 'Rest me weary old legs.' Despite the heat, he was still dressed in the same clothes: green canvas trousers and a tattered tweed jacket. His only concession to the weather was shedding his old oiled gabardine raincoat.

He lit his pipe and we were sitting there in companion-able silence, while Jimmy went off searching for daisies to make a chain, when Henry Blackman drove past in a brand-new open-topped sports car, gleaming red. He was wearing one of those peaked caps, like a naval captain. Two minutes later came another sports car, in exactly the same red, with Blackman's wife Melissa at the wheel, her hair tied back with one of those film star scarves, a white wisp of silk trailing out in the wind behind her.

'Well, blow me down,' old Eli muttered, sucking his teeth.

It took me a moment to work out why the sight of those two cars, one after the other, struck me as slightly absurd, even comical. On one hand, there was nothing really *wrong* with showing off a bit, was there, if you had the money? There was no law against it, after all. But to buy *matching* sports cars? In *red*? After a war when everyone had been required to tighten their belts? Did the Blackmans have no idea how others might judge them? Did they even care? It wasn't just ordinary showing off; it was the equivalent of shouting, 'Look at me! Look at me!' in the loudest, most vulgar way. Like spoiled children.

I watched Jimmy destroying the daisy chain I'd made,

as he tried to add more flowers to the links. 'I can hardly believe what we've just seen,' I said at last.

'Nowt so queer as folks,' Eli commented drily.

Jimmy brought his broken daisy chain back to me and I told him we needed ten more flowers, ones with long, thick stems, to mend it.

Eli relit his pipe. 'Shall I tell you a story, Miss Molly?'

'Yes, please.'

'Once upon a time,' he began, 'there was a little boy whose father was killed in the war.'

'The last war?'

'One afore. The Great War.'

'Is his name Henry Blackman?'

'Mebbe. Why don't you decide, when I've finished? Well, his ma's got problems – you know, up here.' He tapped his temple. 'Took her off to Severalls, they did, the asylum in Colchester.'

'What happened to the boy?'

'Got sent to a children's home.' He sighed. 'But 'e never could get round the shame of it all, you know. Never went to see his ma – not once, as far as I know. She could be dead by now, of course. And he claims his pa died a hero in the first war but us old 'uns knows better. He was a travelling salesman, far as I know. Disappeared off the face of the earth. Anyroads, when the second war comes by, our lad turns out to be no hero, either. He got off the fightin', claiming he'd poorly lungs.'

'Did he? Have poorly lungs, I mean?'

'Who knows, dearie? He gets himself a good little job trading cars, but when that falls flat, cos of petrol rationing, he borrows a bit of money and begins buying up bits of what everyone else thinks is wasteland. What everyone else doesn't know, and he does, is that under that land is tons and tons of gravel. And gravel is what they'll be needing. D'you know why?'

I shook my head.

'Airfields, Miss Molly. Runways. The Yanks built hundreds of 'em round here. The man sells the gravel and buys more land, and so on, till by the end of the war he's got more money than he knows what to do with.'

'Was it illegal?'

'Nah. He's too clever to do anything illegal. Never under-estimate a fellow like that, Miss Molly. It buys him what he's always wanted: a fancy house in the village where he was born, but he always wants more.'

'You *are* talking about Henry Blackman? He was born here in the village?'

He nodded. 'So after the war he starts a property company, buyin' and sellin' and whatnot, managin' houses for letting, and the rest. Employs quite a few locals, so they's on his side anyway. And sets about becomin' Mr Wormley, the life and soul of the village, buyin' everyone rounds in the pub of a Saturday night.'

'But why?'

He shook his head. 'Who knows? To prove he belongs or summat? Because he don't have a father, p'raps?'

'You're saying he's illegitimate?'

Eli shook his head and took a puff on his pipe. 'Well, that'd be tellin', wouldn't it? Who knows, but I have my suspicions. Anyway, he joins them committees and all. Pillar of the community, he becomes. Best pals with the previous fella.'

'The previous vicar?'

'Ran rings around him, he did.'

'What do you mean – rings?'

The old man shook his head, relit his pipe and puffed on it silently for a few moments.

But he'd opened the door to the topic, and I couldn't let it pass. 'But he's upsetting people. You included.'

'Thass true, Miss Molly,' he said, exhaling smoke into a cloud of gnats. 'We never did hit it off, him and me. It's what I knows about his dealings with the previous fella what irks him, I reckon. And he's tryin' to get me off of that land cos he wants to build houses on it and make even more money.'

'Build *houses*?' He'd never admitted that to Pa. 'In those beautiful woods?'

'That's what they say. Been after it for years.'

I wanted so much to ask Eli more, but right then Jimmy returned, wanting to crown me with his daisy chain. After we'd said goodbye and were heading back to the vicarage, I glanced back.

Eli was still sitting there, pipe in hand, staring into space with an expression of such desolation that it broke my heart. He'd always seemed as old as the hills, but there was such a strong spark of life inside him that you never really noticed his age. Was it my imagination, having heard what I'd just heard, or did that spark really seem to be fading? Something had to be done to save Eli's home.

I had to raise it again with Pa, even if it meant adding to his burdens.

'Have you thought any more about the plan to sell the woodland?' I asked him after supper. In the heat, none of us had any appetite, but we'd tried hard to do justice to

Mrs D's efforts. 'Eli is convinced Blackman wants him off the land so he can buy it and build houses on it.'

Pa gestured to the chair beside him. 'Look, my darling, as far as I know, no one wants to build houses there. But there is a level of concern about Eli's safety in that old hut, as he grows older. The idea is to offer him one of those new council houses instead.' I knew what he was talking about – a new development of neat little semi-detached houses being built along the main road a couple of miles away.

I began to protest, but he silenced me with an upheld palm.

'Listen, Eli wouldn't even be considered for a council house unless he was actually in danger of becoming homeless. Think about it for a moment. An old boy like that can't go on living in a hut with no water or electricity. Surely it would be for the best if he was moved into a house with all mod cons?'

I heard myself shouting now. 'How does the church have the right to decide where Eli should live? Surely it's up to him? He loves the woods and having all the nature around him, and he'd hate it in a house up on the main road. Doesn't what he wants count for anything?'

'Hold on, sweetheart,' Pa said, startled by my outburst. 'I think you might be getting the wrong end of the stick. We want to help.'

'Then why doesn't anyone actually ask Eli what *he* wants?'

He became thoughtful for a moment, pulling at his earlobe. 'All right, my dearest. I will ask him. You and Jimmy could take me there. Tomorrow afternoon?'

As we came in sight of the hut, Sarge leaped to his feet, growling menacingly, the hair on the back of his neck standing on end.

Pa stopped in his tracks. 'That animal looks as though it could eat us alive.'

'Don't worry, he's perfectly friendly when you get to know him.' I called out, 'Good boy, Sarge. It's only us.'

At the sound of my voice, the dog's demeanour changed completely and his tail began to wag. Eli appeared at the doorway, doffing his moth-eaten hat. 'Afternoon, Vicar. To what do we owe this honour? Come on up, please do. Don't mind old Sarge. He won't hurt a fly.'

Pa was given the honour of Eli's best chair, while I sat on the bench and Jimmy got the milking stool next to Sarge, who loved to be petted.

'Cuppa tea for you folks?' Eli asked.

Pa was about to refuse, but I jumped in. 'Yes, please.' With Eli, I'd already come to learn, the gentle formalities of hospitality must always be followed before he could feel at ease.

Mugs in hand, and with Jimmy now happily munching on a biscuit and sharing a few crumbs with Sarge, we exchanged pleasantries about the weather – 'too ruddy hot' – and the beauty of the woods – 'some of these trees've been here hundreds of years, Vicar. Make you wonder what they've seen, don't it?'

After a few minutes Pa seemed to decide that the time was right. 'So you live here all year round, Eli?'

'Oh yes, sir. I loves it here. Been here near ten year, since me old cottage got bombed.'

'I'm so sorry. And that was the night your wife died, too?'

'A bad night, it was.' Eli shook his head and then took his pipe out of his pocket. He offered the tobacco pouch to Pa. 'Smoke, Vicar?'

'Not for me, thanks.'

We waited as Eli filled and lit his pipe, puffed it into life and sat back, as I'd seen him do so many times before.

'Was there no chance of saving the cottage?'

'Nah, it'd cost too much to rebuild. So oi come down here.'

'Don't you get cold in the winter?'

'I've got me little stove, and there's plenty of wood around.' He waved his arm expansively. 'And there's the old mutt to cuddle up with.'

'It must be tough, though. Wouldn't you prefer a nice house, if we could find you one?'

Eli's reaction was sudden and frightening. He put down his cup with a clunk and his whole body seemed to tense, the sinews on his neck standing out. Sarge stood up, ears pricked, and gave a low rumbling growl. After a few moments Eli appeared to steady himself. He relit his pipe with a trembling hand and took a few long draws on it.

'Forgive me asking, but is it that Mr Blackman what sent you here, Vicar?'

'No, it was me,' I jumped in. 'I asked Pa to come. They're putting your name forward for one of those new council houses up at the top.'

'I knows all about that, thank you very much,' he said. 'I don't want it, and that's that. But that bast— Sorry to swear, Vicar, but that man is the very devil, spreading poison through our village. He 'ont take no for an answer.'

Eli rose to his feet and disappeared into the hut, returning with the box-file marked 'Land', opened it and took out a sheaf of letters, at least twenty.

'Look at this lot, sir. All from that man and his solicitor fella. Sayin' that if I don't get out, they'll get the bailiffs onter me.'

I tried not to gasp. In London we'd once watched, powerless to help, as the bailiffs arrived at the door of a neighbour and taken almost everything, leaving the poor woman and her two children virtually destitute. Blackman had never mentioned bailiffs. What else was he not telling the rest of the committee?

'He can't do that, can he, Pa?'

'I tell you here and now, Vicar, I ain't going nowhere – and certainly not to no council house. I'll chain meself to this hut before anyone takes it off of me. That, or them'll have to carry me out of here in me coffin. And that's the end of that.'

He plonked down the file and brushed the legs of his old trousers, as though ridding himself of any taint of Blackman troubles. 'More tea, anyone?'

***

On the way home I remonstrated with Pa once more.

'Did you know about this bailiff thing? All those letters?'

He shook his head. 'Must have been before we got here.'

'But don't you see, now? We have to do something.'

He walked on, saying nothing.

'Well?' I pressed.

'My darling, I'm not sure what I *can* do.'

That evening I found him slumped in his office chair,

bottle of beer in hand and another empty bottle beside it. He looked exhausted and old. Coming to the village was supposed to have been a new start, a chance to recover from his war experiences and his grief, to get back to normality. But he was already being beaten down by apparently insuperable problems.

I recalled Eli's phrase about Blackman: *spreading poison through our village*. It made me shiver.

THE UGLY DRAGON
by Molly Goddard

Chapter 4: The dragon hates the taste of human beings

The next time Jimmy and his sister went to call for the dragon, she appeared immediately.

'Hello again,' she said, hauling herself onto the bank. 'Now I've been wondering,' she went on, 'why you don't seem to be afraid of me? Most people are terrified.'

Jimmy didn't know what to say. He wasn't entirely sure himself.

'Didn't they warn you about how I used to eat people?' she asked.

Jimmy told her that he'd heard all kinds of stories, but he didn't believe what everyone said. For example, they said the dragon was killed by a knight called George, which was plainly wrong, because she was still here. The dragon laughed. Deep rumbles from her enormous belly seemed to make the ground tremble, and fountains of water spurted from her nostrils.

'Ha-ha-ha. They sent plenty of brave men with spears and swords, but I hate fighting. I just disappeared underwater for

a while, so they could claim they had killed me, and everyone praised them as heroes.'

Jimmy took out a bag of teacakes and offered her one, placing it on the ground rather than risk being nicked by her sharp teeth. She munched it down in a single gulp.

'Got any more?'

He gave her his last one.

'Delicious,' she murmured, twisting her snout to one side to pick up the crumbs.

'Tastier than human beings?' Jimmy asked.

She snorted. 'I don't eat them any more, gone off them completely – don't think I could even stomach a virgin these days. Some human beings are so wicked it makes them taste terribly bitter, which is why I won't eat them any more. But don't tell anyone. I have my reputation to keep up. If people are afraid of me, they leave me alone.'

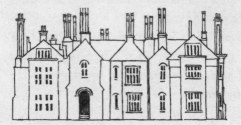

13

I was sitting on the wide windowsill halfway up the stairs rereading *The Man in the Dark Coat* – 'he was like a bright star that seemed to tug at all her senses' – when I spied Kit speeding towards the vicarage on his bicycle, long hair flying out behind him like a dark charger. For a glorious moment I imagined he was coming to visit me, but he rode past with scarcely a second glance.

My head was still filled with contradictory emotions: I longed to see him, but didn't want to seem too desperate; and he hadn't replied to my letter, so should I assume he wasn't interested in me? But then hadn't he told Rob I was pretty? The thoughts went round and round in my head, until I could stand it no longer.

He must have returned later when I wasn't looking, because that afternoon we found on the mat an envelope addressed to me and Jimmy and, inside, an invitation in neat, elegant script on a small card:

Kit Waddington, Esq.
Requests the pleasure of your company
To celebrate his 17th birthday
At: Wormley Hall
On: Tuesday 15th August, 3 p.m.
Bring swimmers
RSVP

Tuesday: just a few days away! Questions crowded my mind: who else would be going? Despite being handwritten, the wording of the invitation – 'requests the pleasure' – sounded terribly formal. Yet we were told to bring 'swimmers', which I took to be boarding-school slang for bathing suits.

Pa found me a blank postcard and showed me how to write an RSVP. My handwriting was nothing like as neat as Mrs Waddington's (for I assumed she had written the invitations – it was surely not a boy's hand), but it looked reasonable enough to me.

Molly and Jimmy Goddard
Thank Kit Waddington, Esq.
For his kind invitation for Tuesday 15th August
And have pleasure in accepting.

Later that morning, Blackman called for Pa in his bright-red sports car and they drove to Sudbury for the meeting with the bank manager. When he got home, Pa rushed through his lunch, barely eating a thing or speaking a word, then closeted himself in his study till mid-afternoon.

I couldn't bear to wait any longer. 'Please, Pa. Please tell me what happened?'

A muffled 'Come in'.

'How did it go – your trip to the bank?'

'It's fine, sweetheart,' he said. Sheaves of paper surrounded him on the desk, all covered in figures. 'It'll be sorted out soon enough.' The drained look on his face told me he was lying.

'You don't have to pretend, Pa.' He looked at me for a long moment. 'You have to trust me. I'm old enough to share things with, you know.'

He gave a great sigh and gesticulated to the papers on his desk.

'I barely know where to start, my darling. Henry's right: there is a third bank account, which up until December was showing a sum of around five thousand pounds. But over a period of a month, starting from when I first became a signatory to the account, that money has been withdrawn, and now it's nearly all gone.'

'But who's taken it?'

He shook his head. 'The bank says it could only have been Henry or me.' Miss Calver's words resounded in my head: *Tell your pa to take care around that man.* 'Henry claims it couldn't have been him, because any transactions he makes are supposed to be approved by me.'

It didn't make any sense. 'I assume you . . . ?' I couldn't finish the sentence.

'You don't think I . . . ?' Pa's face seemed to collapse, and I feared he might be close to tears. 'Look, my darling, I know I'm not the most organised person in the world, but I might have noticed if I'd taken all that money out of a bank account, don't you think? Five *thousand* pounds. What on earth would I spend that sort of money on?'

He dropped his head into his hands. He seemed so

brittle, as though he might fall into pieces right there in his study. A heavy dread slithered into my stomach. 'What's going to happen now?' I whispered.

'We've agreed to keep it between us, while the bank makes further enquiries,' Pa said. 'But after that, Henry says, we have to call in the diocesan auditors. Hence, all of this,' and he gestured to the papers again. 'I need to get my head round who was doing what before I got here, so I'm ready.'

On Saturday our turn on the church rota came round again.

I never minded. It always reminded me of Mum, who would, I hoped, be looking down on us approvingly from her cloud. And I'd heard from Mrs D that our helpfulness had been commented on in the village. 'Earning all kind of Brownie points for your pa,' she said drily. I could never tell whether she was being funny or serious.

The ladies doted on Jimmy, bringing him biscuits, and he glowed in their attention.

Work was in full swing when we arrived, and I asked what needed doing. 'Prayer books for young Jim, please,' one said. 'And you were so good at the ironing last time. I'm sorry it's a steamy sort of job on a day like this.' I didn't mind at all; in this weather the church was one of the coolest places to be.

I was alone in the vestry, spraying and ironing surplices while listening with half an ear to the gossip being exchanged between the ladies who were sweeping, dusting and arranging flowers in the main church, when my ears suddenly tuned into their conversation.

'Shocking, ain't it? Turfing him out of that hut, after all these years?'

'But he's an old boy now. Losing it a bit, they say.'

'Wouldn't he be better off in a nice warm council house with all mod cons?'

'It ain't right, letting him live in the woods at his age.'

'What harm's he doing to anyone? Live and let live, I says.'

I felt an urge to rush out and ask everyone to step in and support Eli. Many of their families had lived here for generations. They knew him better than any incomers, like Blackman or Pa. But as I dithered, the first speaker lowered her voice to a whisper, so that I had to strain to hear.

'But who's going to stand up for him?'

'It's a ruddy scandal, if you ask me.'

'It's you-know-who, of course.'

'Wants to get his mitts on that land himself, I'll be bound.'

'And what's the vicar doing about it then?' My heart seemed to stop. I heard the others shushing her, imagining nudges and fingers to lips as they pointed in the direction of the vestry – and me.

How easily this kind of rumour could get out of hand, and Pa's reputation called into doubt. Surely the information should be out in the open, not being whispered behind backs? I continued ironing until the job was done, but my head was filled with so many questions it was a miracle nothing got scorched again.

There was a meeting of the Church Management Committee at the vicarage on Monday, and Pa was fidgety, unable to settle to anything. Mrs D had laid out a cold supper that evening, and he pushed the food around his plate like chess pieces, barely eating a thing. There was some leftover blanc-mange to finish up too, usually a favourite, but Pa excused himself from the table saying he needed to tidy the dining room, even though Mrs D had already hoovered and dusted, leaving it spotless.

Mr Blackman was first to arrive. He greeted me like a long-lost friend, even though we'd met in church only the day before, patting me on the shoulder and declaring that I was looking well. He thanked me loudly several times for bringing in the tea and cold drinks, exclaiming, 'What a charming daughter you have, John, and growing into a lovely young woman before our very eyes. You must be very proud.'

Why did his presence always make my skin crawl? His appearance was perfectly ordinary. Eli said Blackman had used his fortune to move to the village that he'd felt deprived of, as a child. We should have felt sorry for him. But how can you summon any sympathy for someone so determined to oust an old man from his home and sell off a piece of beautiful woodland?

I was taking the pot of tea, jug of milk, cups and saucers and a plate of biscuits into the dining room when Pa came out to ask whether I would mind taking the minutes. 'It seems Miss Calver is indisposed,' he said. I didn't protest too much, and was genuinely flattered to be asked. Apart from Blackman, the other committee members were generally a cheerful lot, always ready with a kindly word to me and Jimmy. They included the curate, Alistair Thornberry, the twins' mother Mrs Timpson and a couple of other friendly souls.

'It's only a matter of taking notes. I'll help with the writing up, later,' Pa said, lowering his voice. 'You don't get to contribute or vote, of course.' He gave me a warning look.

After agreeing the minutes and 'matters arising', Pa announced, 'Item one. Stained glass. Of course, we are most grateful to Mr and Mrs Waddington for their generosity, and to Mrs Blackman for her charming design. You've all had a chance to view it, I hope?'

'Forgive me if this sounds ungrateful.' This was Mr Abbott, an elderly, pious man who attended every church service and had apparently been on the committee forever. 'But is it right to celebrate what is essentially a heathen legend as part of the fabric of the house of our Lord?'

'Have you seen the dragon on the wall of Wiston Church?' Mrs Timpson piped up. 'Let's not allow them sole ownership of this important medieval legend, part of the wonderful history of our village.' This was met with mutters of 'Hear, hear'.

'Shall we vote?' Pa asked, after the debate had ranged around the table for a few minutes. 'All those in favour.' Five hands went up, including his. 'Those against.' Only Mr Abbott raised his arm.

'Thank you. We have shown the design to the diocese and we are confident they will approve it. We will keep you updated,' Pa said. 'Let's move on to item two: use of church land.'

My ears pricked up and I concentrated on capturing every word as accurately as possible. 'As you know, we are concerned about an elderly gentleman who is frail in both body and mind . . .' Blackman began. Was he really suggesting Eli was going doolally? He seemed to me the sanest person in the village. I tried to catch Pa's eye, but he looked away quickly and by the time I tuned in again, Blackman was saying, '. . . a nice warm council house with running water and electricity.'

Heads around the table were nodding. I felt my cheeks flushing with fury.

'In addition, there are planning laws to consider. It would be a dereliction of our duty if we simply allowed anyone to camp on church land.'

Pa's curate, Alistair Thornberry, piped up, 'Mr Chadwick has been living in this hut for ten years or more. Who are we to tell him he must leave?'

'It is not us, Mr Thornberry. It is the regulations. That hut contravenes planning laws.'

Pa spoke now. 'I have been to visit Mr Chadwick, and he showed me a sheaf of letters he's received over two years, including a threat to bring in bailiffs. Surely it is all wrong, hounding an old man like this? It is his life, after all, and he should be given the choice.'

Blackman was as cool as a cucumber. 'You are right, Vicar. We have been trying to resolve this problem for the past eighteen months. But with respect, colleagues, we have no choice. We have an obligation to obey the law.'

'But why? He has been living there happily, bothering no one, for a decade or more. Why is it suddenly so important to evict him?'

'Because it was brought to our attention, about two years ago, that he has no lease. As a committee, we are duty-bound to make the best use of church land, especially when our finances are in such a parlous state. This irregular situation has been going on far too long.'

As the debate continued, it seemed that only Pa and Alistair – both relative newcomers to the committee – were prepared to stand up to Blackman, and I feared they were losing the battle. If only Miss Calver had been there to back them up. I listened with growing despair: what a spineless lot they were. Eventually Pa invited a show of hands.

'All those in favour?' I held my breath. Four hands went up. 'All those against?' Only two were left. Pa's voice cracked. 'The motion is passed. But if we are determined to move Mr Chadwick, we must do it through persuasion and kindness, not threatening letters.'

'Hear, hear, Vicar.'

Blackman was determined to have the last word. 'I must point out that by allowing this situation to persist for so many years the church has been in breach of the law. In light of this, it is my strong recommendation that this issue should remain confidential to this committee.'

The air felt close, hard to breathe. I longed to say something, but the meeting was already moving on. Pa announced item three, the annual financial report.

Blackman spoke for what seemed like an eternity about what he called 'estimates for upcoming needs': the familiar list of flagstones, organ bellows and vestry roof. An extended debate followed about which of these was the most pressing – of course, it was the roof, but this was also estimated at tens of thousands of pounds, and they would have to launch a special appeal.

'There is another option,' Blackman said. 'We could consider divesting some of the church's assets.'

'Sell off the family silver? I don't think so,' Mr Abbott said.

'There is a piece of land,' Blackman went on, 'on which the aforementioned illegal encampment currently sits . . .'

'Surely, you're not talking about the *woodland*, Henry? That's a village asset. We couldn't sell that,' Alistair Thornberry said. 'Anyway, why would anyone want to buy it?'

But Blackman answered, smooth as silk, 'Of course, of course. It was only a passing suggestion, in case we should find ourselves in very serious financial difficulties in future.' That threat again. Pa seemed to be studying the papers on the table in front of him.

Mr Abbott piped up again, 'Whatever happened to that matter of the missing money, Mr Treasurer? Weren't you supposed to report back to us on that?'

Blackman responded without a flicker of hesitation, 'I'm glad you asked, Charlie. We have been working very hard to try untangle it, haven't we, Vicar?'

'The previous incumbent obviously got everything into a right muddle,' Mr Abbott grumbled. 'I hope you can get it sorted out, sharpish.'

'We went to the bank last week,' Blackman said. 'So we're nearly there, and you will be the first to know what's been going on.'

At the end of the meeting I stomped off upstairs, bursting with fury, unable to face the goodbyes and other pleasantries. After the anger had turned to tears, I felt overwhelmed with a heavy sense of inevitability. My father was defeated. It was no use haranguing him. If I wanted something to happen, it would be up to me.

14

There were other pressing concerns in my life: what to take as a birthday present for Kit. But what does a seventeen-year-old boy want? Especially a wealthy boy who already seemed to have everything? I consulted Mrs D.

'What does he like to do?'

'I don't really know him that well. He likes swimming and being out on the lake.'

'How's about a book?'

'I really don't think he's the reading type.'

'How's about making him something yourselves? Hand-made things always mean more. Some fancy biscuits, say? We've got some sugar coupons, so that shouldn't be a problem.'

I dismissed the idea at first. He'd think it childish, and there would be plenty of food at the party anyway. But then I had an idea. We could turn it into a joke, decorating the biscuits with pictures of boats and . . . pirates, perhaps. Yes, pirate-themed biscuits. Just a bit of fun. And Jimmy would enjoy it, too.

We made gingerbread biscuits, which gave a good flat

surface for the icing, and Mrs D suggested that I should draw the images to size beforehand to create a template, as she called it. I drew a boat – modelled on the *Mary Jane* – a pair of crossed oars, a skull and crossbones, a pirate's face with a bandana, and a parrot. Jimmy wanted one of a dragon, too, to continue the lake theme, and went on about it so much that I gave in, deciding to go with the crocodile shape, as the more traditional dragon was more complicated. After the dough shapes were cut out and baking in the oven, Mrs D made me practise with the icing bag until the outlines looked like they were supposed to.

An hour later, and with only three wasted (though not wasted, as we ate them there and then), we had fifteen perfectly iced biscuits laid out to dry in the pantry. We made up a box and covered it with stripy coloured paper that Mrs D found in the bottom of a drawer, and tied it with a piece of white bias binding, as we hadn't any ribbon. The gift looked better than I could ever have hoped.

There were ten of us altogether, including Kit: me and Jimmy, Rob and the other boys from the village, Ashley, Brian and Peter, and three posh friends from his boarding school, who seemed to be so much older and more sophisticated than the rest of us. I was the only girl, which felt strange at first – where were the twins? I supposed they must be away on one of their holidays, or at Pony Club camp. But it also made me feel rather special.

We all arrived at about the same time and went into the drawing room. Kit opened each parcel – they contained boyish things like pens and scarves – said a cursory thank you and got on with the next one, so you couldn't tell whether he was pleased or not.

By the time it came to our little box I was in a fever of embarrassment. How stupid I'd been to imagine Kit would appreciate home-made biscuits! How humiliating it would be when he opened them. But to my surprise, he actually showed a little more interest than he had in the other gifts; and his mother, watching over his shoulder, commented that the decoration was very artistic. She asked whether they might put them out on a plate to serve them for tea and, of course, we agreed. Jimmy looked especially pleased.

At the meal everyone took a biscuit, and Robert ended up with a crocodile. 'What's a crocodile got to do with the pirate theme?' he asked.

'There's a crocodile who menaces the pirates in *Peter Pan*,' I said, catching Kit's eye. He was smiling. 'And there's one living in the lake.'

'But isn't it a dragon in your lake?' someone asked. 'Not a crocodile?'

'It depends on which legend you read,' I said. 'Some say the Wormley Dragon was actually a crocodile.'

Mrs Waddington offered the plate to Jimmy. He'd been at my side all the time, behaving beautifully, perhaps over-awed in the company of so many older children, who had mostly been ignoring him. 'Look, there's just one dragon left,' she said. 'I think you should have it.'

The conversation was interrupted by Mr Waddington. Tapping a glass with a spoon to bring us to silence, he announced that a surprise would be revealed at the boat-house, and we should take our swimming things and make our way there as soon as we'd finished our tea.

The 'surprise' turned out to be a new boat for the lake:

the most curious kind I'd ever seen, with highly varnished wooden sides and a base of bright-red coated canvas stretched tightly over a wooden frame. It had two seats, two oars and two rowlocks, and didn't look particularly safe. Mr Waddington produced a bottle of champagne. 'What shall we name her?' he asked, glancing around for suggestions.

'*Victory,*' someone suggested. '*The Beagle,*' another said. These boarding-school boys were well versed in their history, right enough. Various other suggestions followed, most of them silly and unsuitable.

'Tell you what,' Kit said eventually. 'Jimmy is such a good rower, I'm going to let him name her.' He gave my brother the sweetest smile. 'Think of a nice name for the canvas boat, Jim-boy,' he said. 'Maybe something that's red?'

It came out almost at once, as though the word had been in his head all along. '*Rob . . . Robin,*' he said, pronouncing it almost perfectly. 'Molly likes robins.'

Mr Waddington popped the cork – it bounced into the lake and floated there – before pouring the fizzy wine over the prow of the boat and announcing in a very pompous voice, 'I name this ship *Robin.*' We all laughed and cheered, especially Jimmy, who clapped his hands and tried to climb into it immediately.

'Not yet. Let Kit try it out first,' I said, holding him back.

The little boat looked so frail and was clearly as light as a feather. But when Kit lifted it into the water and jumped in, fitted the oars into the rowlocks and began rowing around on the lake, it seemed to work beautifully. I remembered reading in a history book about round boats that early man used, called coracles, made of sticks and animal skins. *Robin* was a modern version of a coracle, in a more boat-like shape.

'She's brilliant,' he called. 'Who wants a ride?'

Jimmy put his hand up. Kit came back and helped him climb in, instructing him to step carefully, only on the wooden base, and not on the canvas sections.

'Don't go too far,' I shouted, praying that Jimmy wouldn't try to stand up and capsize them. 'Look after my brother, Kit.'

'I will, don't worry,' he called. As they rowed way, with Kit singing, 'Yo-ho-ho and a bottle of rum', Jimmy waved back, his face a picture of delight, and I loved Kit all over again for his kindness.

'Why don't the rest of you go for a dip?' Mr Waddington suggested. He was still clutching the champagne bottle and I'd spied him swigging from it, when no one was looking. 'You can all swim, can't you?'

The swimming platform had a ladder, so that you could climb gracefully into the water without having to jump in or wade through the reeds. There was even a little hut for changing in, not that the boys bothered. They simply changed there and then, and immediately leaped straight into the water and began shouting and larking about.

How can I describe the feeling of plunging into that lake for the first time? I was used to the turbulence of the sea, to leaping over waves or, on calmer days, floating on my back, enjoying the buoyancy of the salty water and watching the clouds. But I had never swum in fresh water before. I was immediately out of my depth and the cold made me gasp at first, but it was no worse than I'd known in the sea, and I was already warmed up by the time I'd swum a few yards.

The boys were still messing about, so I carried on swimming out into the lake until their voices receded and I could enjoy the relative peace. The water felt wonderfully silky on my skin and had a very slight, but not unpleasant, smell of vegetation. It was clear enough to see my feet, although it gave them a greeny-brown tinge. There was no weed in this area – presumably it was too deep to grow here. I wondered briefly about fish and other creepy-crawlies, but the sensation of being immersed in that cool, silky water was so delightful I put the idea from my mind and carried on.

It was after I'd gone thirty yards or so and was circling back towards land that I saw the 'monster'. Actually, it was only a smallish snake swimming along the top of the water, but coming literally face-to-face, eyeball-to-eyeball, with such a creature is quite as terrifying as meeting a monster. I let out a yelp and the snake slithered away so fast that afterwards I wondered whether I had simply imagined it.

Feeling shaken, I started to swim back towards the shore. Just a few seconds later I felt something brush against my leg. Not the snake – something bigger and rougher-textured. I yelped again and swam away from the area as fast as I could. My heart was beating so fiercely in my chest that it was hard to catch my breath. What on earth could it have been? A fish, or an otter, perhaps? No, it felt solid, larger than that. It couldn't have been a log, because this was clear water, not close to any land. Anyway, a log would float, wouldn't it?

Whatever it was, I didn't fancy bumping into it again.

By the time I'd dried off and changed, Kit and Jimmy were back.

'Anyone else want to have a go in *Robin*?' he asked. 'What about you next, Molly? Come on, she's a sweet little thing. You'll love her.'

'What about Jimmy?'

'You'll keep an eye on him, won't you?'

I looked at Robert and his friends, now out of the lake and sitting around wrapped in towels. They murmured their agreement, although none of them met my eyes, and of course it didn't occur to me until much later that Robert might have been jealous of Kit.

'He mustn't go in the water, though. It's too deep. Promise me, Jimmy?'

He nodded. Even so, I dithered for a long moment: my conscience told me I should stay with my brother, but the temptation of going with Kit was too great.

'C'mon, Molly. He'll be all right for a little while,' Kit said. I succumbed to selfishness. Why shouldn't I have a bit of fun?

'She's so light to row,' he said. 'Why don't you have a go?'

Rowing must be like riding a bicycle: once you've learned, you never forget. I was surprised to find it so easy – in fact, easier than before, because the lightweight boat seemed to skim across the surface of the water like those insects Kit called 'water boatmen'. It was harder to keep it in a straight line than the big wooden boat, but I got the hang of it soon enough; you just had to keep an even, equal stroke on both sides.

'Where do you want to go?'

'The Retreat,' Kit said. 'Let's check out the summer house.'

'Will Jimmy be all right, do you think?'

'We'll only be gone twenty minutes.'

Entranced by the moment, I quickly forgot to worry. My arms worked rhythmically to pull the little boat through the water, the lake spread out before us, and a handsome boy was grinning at me from the stern. It was like a daydream.

We landed and pulled *Robin* up onto the shore. 'Don't want her floating off,' he said, tying the rope to a tree. I wouldn't have minded. Cast away on an island with Kit: what could be more romantic?

The summer house was a large shed painted in peeling eggshell-blue, with French doors and windows all round, in which hung sun-faded blue gingham curtains. Kit retrieved the key from under a stone and opened the door.

'Welcome to my humble abode, sweet maiden,' he said, giving an exaggeratedly dramatic bow.

The shed was furnished simply but charmingly with a small table and chair, also in eggshell-blue, and a scruffy settee covered in soft rugs along the back wall. On the table was a jam jar with pens and pencils, and a notebook browned and curled from the sun. I longed to open it.

A bookshelf held faded paperbacks and magazines, and on the walls were pinned amateur watercolours and children's drawings. It smelled cosy, of warm cedar and dried leaves. A butterfly rested on the windowsill, long dead but its colours still iridescent. If only there was some kind of stove, I thought to myself, you could live here forever. Like Eli.

'It's so pretty,' I gasped. 'The perfect place for writing.'
I sat at the table, took up a pen, pretending.

'Do you write, Molly?'

'Just my diary and a few stories. I'd like to be a proper writer one day, though.' I wasn't going to tell him about the dragon book, not yet.

'Then you can come here any time you want, and we'll be able to say it was where the famous author wrote her bestseller,' Kit said, resting back on the settee.

'Don't tease.' I wanted to move beside him, but decided it was best to wait until he asked.

'I'm deadly serious.' His eyes twinkled in the most un-serious way.

'Does anyone come here much?'

'Not these days. Except me, when I want to get away from things.'

'Is that often? I mean, that you want to get away?'

'When it gets too difficult at home.'

'What do you mean, difficult?'

'Pa's a bit of a brute, you know. They argue a lot. It gets ugly sometimes. It's better when he's in London.' Kit stopped and stared at the floor. I was curious to know more, but didn't want to press him. 'I like you, though,' he said suddenly. 'You're quiet and calm. You talk about interesting things. And your brother's a great kid.'

'You've been so nice with him. I really appreciate it. Not everyone is kind to people who are different.'

He stood and moved towards me. I stood too. We were so close, with barely a foot between us. This is it, I thought, holding my breath, he's going to put his arms around me, and then he's going to kiss me. *Her heart began to thud as she looked into his tanned face and saw her reflection in his eyes. What greater happiness could there be than this?*

My first kiss was just seconds away, inches away. And I couldn't imagine a more romantic place for it. But that is not what happened. Kit moved past me to the door. 'Suppose we'd better get back now,' he said. 'They'll be wondering where we've got to.'

He'd said he liked me. He thought I was pretty. Was my breath not sweet? Did I look at him the wrong way? Did I say something that put him off? I couldn't imagine what I had done wrong.

15

When we returned to the shore the others were lounging about on the grass, drying off, but Jimmy was nowhere to be seen.

I didn't panic, not at first. 'Anyone seen my brother?' I asked.

'He was here for a while, watching us,' Robert said casually. 'But then I looked and he'd gone.'

'Did you see where?'

He looked blank, and the others all shook their heads. Had they not thought to check?

'I'll help you find him,' Kit said. 'He can't have gone far. Come on.'

We looked in the boathouse and along the path leading round the edge of the lake, calling Jimmy's name all the time. I wondered whether he might have followed the path into the woods to find Eli, but then we reached a great iron gate, locked with a padlock and chain.

'He'd never have got through there,' Kit said.

We checked the moat and then retraced our steps through the knot garden and through a door in a long red-brick wall into the largest kitchen garden I've ever seen. None of the gardeners working there had seen a small boy. By now, I was beginning to worry.

'He's probably back in the house with Ma,' Kit said.

We found Jimmy helping to put away the birthday tea. He turned to us with a guilty look, his mouth full of biscuit. I should have guessed that was where he would be.

My first response was to hug him tightly, my face in his biscuit-smelling hair. My second response was fury. 'For heaven's sake, Jimmy. You mustn't run away like that without telling people,' I shouted. 'We had no idea where you were. We were worried stiff.'

My third reaction was to feel guilty; sickeningly, gut-wrenchingly guilty, and ashamed at myself for leaving him alone with the boys. I'd been cross with them, but Jimmy was hardly their responsibility. He was mine.

Perhaps it was the guilt that made it hard to stop being angry. As we walked back to the village I continued to berate him. 'Why did you go back to the house? You know I told you to stay with the boys?'

No reply.

'You must do what I tell you, Jimmy, or you can't come here with me again.'

'Don' want to.'

'You like Kit, don't you? He's been lovely to us. Teaching you to row.'

'They said . . .'

'Said what?'

No reply.

'Kit? Was it something Kit said that upset you?'

No answer.

'Who? Was it Robert?'

'Not Robert. The others.'

We were nearly home. I stopped and made him sit on the low wall of the churchyard. 'What did they say, Jimmy? Come on, this is important.'

'I wanted to play . . .'

He sniffed. I looked at him, shocked to see a tear on his cheek. Jimmy hardly ever cried. I threw my arms round him, holding him tight. It didn't matter what had been said, and who'd said it. I would defend my brother to the death, however annoying he might be.

Through his sobs I heard, 'They said . . . I'm stupid.'

His words were like a stab to my heart. 'You're not stupid, Jimmy,' I shouted. 'You're different, that's all. Whoever said that is the stupid one, because they don't understand what a lovely, special person you are.'

'Said . . . go 'way.'

'They told you to go away?'

He nodded. 'I wanted to play.'

'And they said you couldn't play with them?'

His little face crumpled. I felt helpless, unable to make things better. How wrong it is, that old saw: *Sticks and stones may break my bones, but words will never hurt me.* In my experience, words can cut deeper and hurt for longer, and no amount of sticking plaster will heal the wound. The only remedy is distraction. 'Come on, let's get home. Are you hungry, even after all those biscuits?'

Jimmy nodded, smiling now.

'Okay. I'll make you a sandwich – how's that?'

'Honey?'

'Honey it is.'

It must have been like this all his life, I supposed – feeling different – although I could never be entirely sure how aware of it he was. The only time Jimmy felt really at home was with me and Pa, and with his pals at the special school. And now, of course, with Kit. In other company he was always at a bit of a loss.

And that evening in bed, thinking over the events of the day, it came to me with a clarity I hadn't felt before: Jimmy might seem self-sufficient in many ways; he didn't ask for much, and seemed content with simple pleasures. But when it came to going out in the wider world and meeting new people, he needed to be protected. And that was my responsibility. I'd been so absorbed in thinking about Kit that I had failed to protect my brother.

16

The following Sunday, Pa was due to tell the congregation that he'd got the go-ahead from the diocese for the stained glass. Melissa Blackman arrived in a particularly fetching dress and fancy hat, ready to bathe in glory. Mrs Waddington was there too, unusually, but her husband was missing and so was Kit.

Pa's sermon that day was one of his more engaging ones, I thought. It was all about the importance of cherishing traditions – something the church did very well most of the time – alongside valuing the beliefs of others, something the church was sometimes not very good at. The choice of subject was so transparent I had to lower my face to conceal my smile.

One of the benefits of being in the church choir was having a grandstand view of the assembled congregation. From here, we could spy any new faces and whether anyone was missing; who was attentive and who had a tendency to fall asleep. We saw discreet smiles being exchanged, eyebrows raised, sideways glances. Weddings were rare, but the one service I sang for during our time in the village offered us a special treat, since we were perfectly placed to see the expressions on the faces of bride and groom, ranging from blissful joy to utter terror, sometimes in the same minute.

After the final blessing Pa moved forward between the front pews – his 'I'm a man of the people' position – and invited everyone to be seated for the final notices. 'We are truly grateful to Mr and Mrs Waddington for offering to pay for new stained glass in our beautiful old church. The window will be dedicated to the memory of all those who fell in two world wars, and in particular to Jane Waddington's brother, Captain David Burrows, who died in 1944 while fighting to liberate Italy. I am pleased to tell you that Mrs Blackman's charming design has been given the go-ahead by the diocese. They share our view that the story of the dragon is an important part of our shared history and sense of community. Something we should be proud of, even.'

A familiar voice – Blackman's – boomed a self-important 'Hear, hear'. Mrs Waddington smiled modestly.

Pa went on, 'You only have to look at the medieval carvings on this very church to acknowledge that throughout the centuries we have always incorporated the beliefs and symbols of other, earlier religions and cultures. And this design pays tribute to so many things: medievalism, the history of the Crusades and, not least, Wormley's legitimate claim to its very own dragon. We consider ourselves to be blessed – and our thanks to everyone who is helping to make it happen.'

As we filed out of church I watched people shaking Pa's hand to congratulate him, as well as stopping to thank Melissa Blackman and Jane Waddington. Pa's face was lit with a genuine happiness we'd rarely seen since Mum died. I should have been pleased for him, but at the same time I felt heavy with foreboding: all this hard-won acceptance would disappear in an instant if the matter of the missing church funds wasn't cleared up soon.

It was so hot, that summer, that we'd almost come to dread the sun rising every day. The heat hung over the countryside like a heavy blanket, stifling the breeze and deadening the birdsong. The farmers were afraid the corn would never fill and prophesied an early harvest with poor yields.

Jimmy and I flopped around, seeking every spot of shade or hint of breeze we could find. The garden was drought-stricken and brown, save for the twirling stems and white flowers of the still-rampant bindweed, and the fields on either side of the valley gleamed like bleached gold. Two elderly parishioners had succumbed to the heat, but their burials had to be postponed because the ground was too hard to dig the graves. Pa was even more preoccupied than usual, spending hours alone in his study or at the church, praying.

The heat seemed to compound my state of feverish anticipation about Kit. There had been no word from him since the birthday party five days before. I longed for just a little sign before the school term started again. In my imagination we would exchange witty and erudite letters and then, at Christmas, he would return home to whisk me away in a whirl of glamorous country-house parties.

So when Rob called around to say they were going swimming and would I like to join them, I eagerly agreed. 'Is Kit coming?'

He shrugged. 'Might do,' he said.

'I'll go and get Jimmy, shall I?'

Robert's smile faded. 'The thing is . . .' He hesitated.

'What?'

'Jimmy.'

'What about Jimmy?'

'What will he do? He can't swim, can he?'

'He can sit on the shore and wait for us. Anyway, he'd enjoy paddling,' I said.

Just at that moment my brother appeared at my side. 'Paddle?' he asked, his eyes eager.

Rob kicked the dust with his feet. I was so desperate for an excuse to go to the lake I caved in. 'Tell you what, I'll ask Pa to keep an eye on him for a couple of hours.'

'I come?'

'Not this time, Jim.'

'Want come.'

'I'm going with Robert. We'll go another day.'

Jimmy grabbed my arm. 'Come.'

I shook him off, too fiercely. 'No, Jimmy. I said no. Go away and stop bothering me, for goodness' sake.'

Mrs D heard me and popped her head round the kitchen door. 'Is everything all right here?'

'Can Jimmy stay with you for an hour or so, Mrs D?' I pleaded. She seemed to size up the situation with a single glance: me looking flushed, Jimmy looking crestfallen, Robert shifting his feet with embarrassment in the doorway.

'Of course. Come here, laddie. You can help me with

the baking.' Jimmy's sad little face filled me with guilt, but by the time Rob and I reached the lake, my conscience had disappeared. It was a perfect day and I felt suddenly light and carefree in this beautiful, peaceful place. Even in the furnace of that summer heat, it felt immediately cooler in the shade of the tall willow trees beside that great spread of still, dark water. Willow fluff floated on the air and settled as a haze on the motionless surface of the lake, and the only sound was a hidden coot tick-ticking to warn others of our arrival.

Wormley Hall and most of its gardens were hidden behind the curve of the lake. I could see the boathouse and the swimming platform, but both were deserted. Of the four islands, only Pirate's Lair was in full sight; it made me smile to imagine Kit as a young boy with a red handkerchief round his head and a make-believe sword between his teeth. But where was he now?

Rob interrupted my reverie. 'Coming in, Molly?'

'Aren't we waiting for the others?'

'It's too hot to wait.'

My costume was already under my shorts and T-shirt, so I stripped off and waded in. The water in the shallows was warm, but below the top three inches it became cooler, even cold. Within a few feet of the edge the gravel bottom disappeared, and to save stirring up the stinky mud we both plunged in, gasping slightly at the contrast in temperature.

As we swam, I told Rob about the snake I'd seen on the day of Kit's birthday.

'Sure it wasn't a dragon?'

'Don't be silly. Even I know the difference.'

'How long would you say?'

'Only a foot or so.' I trod water to hold my hands in the air, measuring it.

'It'll have been a grass snake. And it was probably more frightened than you were.'

'Then it was pretty frightened.'

'I'm here to protect you this time,' he said, laughing and swimming away. When I wasn't looking, he seemed to disappear. I twisted round in the water, wondering where he'd got to, when I noticed a huge greeny-white shape appearing below me and remembered the fright I'd been given by the submerged log at the birthday party. Then something grabbed my legs. Although I knew it must be Robert, my terrified scream reverberated across the still water. And then, of course, he emerged beside me, spitting water out of his mouth and laughing uproariously.

'You nearly gave me a heart attack,' I shouted, trying to slap him, but he dodged away and the slap just splashed him instead, so it soon turned into a splashing match, which he won by grabbing both of my arms.

'Let me go,' I spluttered, trying to pull away. 'I'll sink.' I thought we were both treading water but I now understood that, with his greater height, his feet were probably touching the bottom.

'I'll save you,' he laughed, delighted by his own show of strength. 'I'm a qualified lifeguard, didn't you know?' He dragged me closer into his arms and tried to kiss me, but I turned my face away so that he planted it on my cheek. 'This is nice,' he whispered.

It wasn't nice. Not nice at all. Our almost-naked bodies were touching under the water, and I now realised far too late that this was what he'd planned, all along. The other boys wouldn't be coming. Robert wanted to get fresh with me.

'Get off!' I shouted, trying to wriggle out of his arms, but it only made him hold me tighter and I began to panic. 'Stop, Robert. Please. I mean it.'

He let go suddenly and I sank, swallowing a mouthful of water and coming up coughing.

'Here, let me help you.' He held out his arms again, but I turned away and swam as fast as I could to the shore.

'I'm sorry, Molly. I didn't mean to frighten you,' he said, following me out of the water. 'I thought you . . .'

'Well, you thought wrong.'

'Look, I didn't mean it. It was just a bit of fun.'

'I'm not that kind of girl. Anyway, where are all the friends you said were coming?'

Rob began to protest.

'They aren't coming, are they? You tricked me, didn't you?'

I grabbed my sandals, clothes and towel and fled away along the woodland path, brushing away tears of anger and confusion. How different it would have been if Kit had been there, instead of Rob.

After a few moments, satisfied now that he wasn't following me, I stopped to dry off and change back into my clothes. As I sat there, trying to gather my breath and sort out my thoughts, something else caught my attention. It was the unmistakeable gurgle of Eli's chesty guffaw. He had company, by the sounds of it. I started up the path and, growing closer, began to recognise the sound of the other person's laughter: it was Jimmy's. Sure enough, when I came in sight of Eli's hut they were both there, sitting on the steps with mugs of tea in one hand and biscuits in the other, still chuckling.

'Jimmy? What on earth are you doing here? You're supposed to be at home with Mrs D and Pa.'

His little face fell. He'd probably wandered off into the churchyard and down through the woods, without a thought of the worry he'd cause. Now he looked so downcast that I couldn't go on being angry, so I gave him a hug instead.

'You seemed to be having a good joke,' I said. 'What was that all about?'

Eli chuckled again, tapping the side of his nose with a tobacco-stained forefinger. 'Thass between you and me, ain't it, laddie? Can I make you a cuppa, Miss Molly?'

It was tempting. The familiarity of this little porch, the smell of wood-smoke, the chipped enamel cups and ever-present plate of oatmeal biscuits made me feel safe again.

'Oh no, thank you, Eli. We'd better get back. Everyone will be wondering where this naughty boy has got to.'

Jimmy dawdled and complained most of the way home.

'Don't you realise how much Pa and Mrs D will be worrying about you?' I shouted, annoyed with myself, as much as with Jimmy. 'You can't just wander off without telling someone where you are going. Don't you understand?'

'Sorry.'

'What was so important that you had to see Eli this afternoon? You know I would go with you any other time?'

'Help . . . my friend.'

'Yes. We all want to help him,' I barked.

Jimmy stopped on the path, refusing to move, with tears falling down his cheeks. I took his hand.

'But when you run off, we worry about you.'

'My *special* friend.'

All the upsets of the afternoon crowded in, nearly bringing me to tears. I'd shouted at my brother twice and gone alone to the lake with Robert, whom I thought I trusted and regarded as a pal. And the sad truth was that Eli was not simply Jimmy's special friend. He was his *only* friend in the village.

When we got back, Pa was closeted with someone in his study. Later I found him sitting on the bench in the garden with a beer bottle in one hand, cigarette in another, his dog collar loose around his neck. When I sat down beside him, he seemed barely to notice.

The sky was a deepening blue and for some minutes we watched the bats as they swooped above the garden in front of us. They'd frightened me when they'd first arrived that summer, but since Eli told me that each bat could eat several thousand insects every night, I'd decided to welcome them. Wasps, gnats and mosquitoes were new entries in my countryside 'not good' column, so bats were my heroes now.

At last Pa looked up. 'Have a nice swim, love?'

'Lovely, thank you,' I lied. 'The lake was beautiful. And so cooling.'

'No dragons then?'

I smiled, to humour him. 'Who were you with when we got back?'

A shadow fell over his face. 'Mr Blackman, of course.'

'Any news from the bank?'

'The money is definitely missing. We'll have to report it to the diocese.'

'What happens then?'

'I'm not entirely sure, my darling. But no doubt they will have to investigate. It's a lot of money, after all. And after that, who knows?'

'But where's it gone?'

He shrugged and took out another cigarette. As he lit it, I noticed his hands trembling.

'And if they can't find out?'

'Could be the end of our village adventure, my darling.'

'Whatever do you mean, the end?'

He shook his head. 'It's Henry's word against mine, I'm afraid. And he's got the trust of the committee. Not to mention that it seems the money only started to disappear after we arrived.'

'They couldn't think that you . . . ?'

'They might, they might.' His voice seemed to crack and he took another swig of beer, upending the bottle. 'Time for another, I think,' he said, getting to his feet and leaving me sitting in the growing darkness, my thoughts whirling. Whatever would happen if Pa was accused of theft? Could he actually lose his job? Where would we go, how would we live?

❦

We'd been in the village for nine months and my list was growing. It was more evenly balanced now, but some of the negatives were really serious ones:

Good	**Not good**
Kit	Money (very serious)
Mrs D nice (the best)	Eli and his hut (the
Church choir	Blackness in general)
Summer flowers	Jimmy has no friends
Robins	Having to look after
Eli and his stories – nice to J	Jimmy
The lake, especially The Retreat	Wasps and mosquitoes
Learning to row	Robert thinks I fancy
	him; he's wrong

THE UGLY DRAGON
by Molly Goddard

Chapter 5: About friendship

The next time they went to the lake shore they called and called, and their voices echoed back to them across the water but there was no sign of the crocodile, and Jimmy wondered whether they had said something to offend or frighten her.

At last the still surface seemed to move, and the ripples came closer and closer until the lumpy green back of the crocodile emerged from the surface, and she hauled herself out onto the beach beside them.

'Where have you been?' Jimmy asked.

'You're not going to kill me, are you?' The slits in her green eyes grew wider as she looked at him.

'Don't be silly. Why should I want to kill you?'

'You and that boy were talking about killing the crocodile. You didn't mean me, did you?'

Jimmy realised that she must have overheard them talking with Kit in the boat. 'It was just make-believe,' he said. 'They're characters from the book I showed you.'

'Do they want to kill crocodiles?'

It was so hard to explain. 'Captain Hook is a pirate and a bad man and wants to kill Peter Pan. He also wants to kill the crocodile, because it bit off his hand and he has to wear a hook instead. That's why he's called Captain Hook. Fortunately the crocodile has swallowed a clock, so you can tell where he is by the ticking noise. Peter fools the captain by mimicking the sound of the clock. And it all ends happily ever after.'

'Thank goodness for that,' the crocodile said, laughing. 'And you say none of this really happened? It's just a story?'

'That's right.'

'And the crocodile is not evil then?'

'In some ways it's quite friendly. To Peter, at least.'

'Are they friends?'

'Sort of. Not proper friends, like you and me and Molly. And Kit.'

Her face brightened. 'We're all friends?'

'Of course we are. We talk, we keep each other company. Most important of all, we trust each other,' Jimmy said.

'That's wonderful. Thank you.' She danced a little jig on her short stubby legs, kicking up a shower of sand and pebbles. 'Hurray, I've got three new friends.'

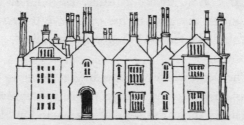

17

Almost every day Jimmy badgered me to take him to see Eli, but the old man seemed to have gone AWOL. We visited twice that following week, but his hut was locked and deserted.

I worried that he might have given up the fight and walked away – heaven knew where. Pa assured me he'd have heard, had Eli already been moved into a council house. But he was nowhere to be seen in the churchyard or around the village, and no one in the pub had any knowledge of him. I began to imagine him dead or dying in a ditch somewhere.

So it was a great relief when, next time we went down the path, I smelled a whiff of wood-smoke and there Eli was, sitting on the step, puffing on his pipe as though he'd never been away. He hailed us like long-lost friends.

'Where've you been these past few days?' I asked.

'Out and about,' he said vaguely. 'Got friends down Bures way.' I didn't press him any further; perhaps he'd just been enjoying a change of air. He turned to Jimmy, patting him on the head. 'And how's life with you, my young friend?'

'There's a dragon,' Jimmy said.

'A dragon? Well, there's a thing.' Eli feigned astonishment, although the glint in his eyes gave it away. 'You've seen it? You lucky fellow. Where? In the lake?'

'For church.'

'Great heavens, whatever's the dragon doing in that holy place?' Eli turned to me, his grey bushy eyebrows raised. As I explained about the stained-glass window design, he began to chuckle so hard it turned into a coughing fit that took some minutes to calm down. 'I'll have to take a look. Give 'em the benefit of my opinion. Not that anyone'll take a blind bit of notice of what I think.'

He made tea and came back to sit down, relit his pipe and took a long draw, which set off another bout of coughing. The rattle in his lungs seemed to be getting worse.

'Have you heard any more about the council-house business, Eli?' I asked, when he'd caught his breath. 'My father tried to dissuade the committee but it didn't make any difference, I'm afraid.'

'Yep, I got a new letter the other day. Says I'll have to move end of next week. For the sake of my welfare, or some such guff. Over my dead body, I says.'

I was shocked. So little time to stop this horrible threat. 'What can we do to help?'

He shook his head. 'You're a good lassie, but there ain't nothing's going to stop that man.'

'What if we ask other people in the village?'

'Huh,' he scoffed. 'That lot don't care a jot about old Eli. They'd as soon have me tidied neatly away as lift a finger to help.'

As we walked home, Jimmy asked me what was going to happen to Eli. He didn't fully grasp all the complications, but he understood enough.

'Must help him,' he said.

'You're right, Jim. We'll make a plan, don't you worry.'

When we reached the churchyard I told him to go home for tea, and I would be back shortly. Sitting on a gravestone in the shade of the ancient yew trees, I tried to think. The committee supported Henry Blackman, but did they really have all the facts? He was such a clever man, so persuasive, so well informed about the law. I got the impression they were all rather in awe of him, and poor Pa was simply outnumbered. Besides which, with the money business hanging over him, he was clearly afraid.

People were fearful for their jobs, of upsetting their neighbours, or perhaps even that Blackman might find some way of persecuting them too. I remembered how he'd urged the committee to keep the matter confidential and told Eli that if he talked, it would be 'the worse' for him.

Blackman's way of operating was so secretive, and so insidious. Perhaps the legend about the dragon was true: if you disturbed it, evil would spread through the village. Last time it was bombs. This time it was a man they called the Blackness. But how could we expose him for what he was doing, or even gather a group of people to oppose him, when so many were afraid of him?

I was deep in thought when a familiar voice hailed me. 'Molly Goddard? It might never happen, you know.'

I'd never been happier to see Kit's broad smile. 'What

do you mean?' I said, trying to ignore the furious pounding of my heart.

'You look so serious. What's up?'

'Long story.'

He waved a bunch of letters in his hand. 'Just let me post these for Ma and I'll come back. Then you can tell me your long story.'

'What a dutiful son you are,' I said, when he got back.

'Doing my best,' he said, plonking himself down beside me and sweeping back the hair from his face. 'I'm in the doghouse at the moment.'

'What've you done, Kit?'

He swatted the air with a hand. 'It's too boring.'

'Have you been away?'

'In London. Bloody hell, it was so hot in town. For once I was actually glad to be back in the country. And it's good to see you, too. I was going to call in tomorrow anyway.'

'What were you up to in London?' I asked.

'Oh, this and that,' he said, kicking the dusty ground. 'But you haven't told me why you're sitting all alone in the churchyard.' He put on a theatrical voice. *"Tis now the very witching time of night, when churchyards yawn and hell itself breathes out contagion to this world.'*

'Whoever said that got it about right. About hell and contagion.'

'Hamlet, I think. But what do you mean?'

'Can I trust you?'

'Pirate's honour,' he said, crossing his hands over his chest. 'My lips are sealed. Fire away.'

He was a good listener, taking in every word as I explained about Eli, the Blackness and the meeting, and what Miss Calver had said.

'What a bastard,' he said finally. 'That old boy's been around forever. He was very kind to me when I was younger. Always giving me biscuits and the rest.'

'Jimmy adores him,' I said. 'We must do something, and soon. But what?'

'Are you really certain that saving the hut is the best thing to do?' Kit asked. 'Would he actually be better off in a council house, like they say?'

'Honestly, it's not as though I haven't wondered that too. But I've seen how Eli loves the place. That glade, the trees, the birds. And he said he'd only leave if they were carrying him out in his coffin. And I believe he's serious. I'm afraid that if they force him to move, he might just wither away and die.'

'Blimey.'

'So don't you see? We *have* to do something.'

Kit went silent for a few moments. 'Look, I think it's brilliant that you want to help the old boy,' he said. 'And whatever you decide to do, you can count on me.'

I could have kissed him there and then, but something held me back, and then the moment had passed. Kit stood up and began to pace the ground in front of me. Suddenly he said, 'We need a demonstration. What about a parade, with white horses and banners?'

'Where are we going to get white horses?' I said, starting to enjoy myself. Somehow, when Kit was around, I couldn't help it.

'And a brass band.'

'We'll chant, "Down with Blackman".'

'Give the bastard Blackman a black eye.'

'The evil Blackness.'

He held his fingers in a cross, as though warding off the devil: 'The curse of the Blackness.'

Turning him into a figure of fun gave me courage. We were still laughing when Jimmy appeared, calling us in for tea. 'I'm hungry,' he insisted, pulling at my arm. 'Come on.'

'Just a few more minutes,' I said. 'Come and sit down.'

I sat on a gravestone. Kit took one opposite and Jimmy sat down next to him. 'Good lad,' Kit said.

'But seriously, what can we do? Any other ideas?' I said.

'A petition might be less controversial.'

'But would people want to sign it? That's the problem.' I told him about the conversation I'd overheard in the church about people not wanting to get on the wrong side of Mr Blackman.

'The very fact of starting a petition would rattle him, surely? And even if we didn't get many signatures, it would at least be a way of telling the village about Eli's plight. Even if they won't give their names, they can put a mark, with "Signature withheld" or some such official words. Like: *We, the undersigned, wish to state that . . .*' Kit dried up. '*We object to the plan to move Mr Eli* – what on earth is his surname?'

'Chadwick. Anyway, there's only one Eli in the village. Everyone will know who we're talking about.'

'*Object to plans to move Eli Chadwick from his shepherd's hut . . . that he's lived in for ten years – to a council house, against his wishes . . .*'

'. . . *threatening the future of the precious village woodland,*' I added.

'What do you think, Jimmy? If we make a petition, you can help me persuade everyone else to sign it. Will you do that?' Jimmy's eager nod helped me decide. At least we'd be doing something.

'There's my boy,' Kit said, ruffling his hair. My brother's face lit up with the most beautiful smile. He loved Kit as much as I did.

Kit was as good as his word. The very next afternoon he came to the vicarage with a bag containing a clipboard – stolen from his father's office, he said with a cheeky grin – and several sheets of lined paper. We drew up columns, finalised the wording, and set out to knock on doors.

We met a mixed reception and lots of difficult questions: who owned the land, why was the church so keen to get rid of Eli's hut, what was the church going to do with the land anyway, and why didn't I get my father do something about it? He was the vicar after all, they pointed out, not unreasonably. When I explained that it was a committee decision, instigated by Mr Blackman, who was in charge of church financial matters, their countenance changed.

Although they were concerned that Eli might be moved against his will, would it not be better for him in the long run? 'If only he could be persuaded it's for the best,' they said.

'But the hut is his home, and he's been there ten years,' I tried to explain. 'He doesn't care about the inconvenience. He loves the woods and the birds. Why can't he live the rest of his life in the place he loves?'

Jimmy always tried to chip in, too, not always successfully. 'Eli my friend.'

By six o'clock that evening our optimism was fading. We'd been to fifteen houses and had no signatures at all. It was quite clear: people were afraid of standing up to the Blackness. Half an hour later I'd all but given up, and anyway Kit said it was time to head home for supper.

'Whatever can we do now?' I said, miserably.

'Come to the Hall tomorrow morning. Ma will be out, so we can talk. Bring Jimmy.'

❈

Of course, the news reached Blackman. Soon after supper the doorbell rang and he was on our doorstep. I showed him into Pa's study and lurked outside the door, trying to overhear what was being said. Before long, I was summoned.

Both men were still on their feet. My father's normally pale face seemed to have taken on a tinge of puce.

'Henry here has been telling me about the petition you've been circulating,' he began, 'about the plan to find Eli a council house. This is confidential church business, for goodness' sake. Why didn't you ask me first, Molly?'

'Because you would have stopped us,' I said, wishing Kit was with me, and cursing myself for not being better prepared for this moment. Here was my big opportunity to tell Blackman the truth, but somehow the words wouldn't come. Pa sighed and sat down heavily on his desk chair.

Blackman filled the silence. 'I understand that you and Christopher Waddington have been fomenting unrest in the village.' What a pompous idiot; we were hardly starting a revolution. 'I think I have the right to see this so-called petition, if you don't mind.'

Actually I *did* mind, and wasn't about to admit that we'd failed to gather a single signature. 'When it is complete,' I said, feeling braver by the minute. Kit would have been proud of me. 'You will of course see it, when we have spoken to everyone in the village.'

There was a knock on the door. Pa ignored it. The knock came again.

'What is it?' he said, irritably.

The door opened and Jimmy walked in, bold as brass, without waiting for permission. 'Want to help Eli. My friend,' he said simply, without a single stutter. Pa stood there, astonished, and seeing my brother being so bold and determined only galvanised me further.

'We both think that trying to make Eli move out of his hut is unfair and wrong. He's been there ten years and, more to the point, he loves it there. He doesn't want to go into a council house, and he would be miserable without the trees, his birds, his woods.'

I stared right at Blackman, but he seemed unable or unwilling to meet my gaze. His eyes strayed to the floor, out of the window or at Pa, as though he didn't want to accept that what I was saying was the truth.

Even when he addressed me directly, he seemed to be

looking somewhere to the side of my face. 'Your passion is laudable, Miss Goddard, but I'm afraid we cannot escape the fact that, as a community, we have a responsibility to look after elderly frail people like Mr Chadwick. This is precisely why we have petitioned the council over several years to build ten council homes in the village, for deserving people like him.'

'What if Eli doesn't want to leave?' I continued to glare, daring him to meet my eyes. He was a bully and a coward, and I felt suddenly powerful, facing him square-on with my arms folded in front of my chest.

'Then I am afraid that the other matter – the legal issue concerning the lack of any formal lease for the hut – will come into play,' he said, looking at my father. Pa's eyes were lowered; he seemed determined not to take sides.

'And you will evict him by force? Don't imagine he will go quietly.'

Blackman hesitated for a fraction of a second. 'We are sure it will never come to that, Miss Goddard. When Mr Chadwick sees the wonderful facilities he is being offered, he will see his old hut in a different light.'

'He has made it perfectly plain that he will never leave his hut of his own free will,' I said. 'You'll have to carry him out in his coffin, he says.'

Jimmy now began to shout, 'No, no, no, NO!' I turned to him to tell him to stop, but his eyes were closed and his hands over his ears. His cheeks burned bright red and he was well on his way to a fully-fledged tantrum. I needed to calm him down. Mother had always drummed into us that, because he had a fragile heart, he must not be allowed to get upset.

'Take him for a walk in the garden, Molly,' I heard Pa saying, over Jimmy's shouts. 'I will be with you shortly.'

As we walked in the cool of the evening, with the sky turning a luminous azure and the stars just beginning to appear, Jimmy's breathing slowed and his face returned to normal. The mosquitoes had largely disappeared – apparently the countryside was so dry they had nowhere to breed – and it was the only place where you could hope to find fresh air.

'We're going to stop him somehow, don't you worry.' I tried to sound confident even though, inside, I felt quite terrified by the storm we had unleashed. Soon afterwards Pa came out too.

'I'm sorry, Pa,' I started. 'But we had to do something to help Eli.'

'I know how much this issue upsets you, and Jimmy. But it is absolutely the wrong time for me to take a stand. The diocese is launching formal investigations into the missing money, starting next week.'

My stomach lurched. 'Oh, Pa, that's terrible.'

'So you'll understand that I have to be very careful until that's been cleared up.' He took a last draw on his cigarette and stubbed it out against the wall. 'Now listen. This is deadly serious. I want you to back off from this business with Eli's hut.' I was about to interrupt, but he held up a hand. 'Let me finish. I need to concentrate on sorting out the church finances, before anything else. And while that is still under investigation, I simply cannot afford to offend Mr Blackman – or anyone. I'm going to need all the support I can get.'

That night the village seemed to be holding its breath.

In the distance we heard the first rumblings of thunder and a few flashes of lightning lit up the sky, but the rain never arrived and the heat felt even more oppressive than before.

18

Next morning was overcast and not a single hint of a breeze tickled the leaves of the trees as Jimmy and I walked down the lane to the Hall. The air seemed weighed down with humidity, and we were soon perspiring from the simple effort of walking downhill. But when we arrived, Kit was bounding with an almost manic energy, so that he could barely keep still, and was grinning from ear to ear.

'Come in, come in,' he said. 'Ma's out, and I've got a treat for Jimmy.'

'The Blackness – he came last night and threatened me about the petition,' I whispered as he led us along a corridor.

'Shh. Let's not spoil Jimmy's surprise. We'll have time later.' He winked conspiratorially, and my heart did a somersault. 'I've got an idea.'

He took us into a back room filled with boots and raincoats and six terrifying-looking rifles on a wall rack.

'That's enough to equip a small army,' I gasped.

'My uncle was a maniac,' he said, laughing. 'Liked to shoot anything that moved. My father's not interested, so these days they just breed pheasants for other people to shoot. It's a profitable business.' He scrabbled under a bench and pulled out an old cardboard box. 'Now, Jim-lad. Take a look at this lot.'

It took a moment to work out that this jumble of red and black fabric was a child's pirate costume, including a tricorne hat with a skull and crossbones embroidered on it, a toy sword with a scabbard and strap, and even a moth-eaten woolly parrot that you could attach to the strap so that it seemed to sit on your shoulder.

'You said you wanted to be pirates, Molly.'

'Said nothing of the sort,' I protested, embarrassed. Did he think I was that childish?

'Okay, so you can be Peter Pan.'

'What's got into you?' I said, feeling uncomfortable.

He shrugged. 'I found this lot in a cupboard and thought Jimmy might like it.' I was still hesitant, but Kit was not to be dissuaded. 'Look, I know you're worried about Eli, but we can talk later. Let's have a bit of fun as well.'

So we dressed my brother in the costume and tied red kerchiefs around our own heads. When we looked at ourselves in the mirror, Jimmy laughed so much that he went red in the face, and his clear enjoyment was somehow infectious. I began to loosen up, too.

'Yo-ho-ho, me hearties,' Kit shouted as we ran to the boathouse – Jimmy holding on to his hat and the parrot with both hands. 'I'll take Captain Hook here with me in the *Mary Jane*, though of course she's the *Jolly Roger* today,' Kit said. 'You take *Robin* and try to find us. You'll have to wait ten minutes to give us a head-start, though, cos this old thing's so slow.'

He put a hand on Jimmy's shoulder. 'Come with me,

Cap'n. Let's weigh anchor and hoist the mainsail.' As they rowed away, Jimmy waved his sword and, noisily encouraged by Kit, approximated shouts of 'Yo-ho-ho and a bottle of rum' over and over again.

It was obvious that they were heading for Pirate's Lair, and after five minutes I climbed into *Robin* and began rowing in that direction. Sure enough they had already landed, and I pulled up *Robin* and pretended to corner them. Kit and I had a sword fight with sticks, with Jimmy excitedly shouting encouragement from the sidelines, before Kit surrendered and we all fell to the ground in a heap, laughing uproariously. I was exhausted, hot and sweaty, but hadn't had so much fun in years.

Once we'd recovered, Kit sent Jimmy searching for the treasure he swore he'd buried on the island some years before. 'Look for the pile of pebbles,' he said. 'It'll be under that.'

'Really?' I asked. 'Is that true? I hope you're not teasing him.'

'Yes, really. I buried some old bits of jewellery my mother gave me in a cigar box, and marked it with stones. That was a few years ago, but I expect it's still there somewhere.'

With Jimmy gone, we were alone, sitting side-by-side on the rickety old landing stage, our feet dangling in the water. It was so hot that even the birds seemed to have taken cover: not a single coot, moorhen or duck was to be seen, and there was no song from the trees. Willow fluff floated, barely moving, on the air. Insects skimmed across the surface of the water below us; the ghostly forms of tiny minnows approached our toes and disappeared in an instant with the slightest twitch.

We sat in complete silence for a few minutes. Kit's fingers rested on the boards beside me, and my fingers itched to creep forward and touch them. At any second, I felt certain, he would turn his face, his dark eyes would meet mine in a soulful gaze and he would kiss me.

What he said was: 'So, tell me about the Blackness.'

I wanted to forget about the whole wretched affair and just enjoy this perfect, idyllic moment with the boy I loved.

'Molly?'

I pulled myself together, took a breath and began to tell him about Blackman's visit and Pa asking us to drop the whole thing, although I didn't explain why. The issue of the missing money was too terrifying – as though putting it into words might be implicitly accepting that Pa had some guilty part in it. 'There's no smoke without fire,' I'd heard Mrs D say once about something else, which I understood to mean that however innocent someone is, people will associate them with the problem. Deep down, I was really beginning to wonder whether Pa would ever be able to clear his name.

'So that's it then. We simply give up on saving Eli's hut?' Kit said.

'I don't know. I feel awful about Pa, but I don't want to let Eli down, either.'

Just then we heard Jimmy crashing through the undergrowth towards us, panting as though he'd run a mile, even though the whole island was less than a hundred yards long, and holding out empty hands.

'No treasure?' I asked.

'You haven't looked hard enough,' Kit said.

'Have so.'

'Go and look some more, Jimmy,' I said. 'We're having a talk, Kit and me.'

He put on a sulky face.

'Then sit down and catch your breath for a few seconds, Jim-boy, and we'll come and help,' Kit said. 'But I have to finish talking to your sister, first. Understand?'

Jimmy sat down on the landing stage to the other side of Kit and looked up at him like an adoring younger brother. He'd do anything Kit asked him, I thought, rebelliously. If only we could tell him to row away and leave us alone.

'Okay, so what about this for an idea?' Kit said. 'You told me Eli talked about chaining himself to the hut?'

I nodded, wondering where this was going.

'That's what the suffragettes did – chaining themselves to the railings of Parliament when they were campaigning to get the vote for women. So why don't we suggest that we join Eli, by chaining ourselves up too? If he doesn't want to, we'll do it without him.'

'What would be the point of that? No one would see us.'

'The newspapers printed photographs of the suffragettes. It was a brilliant way of promoting their cause, and it worked. They got the vote in the end, remember?'

'You think the local newspaper would take our photographs?'

'Why not? We'd have to tell them, of course, so they could find us. Your friend Miss Calver would help us with a press release.'

'My father would hit the roof.'

'My parents too,' he said. 'But isn't Eli's hut the important issue here?'

'We should only do it if he agrees.'

'Of course. But the point is that while we're occupying the hut, they can't destroy it.'

The idea was so bold, so daring, so terrifying. Being chained to a hut in the middle of the woods, with press photographers milling around? Pa would be furious. He might never forgive me. And what might the Blackness do? Could we even get hurt? But Kit was looking at me with bright, expectant eyes. How could I disappoint him?

'Let's go and visit Miss Calver and see what she thinks.' I was secretly beginning to hope she would say the newspapers wouldn't be interested, so that we could drop the whole idea.

Kit leaned across and put his hand over mine. I squeezed his hand back and we sat there, holding hands, for a long, beautiful moment. Was his touch thrilling, electric, like those novels said? Did it sear my skin? Well, perhaps not, but it certainly made my pulse race, and it felt so right, so perfect, that I wanted it to go on forever.

'Are you getting cold feet?' he asked. I was wondering how to respond when Jimmy interrupted.

'Find treasure now?' I'd almost forgotten he was there.

'Go and look again,' I said.

But Kit was already on his feet. 'Come on, laddie. Let's go and find it.'

After some searching we eventually found the small pile of stones, concealed under an tuft of overgrown grass, and dug into the hard, dry earth with the trowel Kit had packed. All that was left, after years beneath the earth, was a broken box and some pieces of rusty metal, but Jimmy seemed perfectly satisfied.

As we were rowing back, I glanced across at Kit and Jimmy in the other boat. My brother had never seemed happier than when he was with Kit. They were sharing a joke and laughing out loud – I felt a little pang of jealousy. Kit was such a mystery. I could still feel the imprint of his hand on mine, but he gave no sign that he wanted to be closer. I hated myself for resenting my brother, but how would I ever get a boyfriend with Jimmy hanging around all the time?

Later, when we got back to the Hall, Kit said, 'Where's your parrot, Cap'n?'

Jimmy looked round, checking the jacket and the strap the parrot had been attached to. It was gone – probably lost somewhere on the island. His face crumpled and he looked close to tears. But Kit wasn't bothered. 'Not to worry, Jim-boy,' he said, ruffling his hair. 'It'll be happy enough flying around and enjoying its freedom till we find it again.'

***

'Miss Molly, Master Jimmy, Master Waddington: treble trouble. To what do I owe the pleasure?' Miss Calver said, opening the door.

'We need your help,' Kit said.

'I'll do what I can.' She ushered us inside. 'Forgive the mess. I've been away staying with journo friends in Ipswich. Come through.'

She cleared three chairs and invited us to sit down.

'Well, I don't know about you, but I've had a rather long, hot and tiresome journey, so I think we deserve a little drink. Lemonade?' She checked the man-sized wristwatch that swamped her narrow wrist. 'The sun's nearly below the yard-arm, after all.'

It was only four o'clock – teatime really – but that didn't seem to bother her. She returned with the drinks and took a long swig of whisky.

'Now, how can I help?'

Kit and I glanced at each other. 'You go first,' I said.

'No, you,' he said, nudging me.

'Have you heard about our petition?' I started.

'Petition? No, I haven't. But as I said, I've been away the past week. What's it about?'

'We wanted to get people's opinion about Eli's hut,' I said. 'Because the church committee has been persuaded that he'd be better off in a council house.'

'And what does Eli think?'

'He hates the idea,' I said.

'And your father?' She peered at me over her glasses.

'He's opposed to it, but got voted out,' I said.

'And how did the petition go?'

'No one wanted to sign it,' I said. 'Because they know who's behind the plan.'

'Hmm. Doesn't surprise me,' she said, lighting a cigarillo.

I explained about the meeting and the vote, and the file of letters Eli had shown me and Pa. 'That wretched man,' Miss Calver spluttered. 'Everyone knows he's trouble, but no one's prepared to stand up to him.' She poured herself another generous glass of whisky and swigged most of it in a single gulp. 'So, how can I help?'

'You mentioned that Blackman and Eli had their differences in the past. Do you know what it was about?'

'Ah, they go way back. This isn't the first time Blackman's

tried to get him off that land. Before he even came to live here, just after the war, Henry tried to buy it, planning to build houses there. He knows full well that if you cut down the trees, it would have a wonderful view of the valley.'

'What happened? Did the church refuse to sell it?'

'I don't rightly know, except that Blackman was in cahoots with the previous incumbent, before everything seemed to go very sour and the poor man lost his mind. Eli knows more about it than anyone, so perhaps he threatened to tell. Who knows?'

'And your own disagreement with Blackman?'

'A stupid thing, really. Where I park my car is actually common land. I've used it forever. But they decided to start charging me for the privilege.'

'And what did you do?'

'I couldn't afford the legal fees, so I threatened to go public. In the end we agreed to compromise.'

'That's the thing, Miss Calver,' Kit said now. 'What do you think would happen if we went public about Eli's hut?'

As he explained our plan to occupy the hut, she became increasingly animated. 'My dears, what a simply splendid idea. I'm all ready to join you. My goodness, I love a bit of practical protest,' she said, rubbing her hands with evident glee. 'You've come to just the right person. We'll write a stonking press release they won't be able to ignore.'

She poured herself another generous slosh from the whisky bottle and pulled out, from beneath a mound of papers, a spiral-bound reporter's notebook and a pencil.

A fluent line of spindly hieroglyphs – shorthand, she called it – spooled out from the end of her pencil across the page as she talked. '*Protestors in Wormley near Colchester are chaining themselves to a shepherd's hut* – note the present continuous, always makes it sound more urgent – *to save the home of an elderly war veteran.*'

'That's brilliant,' Kit said, as I quailed at the thought of Pa's fury. '*The hut, on church-owned land, has been inhabited by Mr Eli Chadwick . . .*' She looked up. 'Any idea how old he is?' I shook my head. She wrote, 'Check age' and then continued '. . . *since tragedy struck the village in December 1940. His cottage was bombed and his wife killed. Now the church committee wants to rehouse him in the new council estate being built on the Colchester road. They say the hut is not fit for year-round occupation.*'

'Eli told Molly they'd have to carry him out in his coffin,' Kit said.

'Excellent. Always paint a picture with words. "*They'll have to carry me out in my coffin,*" *Mr Chadwick says.*' She sucked the end of her pencil. 'I suppose you've checked with Eli that he's okay with this?'

'We will, of course. Tomorrow morning.'

'Then we can press the Go button. I might even drive into the newspaper offices and drop it in.' She emptied her glass and plonked it down on the table with a thud. 'Ooh, we're going to have such fun. Feels like old times.'

As we walked back down the street, Kit said, 'Good old Miss Calver. Coming up trumps like that. What do you think, Molly?'

My head was filled with confusion, my loyalties divided. On the one hand, Eli needed our help. On the other, it could all turn out so very badly for my father. But Kit's enthusiasm was infectious. This was our secret shared plan.

Together we would save Eli's hut, so that he could live out the rest of his years happily in his woodland grove.

'So long as Eli agrees, we'll go ahead,' I said.

When we parted that afternoon, Kit took both of my hands in his and looked into my eyes. 'You're a great kid, doing this for Eli,' he said. 'And a good mate. Makes me realise how selfish my life has been up to now.' He let go and turned to leave, touching me lightly on the shoulder. 'Okay then. See you tomorrow, ten-thirty? It's going to be amazing, Molly.'

''Till tomorrow,' I said, near to tears. I didn't want to be a great kid or a good mate. I wanted to be his girlfriend.

At home, Pa was nowhere to be found, and Mrs D was anxious.

'Forgive me, Miss Molly. But has he talked about feeling poorly, lately?' she asked, shaking flour into the large cream mixing bowl she used for making bread.

'Only that he's got a lot on his plate,' I said. The truth was that my father was looking increasingly worn around the edges, like a frayed scarf. 'Why do you ask?'

She demurred, peering down at the dough. 'Well, it's not really my place . . .'

'You can tell me.'

'It's what the hubby said last night.' She carried on kneading.

'Go on.' What new revelation was this?

'George heard him, late last evening, in the church. He'd dropped in to replace the candles . . .'

'Pa often goes over there to pray, of an evening.'

'This wasn't praying, my dear. He was . . .' She stopped her kneading.

'You can tell me, Miss D.'

'The word George used was . . . babbling.'

'Babbling?' Like a brook? Such a strange word. 'What about?'

'None of it really made sense, Hubby said. But there was something about the bank managers and being afraid of the shellings, and the world being out to get him, and someone called Sarah.'

My mother. I felt like crying, but somehow I needed to hold it together to protect my poor father. 'It's the shell shock,' I heard myself saying. 'He gets these turns from time to time. It will pass. And Sarah is my late mother, by the way. In case you were wondering. We all miss her terribly.'

Mrs D brushed her floury hands on her apron, walked over and took me in her arms. It was the first proper hug I'd had from an adult in months. For a second I resisted. But then the dam in my heart gave way, and I found myself falling against her, sobbing.

'You poor child,' she said, stroking my hair. 'So young, and so much to contend with. But I'm sure it will all settle down for your father before long. Just a few teething problems. Only to be expected, in a new parish and all.'

I longed to believe her.

❧

That evening I showed Jimmy my dragon story. I'd copied it out neatly and stitched it between two pieces of cardboard, on which I'd rather ineptly painted a fierce dragon on the front cover, and a crocodile on the back. Jimmy was utterly delighted with it, insisting that I read the whole thing to him.

But as I turned to go, his face fell. The smile had disappeared and his eyes, normally so bright and cheerful, seemed to droop at the edges. It was usually only when he was unwell that we ever saw him like this. I went to sit down beside him on the bed again and put my arm round him.

'What's up, Jimmy?'

'Eli.'

'I know. I'm worried too.'

He looked doubtful. 'His hut?'

'But we're doing what we can, all right?'

He shook his head violently, screwing up his face. 'No, no, no . . .'

He began to sob. It was all I could do not to burst into tears again too. I couldn't bear to see him so unhappy. With Pa so preoccupied and absent, it felt as though the troubles of the world were resting on my shoulders and everything was falling apart.

I took a breath and pushed down my tears, summoning the most reassuring tone that I could muster. 'Look, we're doing our best, Jim. We just have to wait and see.'

19

After that, everything changed.

It started with the weather. Next morning we woke to discover that a curtain of heavy grey cloud now covered the sun, which had shone almost unceasingly for weeks on end. It should have brought relief, but there was still not a single breath of wind. It was swelteringly hot and so humid that the slightest activity brought you out in a sweat.

Mrs D prophesied that a storm was on its way, and it certainly felt as though the world was on hold, just waiting for something to happen. 'Heaven knows, we need something to clear the air around here.' She turned to me. 'Cheer up, Molly. You look like a thundercloud yourself.'

'Sorry. I didn't sleep very well.' I'd lain in bed for hours, thinking about Kit. Our plan had seemed so exciting when we'd been talking about it together, but now it felt as though we were about to step off a cliff into the unknown. Most of all, I worried about Pa. The more I thought about it, the more I was coming to think that occupying the hut was a really bad idea, but having started it, I felt duty-bound to Kit, Miss Calver and Eli to see it through.

'C'mon, Jimmy, get your shoes on. We're going to meet Kit and visit Eli,' I said after breakfast.

When we reached the stile, Kit was already there.

Jimmy ran towards him, holding up his arms, shouting, 'My friend.'

Kit lifted him in the air and swung him round. 'You're looking great, Jim-boy.'

Jealousy welled up in me again, resenting their obvious ease and affection.

As we began walking towards Eli's hut, I started to sense that something was wrong. There was no smell of wood-smoke, no sound of Eli whistling, no Sarge barking. And when we reached the glade, it seemed that my instincts had been correct. Not only was the hut locked and deserted, but on the door was pinned a piece of paper. We climbed the steps to read it. Typed in large red capitals, it read:

EVICTION NOTICE

WE HEREBY NOTIFY THAT THESE PREMISES
ARE DEEMED UNSUITABLE FOR OCCUPATION
AS A DOMESTIC DWELLING
BY ORDER: HENRY BLACKMAN, TREASURER
WORMLEY PARISH MANAGEMENT COMMITTEE

'Bloody hell,' Kit said. 'He's done it. Already.'

Jimmy tugged at my hand. 'Done it?'

'Don't worry, Jim-boy. We're going to stop them.'

'How stop them?'

'We're going to lock ourselves inside the hut, to stop them knocking it down,' Kit said.

'Can I come?'

'No, my love,' I said. 'It's not safe for small boys. Anyway, we need to try and find Eli first. Make sure he's all right.'

Kit was on tiptoe, peering in through one of the windows.

'What are you doing, Kit?'

'Seeing whether he's taken his things.'

It was then that I remembered seeing Eli hiding his key in the arch of the left-hand wheel.

'No need.' The key was still there, and the door unlocked easily. As soon as we stepped inside, its warm, smoky smell brought back all the happy times we'd spent there. All of Eli's possessions were still neatly in place, the bed quilt straightened, the books on their shelves, the kettle on the hob, carefully cut kindling and old newspapers on top of the logs in the basket. It was as though he'd just stepped out for a few moments. Nothing seemed to have been touched, and this made me even more worried than ever.

'No fire,' Jimmy said, peering into the stove. 'Where Eli?'

'They said they were moving him to a council house, up on the High Road.'

'Let's go and find him,' Kit said.

I locked the hut and replaced the key carefully, hoping against hope that Eli was safe and would come back soon.

It was a long, sweaty walk up the street to the High Road – at least a mile, and most of it uphill. Then we had to traipse another half-mile to the council houses.

Halfway there, Jimmy began to sniffle. I took his hand and dragged him along, so roughly that he started to stumble. 'Come *on*, Jimmy,' I snapped at him.' We haven't got all day. Once we've found Eli, we can ask him where he wants to live.'

How I wished, looking back on that moment, that I'd shown more patience, more compassion. What I failed to realise was that Jimmy was as worried and upset as I was – and just as determined to fight for his friend – only he didn't know how to show it.

The place was still a building site: dusty, bare ground was littered with concrete mixers, bulldozers and other rusting equipment, with no greenery and scarcely a tree or bush within a hundred yards. I couldn't imagine a greater contrast with the beautiful woodland glade Eli loved so much. Although four of the ten semi-detached houses looked finished, none of them seemed to be occupied. Bare windows stared at us like the blank eyes of empty souls; it made me shiver.

The place was deserted. And Eli was nowhere to be seen.

'Don' like it here. Want to go home,' Jimmy said.

On the way back down the hill, we argued. Kit was all for going ahead with the sit-in, regardless. 'They've issued an eviction notice, Molly. What other proof do you need?'

I insisted that we must wait until we'd found Eli. 'What if he's changed his mind, found somewhere else to live? We'd be dragging his name through the newspapers when he'd rather be left alone.'

'But it's *wrong*. Immoral. Didn't you say so yourself? The Blackness wants the land for himself, to cut down the woodland and sell for more housing. And that's not enough to demonstrate against?'

I had no answer.

'Where's your passion gone, Molly, your *fire*? I thought you were so brilliant: determined to stand up for the underdog against the evil forces of the Blackness. And now we have genuine proof, with his signature on that eviction notice and all, you've gone soft.'

'Not soft, just cautious,' I muttered, trying to hold back tears.

We parted in ill humour, agreeing that he would come to the vicarage the following morning. I was going to ask Mrs D and other people where Eli might have gone, and Kit reluctantly agreed, although I could see he was disappointed in me. I'd been so flattered that he had agreed to help me – thrilled and perhaps a little blinded by his energy and enthusiasm. And the fact that I adored him. Now I was filled with doubts.

❖❖❖

When we got back to the vicarage I discovered my father in our bleak front room, perched on one of the sagging armchairs with his head in his hands, cigarette between his fingers. The ashtray at his feet was already full, the air muggy with stale smoke.

'What's going on, Pa?' I said.

He tipped his head in the direction of the study. 'Diocesan men are here,' he whispered. 'Close the door. They're going through the accounts with Mr Blackman.'

'Why aren't you helping them?'

He shrugged. 'They asked me to leave.'

As I went over to put my arm round him, their reason became obvious. Tucked down beside Pa in the armchair was an empty bottle, and two further bottles lay on the floor beside him. The stink of alcohol was unmistakeable. At midday on a weekday morning, my father was drunk. My world seemed to crumble around me, but I took a breath and tried to gather myself.

'What on earth, Pa?' I said, holding up one of the bottles.

He looked up at me shamefaced, his eyes bloodshot. Like a scolded dog.

'I'm going to find Mrs D, and make you some coffee.'

'Gone to the market.' Of course, it was market day. Perhaps it was just as well she was not here to witness my father's humiliation. But her absence meant Pa had had free access to the pantry where the beer was kept, without her vigilant eyes to deter him.

There were voices in the hallway outside, and a knock at the door.

'Mr Goddard? Are you there?'

I went to the door and came face-to-face with a tubby grey-haired man in a dog collar and a smart suit.

'My father is not feeling well,' I said, standing in the doorway to block his view. 'I'm his daughter, Molly.'

'Pleased to make your acquaintance, Miss Goddard,' he said, holding out a pudgy, sweaty hand. I shook it, reluctantly.

'Can we talk to him?' Behind him stood Blackman, his face twisted into a smirk, and a younger man holding a large black briefcase.

'I'll ask.' I closed the door and went back to Pa. 'They want to talk to you. Do you feel up to it?'

He shook his head, and I returned to the door.

'I'm so sorry. My father is feeling quite poorly. We've all been down with a bit of a stomach bug,' I lied.

'I'm sorry to hear that.' His expression of compassion, a small frown with eyes briefly downcast, was well practised and clearly false.

'Perhaps you could come back in a few days' time?' I added.

He sighed. 'I suppose so. It's very inconvenient, having to travel from Bury St Edmunds. But please tell your father that we will return early next week. Ah, and we'll be taking the account books with us.'

After the other men had gone, piling into a sleek black motor, polished until it gleamed even in the grey light of the day, Mr Blackman lingered.

'Is there anything I can do to help, Miss Goddard?' he asked, peering round me. 'We are a little, shall we say . . .' he paused for dramatic effect, 'concerned for your father's, erm, welfare.'

Yes, he's drunk, I wanted to shout. *And why do you think a man who never normally touches alcohol, beyond the odd sociable beer, is drunk at midday on a Wednesday? Because of you, Mr Blackman, and your meddling – and the way you have no feelings for anyone other than yourself.*

Of course I said none of that. What I did say was, 'Would you like some coffee, Mr Blackman? I'd like to ask you something. Do come through to the kitchen.' I turned back to Pa, whispering, 'Stay here, I'll bring coffee', and then closed the door behind me.

'And what is this mysterious matter, Miss Goddard?' Mr Blackman said, after I'd made coffee. I took a glass of orange juice up to Jimmy and told him to stay in his room until the coast was clear.

Once again, having spent so many hours imagining him

as a dark, menacing evil, Blackman's very ordinariness took me aback. He was really rather average in every way, the sort of man who might pass unnoticed in a crowd. There was not a single pair of horns, curly tail or fearsome trident in sight.

'It's good news about your friend Mr Chadwick, isn't it?' he said with a false air of brightness. 'We were fortunate enough to persuade the council to allocate him one of those lovely houses on the High Road, and he's moved in. They've got all mod cons, you know? Hot water and electricity, flushing toilets – the lot. He seemed delighted. As surely anyone would be?'

He smirked, showing all his teeth. *How cheerfully he seems to grin, how neatly spreads his claws.* Blackman was lying, and he really didn't care that I knew it. He was operating on a whole different level of truth and morality. It felt like walking on quicksand.

'I went up there this morning, and none of the houses were occupied,' I said. The hint of a frown shadowed his face.

'A man has the right to leave his home from time to time, Miss Goddard, does he not? No doubt Mr Chadwick has gone a-visiting. As people do.' His self-satisfied tone made me want to grind my teeth.

'He didn't *want* to leave. He loved his hut, and said he'd only ever leave it if they took him out in his coffin.'

Blackman sighed. 'Dear Miss Goddard. I realise that you have the best of intentions but, forgive me, I wouldn't expect someone of your tender years to entirely understand the complexities of society. Mr Chadwick is suffering mental-health issues,' he went on. 'When you are older, you will surely see that our actions were very much in his best interests. We are all prone to sentimentality on occasion, are we not?'

Why did he always end his sentences with a question?

'I am perfectly certain that once Mr Chadwick has had a few days to grow accustomed to his new home, he will realise how convenient it is, how warm and well insulated, how nice it is to have running water and electricity. When we get older, our creature comforts become more important than ever and, of course, he's no spring chicken, you know?'

The anger was rising hotly up the back of my neck. 'Eli has lived in the village all his life, Mr Blackman, and although he's suffered much tragedy and loss, he seems to me to be one of the sanest residents of all. It is wrong, and inhumane, to make him leave his hut.'

'The bottom line, my dear, is that hut was neither suitable nor safe for a man of his age and frailties. The parish must take responsibility for the welfare of its parishioners. Winter is on its way, and whatever would people say if we let him freeze to death?'

'Surely it should be his choice where he lives?' I heard myself shouting.

He still seemed unruffled. 'We have no reason to believe that this is not his choice. As I said before, he seemed perfectly happy when we moved him to his new house. And why wouldn't he be?'

It was no good trying to win this argument. He simply wasn't interested in any other point of view. I stood up sharply, knocking over my chair with a crash. 'I think it is time for you to leave, Mr Blackman. I know you've told

Eli and the church committee to keep quiet, but just you wait and see. The newspapers are going to hear about this.'

His smile evaporated, the eyes hardened, his jaw tightened.

'I would think very carefully about that, Miss Goddard.' His eyes were as sharp and menacing as any weapon. 'You cannot have failed to notice that your father has rather more serious issues on his plate at the moment.' He paused, raising a meaningful eyebrow. 'As today's visit from our diocesan friends has made perfectly clear.'

After I'd seen him out of the front door, my legs went to jelly. Using the wall for support, I managed to get back to the kitchen and sat down at the table, with my heart racing and my head whirling. I had confronted the man and tried my best. But right now Blackman held all the cards. I was completely powerless.

After a few moments, when I'd gathered my wits, I went back into the living room to find Pa. He was sound asleep, head back, mouth agape, snoring loudly. Oblivious.

'What have you done, Pa? They think you've stolen the money,' I whispered. 'But why would you do it? We don't want for anything – don't have any big bills or debts. Have you been negligent somehow? Taken your eye off the ball?'

He didn't stir.

***

The rest of the afternoon passed in a state of listless anxiety. Our wonderful father, the man on whom Jimmy and I depended entirely for our livelihood, our support and our happiness, had been reduced to a pitiful husk of himself, all shreds of his growing confidence now drained away. Who could have predicted that such an idyllic-looking village, home to so many genuinely nice people, could have brought a good man so low? And all of Pa's problems – Eli's hut, the fate of the woodland, and the missing five thousand pounds – led back to one individual: the Blackness.

Eventually I encouraged Pa to go up to bed. Jimmy and I sat down to eat the cold supper Mrs D had left out for us, but he seemed strangely unsettled, pushing the food around on his plate, when he would normally have wolfed it down in half the time it took me to finish.

'What's up, Jim?'

'Parrot,' he said.

'Oh, don't worry about that,' I replied, relieved it wasn't anything more serious. 'Kit will find it soon enough. And if he doesn't, we'll go and look for it ourselves, shall we? I'm sure it will be safe on the island. Birds like being outdoors. Now, eat up and we'll run you a bath.'

He seemed satisfied enough and ate a few mouthfuls of ham and hard-boiled egg, followed by some leftover bread-and-butter pudding, one of his favourites.

I ran a bath and scrubbed his back, which Jimmy loved; and then, at his insistence, I read the dragon stories all over again. And as I read, I realised what the next chapter should be about.

THE UGLY DRAGON
by Molly Goddard

Chapter 6: About evil

Jimmy and the crocodile were eating currant buns that Mrs D had declared were too stale, but he liked them anyway. So did the crocodile.

'Goodness, these buns are tasty. Got any more?' she asked. He passed them over and then realised that if he wasn't careful, she would eat the lot – paper bag and all. So he took out a couple of buns and put them on the ground beside her. In two great chomps and with much clattering of teeth, they were gone.

'Can I ask you a question?' Jimmy said.

'Feel free,' she said. 'Any more buns?'

'Some people say you bring evil to the village if you are disturbed, and they're blaming us children for playing on the lake and disturbing you.'

'Ha-ha-ha-ha,' she laughed. 'Fancy me having the power to bring evil to the village.'

'So it's not true then?'

'Of course not. I'm only a small ugly drag . . . I mean croco-dile. Although there is an old legend about a black serpent who

lives at the bottom of the lake and comes out to flick poison from his tongue. But tell me, what evil am I supposed to have caused?'

'Well, there's a man in the village who's been trying to make my friend Eli move out of his hut in the woods. He doesn't want to leave, but the man doesn't seem to care. And it's not the only thing he's done, but everyone seems to be afraid of him and no one is prepared to speak out.'

Her smile disappeared. 'Listen, Jimmy,' she said. 'Men do evil things for many reasons. None of them have anything to do with dragons, or serpents, for that matter.'

'But why do they do evil things?'

She snorted. 'It's about power. Men who feel weak or inadequate feel they have to prove themselves somehow, trying to get power over others and bullying people who can't fight back.'

'Like Eli.'

'Like your friend Eli.'

'But how can we help him?'

'By standing up for him,' she said. 'By showing the world that you care about your friend. You won't always succeed, but at least you will have tried. And that's what matters most.'

20

After writing that chapter I still couldn't settle, and found myself wandering through the house and garden, trying to work out what to do. Every way my thoughts turned they seemed to reach a dead-end: Eli ousted from his beloved hut, Pa under suspicion from the diocese.

Outside, great bursts of lightning lit up the sky again and again, behind the clouds. No rain, no thunder, no visible flashes, just a sudden brilliant brightness in the western sky, gone in an instant, followed by another, and another. Then I heard thunder: a long, deep rumbling that seemed to shake the ground beneath my feet. A storm was definitely on its way.

What made everything worse was my disagreement with Kit. He was my only ally, the only person I could really talk to and trust, and I hated the fact that we'd parted on ill-tempered terms. What I most wanted to do was run down the lane to the Hall and fall into his arms. He would make everything right, I felt sure.

I should have waited until the following day, of course. But once the idea had lodged itself in my head, I couldn't dislodge it. Everything now felt terribly urgent. A storm was coming and somehow that galvanised me; Eli had been locked out of his hut and was nowhere to be found. I couldn't bear to think of him lying in a ditch somewhere, sodden and cold.

Pa was still snoring, dead to the world. When I went to check on Jimmy, the light was out and he was fast asleep. I would only be half an hour or so. Neither of them would even notice I was gone. I prayed the storm would hold off until I got home. My footsteps seemed to guide themselves, and it felt like only moments before I found myself walking up the gravel driveway to the Hall.

I knocked on the door, hearing it resonate inside the huge hallway, mirroring the sound of my heart hammering inside my chest. The words were ready in my mouth: 'Hello, Mrs Waddington, I'm sorry to call so late. It's fine – nothing wrong. But could I have a quick word with Kit?'

There was no answer. My second knock resounded even more loudly. I was about to give up when I heard his voice: 'Hang on, hang on. Who is it? I'm coming.'

The latches went back, the door opened and there he was, my lovely boy, in stripy pyjamas and a velour dressing gown, his hair tousled, feet bare.

'Molly? It's nearly ten o'clock, for goodness' sake. I was getting ready for an early night. Has something happened?'

'Where are your parents?'

'Pa is in London and Ma is at some black-tie charity affair in Sudbury, I think. You know these do-gooders, they like to enjoy themselves. Well, look . . .' He hesitated. 'I don't reckon they'll be back for an hour or so. Do you want to come in?'

We went through to that beautiful drawing room, the one where we'd first had tea all those months ago, where Jimmy had spilled his drink and we'd witnessed Mr Waddington's short temper for the first time. Kit sat in an easy chair and I took the sofa.

'What is it, Molly? You can tell me, you know.'

'I know. That's why I'm here. You're the only person I can trust.'

'Well then, tell me.' The yawning stretch of deep carpet between us made everything so formal.

'I'm so worried about Eli and I really want to help him, but my father's in so much trouble, I don't know how we are going to survive it, and I just can't, I just can't . . .' My voice broke and the tears began to run down my cheeks.

'I'm so sorry, but I'm sure it's not the end of the world, you dear old thing.' Kit reached into his dressing-gown pocket and pulled out a crumpled linen handkerchief embroidered in navy blue at the corner, with the initials CMW. I wiped my face, distractedly wondering what the M stood for.

When he sat down beside me and put a hand on my shoulder, the tenderness of the gesture seemed to open the floodgates and I began to sob. I felt Kit's arm round my shoulders and he pulled me to him, my head on his chest, stroking my hair. After a few moments I managed to pull myself together. I turned my face and looked up. Our lips were just inches apart, and I thought for a brief, glorious moment that he might actually bend his head to kiss me.

Instead he said, 'Let me get you a drink of something. Whisky or brandy?' He took his arm away and stood up.

'A glass of water – or lemonade, perhaps,' I said, feeling

even more stupid. I tried to tidy my hair, wipe my face. What was I thinking of, coming here so late at night and weeping all over him? I must look a fright.

Kit returned with the drinks, sat down beside me and we sipped in silence for a few moments. At last he said, 'Look, Molly, you don't have to do anything you don't want to, you know. If there are problems with your pa, then you must put them first. Yes, we both want to help Eli, but if it's making you so upset . . .'

He put down his glass. 'And to be honest, there was something I needed to tell you anyway.'

My heart seemed to hang in my chest. Was he about to make some kind of declaration?

'The truth is that I've got to go away – to London – tomorrow.'

Panic gripped my breath. 'Tomorrow? What's happened? Is it something I've done?'

'No, not that. It's my father. My bloody father. My bloody bastard father.' The words came out like bullets now. He turned to face me. 'I've been keeping it to myself all summer, hoping that if I don't think or talk about it, then it won't be real. But I'm not going back to school. Not now, not never.'

'Not going back?' I repeated, stupefied. 'But I thought you liked your school?' Kit nodded miserably. 'What on earth are you going to do instead?'

He shrugged. 'Dunno. Ma and Pa want to send me to a crammer.'

'What's that?'

'Where they force-feed you, to pass your exams.'

So he'd been slacking and this was his punishment. 'Is that what you want?'

'Nope.' He shrugged again, picking at a loose thread in the upholstery. He looked so fed up – no, not fed up, but blank and distracted.

'Isn't that what they're supposed to do at school?' I asked. 'Get you through exams?'

'It's no good, Molly. I've been through all the arguments, but I'm not allowed to go back.'

'Not allowed?'

He gave a great sigh. 'I've been expelled.'

I could hardly believe it. A boy like Kit, who seemed to have everything: good looks, sporty, clever in his own way. What terrible offence had he committed?

'For good?'

'That's what "expelled" usually means.'

'Sorry.'

'No, I'm sorry. I didn't mean to snap. It's just that, oh, I don't know . . .' His legs jiggled with pent-up energy.

'And you've been keeping this to yourself all this time?'

'I thought – oh, I don't know – that if I put it to the back of my mind and got on with other things, it would go away somehow.' I remembered his sudden, intense focus on the plans for our protest; his almost manic energy at the birthday party and when we were playing pirates; the way he'd seemed so distracted when we were together on the island. It was all beginning to add up.

He dropped his head into his hands. 'Oh God, I'm so miserable.'

'But what did you do that was so terrible?'

He shook his head.

'Tell me, Kit. I'm the best keeper of secrets in the world.'

'It's no good, Molly. I just can't tell you. I'm sorry. You wouldn't understand.'

'Try me.'

'You're the ruddy vicar's daughter, for heaven's sake.'

'But you know I'm not the churchy type, Kit. I won't judge you, whatever it is you've done. I promise.'

He took a deep breath and sighed. He started to speak, and stopped. 'No, I can't tell you. It's hopeless, Molly. Perhaps one day I'll explain.' He turned to me with tears in his eyes and buried his face in my shoulder. 'Oh God, whatever am I going to do?'

I wrapped both of my arms around him, and he reciprocated. This was the physical contact I'd so longed for, but not in this way – not as his comforter.

After a short while Kit sat up and wiped his face with his hands, leaving dirty smears. 'You must think I'm ridiculous, snivelling away like that.'

'I suppose you'll just have to do what your parents want you to do.'

'But what about Eli and his hut – all of that? I'm so sorry for letting you down.'

'Don't worry. We need to find another way of helping him, I think.'

A distant clock began to chime and we paused, counting to eleven. 'Cripes, is that the time already?' he said, leaping up. 'My parents will be back soon. Will you be all right, going up the lane in the dark?'

'I'll be fine,' I said, my heart breaking. My friend, my love, was leaving and my world was falling apart around me. As we stood by the open front door, Kit took my face in his hands. I will never forget that expression: his eyes darkened with sadness, but were still so beautiful. In that moment I so badly wanted to kiss him.

'Thank you, Molly. We'll get through this, somehow.'

'I'll miss you.'

'I'll miss you too. You're a really good mate.' Then, just as I turned to go, he handed me a rucksack. 'Just in case you decide to go ahead.'

It weighed a ton. 'Crikey, what's in here?'

'Things I promised to bring for the protest: the chains from the boathouse, with padlocks, a tarpaulin and a sleeping bag. Good luck. And give my love to Jimmy.'

'But . . .'

'Just in case . . .'

※❀※

I ran most of the way home, with tears streaking my cheeks. My romantic dreams were shattered. Kit was going away, and heaven knew when we might see each other again. All the plans we'd made together were lost. There was no one else to turn to, no one else I could trust. Being a 'really good mate' was no consolation at all.

A breeze was stirring the trees. The rumbles of thunder were more frequent now, and louder, the lightning flashes lighting my footsteps. The storm was definitely coming and I welcomed it. At least it might clear the air. As I reached the vicarage I felt the first drops of rain.

21

There was little sleep to be had that night.

The wind howled like a tribe of banshees, whistling through the window casements and lifting the curtains with ghostly hands. The storm seemed to pause right over the village for a full half-hour. I tried counting the seconds between the lightning flashes and the bangs of thunder, but gave up. There were just too many of them, and at times they were almost simultaneous.

At its height a series of deafening cracks seemed to shake the house. I huddled under the bed covers, expecting Jimmy to join me at any moment: he hated thunderstorms, and no amount of explanation could persuade him that they were just a natural phenomenon and very unlikely to cause any harm. But he never came, and I assumed he was in a deep slumber, dreaming of dragons and perhaps parrots. At last the storm seemed to abate a little, and I managed to get back to sleep.

Jimmy was late down the next morning, and no one was surprised; we were all rather short of rest. The rain had stopped and the sky was already beginning to clear, but the street outside the vicarage was a lake of puddles. The garden was a mess, with shrubs and trees destroyed by their pummelling from high winds and torrential rain.

Father appeared, hungover and hollow-eyed, just as Mrs D bustled in.

'What a terrible to-do last night. Didn't get a wink,' she said, hauling off her rubber boots and hanging up her mackintosh in the scullery. 'They say the wind was hurricane-force at times. There's a load of trees down in them woods – they takes it bad when they're still so heavy with leaves. The river's flooded its banks at Bures and there's talk of a lightning strike up Assington way. But our church looks safe and sound, leastways from what I could see from the road. Thank the good Lord we was spared, eh, Vicar?'

It was just a five-minute walk from her house to ours, yet somehow she'd managed to gather all this information by half past eight in the morning.

'Where's the little laddie then?' she asked.

'Sleeping in, I expect,' I said. 'After all that disturbance, it's not surprising.'

After a few more minutes I decided to check. Jimmy was not in his bed. The covers were disturbed, but the mattress and pillow were cold. Downstairs in the scullery his wellington boots and mackintosh were missing.

'Not to worry. He'll have gone out to play,' Pa said.

I was certain he was right – jumping in puddles was one of Jimmy's favourite occupations – but somehow it didn't reassure me. While Mrs D rabbited on about the storm and the damage to the apple and blackberry harvest, I couldn't help worrying.

'I'm going out to find him,' I said.

'Finish your porridge, dear, while it's hot,' Mrs D said. But I had no appetite and excused myself. Jimmy should be easy to spot, I thought, in that red mac. But he wasn't in the garden, nor did he appear when I called his name. I went to the church and walked all round the graveyard, even into its furthest recesses; I knew he liked to hide in the shed where Eli and the volunteer gardeners kept their tools, but he wasn't there, either.

Everywhere was sopping wet; the puddles linked into small streams. It had stopped raining, but the trees were so laden that each gust of wind brought further torrents of water down on my head. I was glad of the rubber boots Pa had insisted we bought before moving to the country. I'd mocked him at the time – when would I need such ugly, uncomfortable footwear? How wrong I'd been. They'd been useful right up until the hot weather began and sandals became the only option, and now here I was wearing them again.

Pa came out to join me and we continued searching together, agreeing that the most logical explanation was that Jimmy had got up and gone out early, for some reason known only to himself. He couldn't be far away, surely? Neither of us spoke about the previous day: the diocesan visitors, his humiliation. His drunkenness. Nor the fact that I had crept out without telling anyone.

We stopped everyone we passed – there weren't many at this time of the morning – but no one had seen any sign of Jimmy.

'Should we knock on doors?'

'Let's not trouble people so early. It's been such a rough night. We'll find him soon enough.' Pa didn't sound convinced. We reached the last house, then retraced our steps along the street, back to the church.

'Could he have gone into the woods?' Pa asked.

'It's possible. He was quite upset when we found Eli's hut locked up and barred yesterday. He's his special friend, Jimmy always says.'

Just as Mrs D had warned, the wood was a scene of devastation: trees had fallen everywhere, and it was impossible to keep to the usual paths. The normally dry, springy floor was heavy going and in places so muddy that we struggled to stay on our feet. We hurried on, calling Jimmy's name every few seconds. Towards the bottom of the hill, as we reached the path that led up to The Pines, I said, 'Stay here, Pa, while I just nip to the top. It won't take more than a few moments, and from there I might catch sight of that red mac of his.'

The once-proud stand of pines looked as if they'd been hit by a bomb. Of the ten or twelve ancient trees only three were left untouched and still standing. The others had either been felled completely, their great roots upturned, or their trunks snapped into sharp shards pointing accusingly to the sky, as though a giant had trampled through the copse wielding an enormous axe. The sight brought me close to tears: those trees had stood there for hundreds of years, marking the site of something important to the early inhabitants of the area. And now, overnight, they were gone.

There were further scenes of devastation in the other direction. The river had flooded, turning the water meadows into wide lakes. The woodland was ragged, as though that same giant had pushed the trees aside as he strode through it. I scoured the landscape until my eyes burned, but there was no sign of a red mac.

We set off again along the other path through the woods, still calling Jimmy's name. When we reached Eli's glade, another horrible shock awaited us. Where the hut had once stood was a pile of charred timbers and sodden grey ash. All that was left of the structure were the four metal wheels, now fallen at crazy angles as their wooden axles had burned away; and the cast-iron stove, which now stood upright in the centre of the devastation, as though wondering what all the fuss was about. It would have looked comical, had it not been so terrible. The hut's metal chimney had been felled like a tree and now lay in several charred and crumpled sections, strewn around the glade. We stood for several moments, stunned into silence.

It was Pa who broke it. 'Lightning strike, do you think?'

I could hardly speak. My stomach churned, and I felt sick and shivery. The place I'd come to see as some kind of haven was now showing all the signs of hell. The blaze had clearly been so ferocious that it had consumed almost everything, even metal items. The large milk churn in which Eli kept his water lay on its side, partly melted. Enamel mugs had apparently been thrown by some fiery force – I spied one several yards away from the main blaze. Saucepans had taken on crazy shapes; a frying pan was folded in two, like an omelette.

Blackman would be pleased. This is what he wanted, wasn't it, getting rid of the hut? And now the storm had saved him the bother. At the back of my mind was something Blackman had said. It had sounded slightly odd at the time, and now I remembered. 'That hut was neither suitable nor safe,' he'd said. Was. Past tense. Could he have torched it himself? Or got someone else to do his dirty work?

We retraced our steps to the vicarage, feeling certain that Jimmy must, surely, have grown hungry and decided to come home by now.

Mrs D was waiting by the front door, her face pale and strained. 'No sign of the little laddie?'

'You haven't heard anything?'

She shook her head. 'I'll get Hubby onto it, shall I, Vicar? The more eyes, the better?'

'Oh, I don't think we need to mobilise the troops yet, thank you, Mrs D,' Pa said. 'Jimmy's so well known in the village that surely someone will have seen him.' He seemed quite convinced that Jimmy had strayed away unthinkingly and would turn up at any moment now. I prayed he was right.

Mrs D persuaded us to take a cup of her hot chocolate and, after drinking it, we took to the street again. More people were out and about now, gathered in groups, sharing gossip about the storm. I found myself burning with irritation, as Pa listened patiently to their stories of narrow escapes from flying slates or falling trees, how outhouses had been demolished and gardens devastated, until he could find a moment to interrupt: 'You haven't seen Jimmy, have you? He went out before breakfast and hasn't come back.'

The answer was always the same. 'Sorry, Vicar. Not this morning, we haven't.'

'If you could check any sheds or outhouses where he might have taken shelter,' we asked each one.

'Will do, Governor,' they'd say, or something similar.

'We'll definitely keep an eye out and be sure to let you know. He can't have gone far, can he? Lovely little fella. He'll turn up soon enough.' They would return to talk of the storm and we would struggle to get away.

'Yes, yes. It's terrible. Of course. Thank you. Thank you.'

And so it went, all the way up the street and back down again to the end of the village. No one had seen Jimmy.

※

'Good morning. What a terrible storm last night,' Mrs Waddington said as she opened the door. 'My husband is in London and we haven't been able to contact him. The telephone lines must all be down. Do come in.'

'Sorry, our boots are so muddy. It's just that . . .' Pa began to explain, when Kit appeared.

He looked shocked and seemed to read the anxiety in my face. 'What's happened?'

As soon as we explained, they both immediately went to get coats and boots and then, in unspoken agreement, the four of us began walking towards the lake. The gardens, with their low box hedges and neatly trimmed borders, seemed to have been relatively untouched by the storm, but as soon as we rounded the corner and the full stretch of water came into sight, the destruction was evident: willow trees had fallen like ninepins into the water all round the shore and along the edges of the islands. It became clear that, in the waterlogged ground, their roots had been unable to provide a strong enough anchor against the hurricane.

'Oh my Lord.' Mrs Waddington clasped her hand to her mouth. 'What a terrible mess.'

Kit took my hand and squeezed it. 'Don't worry, Molly. It looks bad, but I'm sure Jimmy's not far away. We'll find him soon enough.'

The boathouse appeared intact from the outside. I noticed the padlock was missing, but said nothing. It was only when we went inside that we discovered how, even here, the storm had taken its toll. The double doors leading out onto the lake had been blown inwards and one of them partly wrenched off, now hanging lopsidedly from a single hinge. The sturdy *Mary Jane* rocked safely at the end of its mooring line, but the canvas boat was nowhere to be seen.

'Bloody hell, where's *Robin*?' Kit said.

'Language, Christopher,' his mother muttered.

'Sorry, Vicar . . .' He need not have been so embarrassed, as Pa often said worse than that.

'Did you tie it up properly?' she asked.

'Of course I did,' Kit snapped.

'It's not your fault,' I whispered. 'She'll have just blown away across the lake. I'm sure you'll find her.'

'Surely Jimmy wouldn't have taken her out all on his own?' Kit said.

'He can't row,' Pa said.

Kit and I exchanged glances, but neither of us corrected him. 'He was really worried about that lost parrot,' I said. 'You don't suppose . . . ?'

'What about the oars?' Mrs Waddington asked.

'Left them in the boat,' Kit said.

'For goodness' sake, why do you think we've put up these brackets? You know you're supposed to stow them away every time?'

'Leave me alone, Ma,' he snapped back. The tension was

getting to all of us. 'I'll take *Mary Jane* and look. I expect *Robin*'s blown away in the wind.' I wanted to hug him for his decisiveness. It gave me strength, too.

❧

By the time we got back to the vicarage it seemed as though the whole village had been mobilised. A large group was gathered at the church gate.

'The wife told us about Jimmy, Vicar,' George Diamond explained. 'Mr Blackman's been getting everyone organised. There are three search parties out already – one group's gone up to the main road, another is covering the woods, and we're searching houses and gardens. We'll find the little fella, don't you worry.'

'That's very reassuring. Thank you, everyone,' Pa said. Somehow I didn't find the idea of search parties at all reassuring. In fact, it made everything frighteningly real. The need for search parties meant that my brother was properly missing.

My guilt was hardening into something so painful that it seemed to grip me by the throat, threatening to throttle me: I was probably to blame for Jimmy's disappearance. How could I admit that I had gone out last night, when Pa was asleep in a drunken stupor? Suppose Jimmy had been woken by the lightning, tried to wake Pa, then went out searching for me and somehow got hurt? Because of me, he would have been out all night in that terrible weather, cold and wet and afraid. If only I'd checked on him properly after I got home, then we could have found him sooner and brought him home. But now . . .

'Thank you so much, everyone,' Pa was saying. 'But we don't want any fuss. Jimmy will back before we . . .' He seemed to sway slightly, and I caught his arm. His cheeks were hollow, his hair stuck thinly to his scalp and he seemed to have aged two decades.

'Come on, Pa, we should get back,' I said. 'Let's hand over the search to the others for a little while.'

Mrs D was waiting for us with more hot chocolate. Less welcome was the arrival of Mr Blackman, bustling with self-importance. He needed to be at the centre of everything, even the hunt for a missing child.

'Henry,' Pa said, shaking his hand. 'They say you've set up search parties. Really, there's no need. Jimmy'll soon be—'

Blackman interrupted. 'You're not to worry, Vicar. You look all done in, the pair of you, if you don't mind my saying so. You stay here in case he turns up, and we'll look after the search. We'll find him soon enough, safe and well, never fear.' He thanked Mrs Diamond, turning down her offer of hot chocolate, and let himself out of the door.

***

The rest of the day was a blur. Waiting was pure agony. The minute-hand on the clock ticked around so slowly it felt as though time had stopped. I'd rather have been out searching, but Mrs D persuaded me that Pa needed someone to stay with him, and he certainly looked too exhausted to carry on.

Reassurances felt hollow and meaningless, but talking

about anything else seemed irrelevant and unimportant. So we sat, wordlessly, with nothing to say to each other, straining our ears for the sound of the front-door latch. Jimmy could breeze in at any moment, calling out, 'Home,' in his usual way, and the torture would be over. But the moments slipped into minutes and then into an hour, and then two, then three. It felt as though the walls were leaning in, threatening to suffocate us.

'Let's pray together, darling,' Pa said at last. I'd been hoping he might suggest it, surprised that he hadn't done so already. Not that I believed it would make an ounce of difference, but by then I was prepared to try anything.

We slipped onto our knees.

'Dearest Father,' Pa said, after a very long pause. 'We beseech you to hear our prayer today and return our dearest Jimmy safely to us . . .' His voice cracked and he seemed unable to go on. I waited. He sat back on his heels, head in his hands. 'Oh God, answer me,' he groaned. 'Just tell me you're there.'

I squeezed my eyes shut and took up the prayer, trying not to think about Pa and his failing faith. 'Dear God, please bring my brother back home. We love him so dearly. He's done nothing wrong and we are worried for his safety. If you have any mercy at all, please, please, please do this for us.' In my head I added: *If you actually exist, then for heaven's sake help us now.*

'Amen,' we said.

'Thank you, my darling,' Pa said, hauling himself back into his chair.

Kit arrived on his bicycle, panting from his ride up the hill. 'No sign, I'm afraid. But I've found *Robin*. She'd been blown right across the lake and into a tree. There's a ruddy great rip out of the canvas. Not sure whether we'll be able to fix her, to be honest. Pa will be furious.'

'Thank you for looking, Christopher,' Pa said. 'We are most grateful.'

'And I found the parrot,' he added. 'On Pirate's Lair, just as we thought.'

'Jimmy will be pleas . . .' The words died in my mouth.

'Yes, he will,' Kit said firmly. 'And I'm sure he'll be back soon enough, so you can tell him. Should I stay?' he whispered as we returned to the hall. 'Or join the search parties?'

'That's kind, but I'm not sure we . . .'

'I understand. But I don't suppose I'll be going to London after all – not for another day or two. I'll drop by later to see if you need me.' He gave a sweet smile. 'He'll turn up soon, I'm sure of it.'

'I'm just so afraid, Kit.'

A knock on the door made us both jump. My heart leaped, of course, but it was only Blackman again. Behind his back, Kit pulled a face of mock horror that, for a brief second, made me smile.

After Kit left, I showed Blackman into the living room. As I left him and Pa, to fetch a fresh pot of tea, I heard him say, 'Whatever is that boy doing here?' I could have emptied the boiling kettle over his head. He sounded so contemptuous, and I couldn't understand why. Whatever had Kit done? He'd been nothing but helpful and kind.

I spent some time searching Jimmy's bedroom looking for clues, but nothing was out of order. This very normality made his absence even more painful. I lay down on his bed, desperately trying to summon up his presence. After a few moments I became aware of something hard beneath the covers, digging into my ribs. It was *The Ugly Dragon*.

Even though I knew every word by heart, I began to read. My heart seemed to shrink: although I'd made sure that in the story we were always together at the lake, had I inadvertently encouraged Jimmy to go there on his own? And had the story somehow inspired him to do something dangerous, like taking a boat or climbing a tree, or trying to paddle out of his depth? By the time I reached the last page I was sobbing again.

When Mrs D called us for lunch, I dashed my face with cold water and went downstairs. Pa and I sat obediently at the table, looking at our sandwiches. Neither of us could bring ourselves to eat, even to please Mrs D.

Pa stood suddenly, pushing his chair back so violently that it tipped over, falling with a clatter onto the floor. 'I'm going to call the police.'

Suddenly everything became deadly serious.

22

If only. The two little words went round and round in my head, like a scratched record, until I feared they might send me mad.

If only I hadn't gone to see Kit last night; if only I'd checked on Jimmy when I got back; if only I'd warned him more often about the lake; if only I hadn't been so absorbed by my concern for Eli. *If only, if only, if only.*

Pa told me not to be silly – Jimmy's disappearance wasn't due to anything I'd done or not done. 'It is my fault, if anything,' he said. 'For getting so drunk yesterday. I'm your father, and it is my responsibility to care for you both. I've been so wrapped up in my own concerns that I've neglected you.' So then it was my turn to try and reassure him. And so we went on, until the police arrived.

In any other circumstances the two men might have made a comedy duo: one tall and thin, with a weasel-like face; the other short and tubby, his trousers clumsily shortened by at least six inches. Yet despite their appearance, the two men were alarmingly businesslike. After a preliminary conversation with all of us, they asked to speak to Pa and me separately. Then they would talk to Mrs D.

Pa took Weasel Face into his study, while PC Stubby stayed with me in the living room and grilled me so hard that by the time he'd finished, I felt as though I'd hidden my brother all by myself and simply decided not to tell anyone. He wanted to know every detail about my relationship with Jimmy, our relationship with Pa, our move to Wormley, Mrs D, my school friends and my village friends, and the exact timings of our movements. He pressed me for what I knew about Pa's service in the war – which wasn't much, because he never spoke of it – and his 'illness' afterwards, by which I supposed they meant his mental state.

But most of all he homed in on the events of the past twenty-four hours.

'Would it be your normal practice to leave the house late at night, Miss Goddard?'

'Erm, no. But Pa was here, and I was only out for a little while.'

'And we now know that he was in no fit state to take care of a child. Do you mind my asking where you went?'

I faltered then, anxious not to get Kit into more trouble. But this was serious; it was no time to tell untruths.

'To see Kit Waddington, down at the Hall. He will confirm that, but I'd rather you didn't tell his parents.'

PC Stubby nodded. 'Hmm. Yes. Kit Waddington. Someone else mentioned that name.' He looked up from his notebook with a sly smile. 'Like that, is it?'

'Not at all. We had something urgent to discuss.'

He cleared his throat meaningfully, and shook his head. 'And what exactly is a "little while"?'

'An hour or so. Perhaps a bit longer.'

He frowned and noted this in his notebook with a stubby pencil. He wrote so slowly and laboriously, his tongue peeking out at the corner of his mouth in concentration, that I felt like screaming.

'And what time was that?'

I told him.

'And you got back when?' I guessed at quarter past eleven. It seemed too careless to tell him that I hadn't actually looked at the clock.

'And it was during that time that your brother decided to leave the house?'

'I can't be entirely sure when he went out, I'm afraid.'

'Did you check whether he was here when you arrived home?'

A lump stuck in my throat.

'I'm sorry, Miss Goddard, but we have to ask these questions.'

I swallowed hard and wiped my eyes with the back of my hand. 'Yes, I know. Sorry. No, I didn't look in on him when I got back.'

'What time did you get up this morning?'

'About eight. We had a very disturbed night because of the storm.'

'Of course. And did you check on him then?'

'Not immediately. We assumed Jimmy was asleep and would come down in his own time, which is perfectly usual during school holidays. I went up to his room at about a quarter past nine, when he hadn't turned up for breakfast. His bed had been slept in, but it wasn't warm any more. He'd been gone for a while.'

'Thank you. That is helpful. Now, does your brother have any friends of his own in the village, or at school? Who does he play with?'

'No one really. He comes with me most of the time.' I sent up a silent, guilty prayer: *Bring him back safely, God, and I will never be grumpy about having to take care of him, ever again.*

'And what do you do, when you go out together?'

'We go for walks, or picnics – you know. To The Pines, or into the woods. Sometimes down to the lake and the Hall. We are friends with the family.' He was scribbling so fast now that I paused to give him time to catch up. 'Kit taught us how to row.'

He looked up sharply. 'On the river?'

'On their lake.'

'Any other friends?'

'The Timpson twins. We see them sometimes. Or the other lads: Robert Parsons, Ashley, Brian and Peter.'

His next question caught me off-guard. 'How well do you get on with your brother?'

'We get on fine. I love him, of course. He's my brother.' It sounded so defensive. 'His language is a bit limited and he might never be able to look after himself, but he's such a happy boy, always smiling.'

'He's a Mongol, I understand?' That terrible, shocking word. It had been used by the hospital when Mum first had Jimmy, but after that she'd banned it.

'No,' I said angrily. 'Well, yes. But it's such an ugly term that we don't like to use it. He has a mental disability.'

I watched him writing: *Mental disability.*

'Your mother . . . ?'

'She died. Nearly two years ago.'

'I'm sorry to hear that, Miss Goddard. So it's just your father looking after you?'

'And Mrs Diamond, our housekeeper. We couldn't do without her.'

'Indeed. Thank you. Now, have you got any idea why your brother left the house, and where he might have been going?'

'He was anxious about a toy he'd left on an island when we were out rowing with Kit. We told him not to worry, but . . .' Wondering was so painful.

'A toy?'

'A stuffed parrot. Part of a pirate's costume.'

Watching him write *Check lake* and *Stuffed parrot on island* so painstakingly in his notebook, I felt a hysterical urge to giggle.

'Thank you, Miss Goddard. We'll get our people on to that right away.'

'Kit checked the island this morning. He went out in his boat. He found the parrot.'

Stubby nodded. And then the oddest thing happened. From a brown paper bag he produced what I thought at first was a home-made scrapbook. And then, as he held it up, I realised that it was my book, *The Ugly Dragon*.

'Do you recognise this?'

I wanted to grab it from his grubby hands. 'Please give it back. It's private, and very precious. They're stories I wrote for my brother.'

'That much is obvious. But I am intrigued. Why this obsession with a crocodile and a lake?'

'It's just a local legend. A bit of fun. That's all.' I sounded defensive, despite my best efforts to speak in a neutral tone.

'But this notion of evil that the dragon goes on about . . . ? The, erm, black serpent?' He opened the book and began to read. '*Men who feel weak or inadequate feel they have to prove themselves somehow, trying to get power over others and bullying people who can't fight back.* And then there is a reference to Mr Eli Chadwick. That doesn't sound like a "bit of fun", Miss Goddard. Would you like to tell me about Eli Chadwick? He lives in a shepherd's hut in the woods, I understand?'

'Not any more. He's been evicted. And the hut's been burned down.'

He looked up. 'Are you suggesting he burned it?'

'No, he'd never destroy his own hut. It was his home. It might have been lightning, but that seems a bit unlikely, since it's surrounded by tall trees.'

'I sense, from your tone, that you are concerned for Mr Chadwick, Miss Goddard?'

'I am. He's a lovely old man who wouldn't hurt a fly, but some people seem determined to force him out.'

'Some people?' He fixed me with a piercing look.

'That is a private book, and a private matter,' I said, annoyed now. What on earth did any of this have to do with finding Jimmy? 'Now can I have it back, please? It is very precious to me and my brother.'

'Of course you may,' he said, putting it back into the paper bag. 'I will return it just as soon as we are finished with it.'

When they'd finally gone, Pa and I compared notes.

'They made me feel like a criminal.'

'Me too. People have been talking about me, Molly. Saying I've been acting oddly, saying they've seen me out at all times of the day and night. It's horrible.'

'But the police have to ask questions. They're only doing their job,' I said. 'What are they going to do next?'

'More search parties, interviewing other people – Mr Blackman, I understand. I hope to God he doesn't tell them about the money. And Eli, I think.'

'If they can find him.'

'They seemed particularly keen, so I expect they will.'

'Keen? What on earth has Eli got to do with anything?'

'Well, you did say Jimmy thinks of him as a special friend.'

'You told them *that*?'

'Yes. Why not?'

'Don't you see, Pa? They'll think Eli was interested in Jimmy because . . .' I didn't have the words for it, just a nasty feeling. 'A young boy says that an eccentric old man is his "special friend". What does that suggest to you, Pa, especially if you are a policeman with a suspicious mind?'

Pa looked shocked. 'Surely they wouldn't think . . . ?'

'Well, whatever they think, they will suspect Eli might have had something to do with Jimmy's disappearance. And he's done nothing wrong. He's completely innocent.'

'You don't know that.'

'What do you mean, "You don't know that"?' I spluttered. 'You don't honestly think Eli would have harmed Jimmy? For heaven's sake.'

'Don't let's argue, darling.'

I stomped up to my room and wept into my pillow. Everything seemed so bleak and hopeless.

At some point in the afternoon the police returned. They'd talked to a number of other people, but hadn't come up with anything yet and would resume their searches in the morning, with dogs and divers this time. *Divers.* The very thought made me feel dizzy and sick.

'Please don't worry too much,' Weasel Face said. 'If Jimmy's just got lost, he'll be perfectly fine for a few days in this warm weather. We are still optimistic of finding him safe and well.'

Henry Blackman arrived with a shepherd's pie made by his wife, and seemed to delight in reporting the day's events: how the police had complimented the way he'd organised the search parties; how he had been up to see Eli in his new home and found him wandering around the building site, looking for firewood.

'Had to show him the electric cooker in his house. Poor old fellow seems to be losing his mind,' he said. 'The police have already interviewed him once, and I got the impression they think there's something he's not divulging.' He tipped his head confidentially.

My guilt had hardened into a permanent painful lump in my chest. Now I felt even guiltier than ever. Why did I tell Pa about Jimmy calling Eli his 'special friend'? It seemed such a harmless, even charming thing to say at the time. But now Jimmy had gone missing the phrase took on a sinister meaning, bringing the poor old man under suspicion. And this, too, was my fault.

By nightfall, Pa and I had held each other and cried together many times. We'd joined search parties, been to the church to pray, talked endlessly between ourselves and to the police. Nothing could bring us any peace. It was like a living nightmare, and I wished so much that I could pinch myself and wake up.

23

I slept in Pa's room that night. Or, rather, we lay together, holding each other throughout the long hours of darkness. Neither of us slept much, if at all. Mrs D stayed too, making up a bed for herself in one of the unused rooms.

At some point in the night I went off to sleep in Jimmy's bed, imagining in my confused mind that I should keep it warm for him. I missed him with a fierce pain that no drugs could dull: his hot, clumsy little body, his crazy smile, the way he hummed tunelessly to himself, how he would tug at my arm if he wanted attention. All the things I'd usually found irritating I now desired more than anything else in the world. I prayed shamelessly to a God I didn't believe in.

Dawn crept in and Jimmy was still missing. And that morning something else had gone, too, although at first I wasn't able to figure out what. It was just a feeling, as though a malign, unseen presence had slipped into our lives, sucking from us all the comfort and strength that our depleted little family had somehow managed to create in that unfamiliar house, this new place, these new circumstances. The ground beneath my feet felt no longer solid but shifting, uncertain, unpredictable. Normally I would have turned to Pa, finding solace in at least being able to talk through my feelings. But how could we look to each other for strength, when both of us were so weak and powerless to bring Jimmy back?

Mrs D went home to change and get her husband his breakfast, and at around ten o'clock Weasel Face and Stubby returned, telling us about their plans for the day's renewed search. They also brought back my book.

Shortly after they left, Mrs D arrived with a face as long as a barn door. Her normally healthy complexion was deadly pale and her voice trembled. 'Oh, my poor dears. I'm sorry to bring you more sad news.'

We immediately assumed the worst. 'Spit it out, woman,' Pa snapped. I shushed him gently. He was on a knife edge.

'Poor, poor Eli.' She began to weep, trying to stem the flow with a totally inadequate lacy handkerchief. Pa produced a man-sized linen version and I put an arm round her.

'Come and sit down,' I said. 'We'll put the kettle on.'

It turned out I wasn't the only one worrying about Eli. At Mrs D's insistence, her husband had walked up to the council houses first thing in the morning to see if he was all right. When there was no answer he'd checked around the building, looking in through windows to see whether he could detect any signs of habitation, but he could find nothing. So he went back down and into the woods to see whether Eli had tried to return to his hut.

What he'd discovered there Mrs D found difficult to put into words.

'Oh, my dears,' she said, lifting her cup with a trembling hand. 'Such a shock. Who'd have thought he'd . . .'

'He would *what*?' Pa snapped. He didn't sound like my father any more. His tone was brusque and impatient, because really the only news we could cope with was whether Jimmy had been found, safe and unharmed.

'I mean, wherever did he get that rope?'

A chill went down my spine, and everything in front of my eyes seemed to shimmer and swim.

Mrs D turned to me. 'My poor dear Molly. You were so fond of him, weren't you?'

'Was it Jimmy?' I almost shouted.

'Your brother? Oh no, darling. Not Jimmy. It was Eli. He's only gone and hanged himself. From a tree. Right by his hut, or where it used to be.'

'Was he . . . ?' My father faltered, unable to say the word.

'I'm afraid so.' Mrs D shook her head. 'He'd used a ladder, you see, and kicked it away. George climbed up and cut him down, but he was long gone, poor old boy. There was no saving him. We called the police, of course, and a doctor. He pronounced him dead at the scene.'

Neither Pa nor I could find anything to say. We were already in shock, and this just doubled it. I found myself shaking uncontrollably and had to sit down. Eli must have been distressed at being moved out of his hut and then finding it burned down, but I never realised that he would give up hope so completely.

And then an even darker thought arrived, dizzying in its obvious clarity. We knew that the police had been to see Eli the previous day and interviewed him about Jimmy. Knowing from my own experience how their questioning could make you feel guilty for no reason at all, it was reasonable to assume that poor Eli would have felt they

THE SECRETS OF THE LAKE

suspected him of having something to do with Jimmy's disappearance. He might even have thought they were going to arrest him.

I felt utterly certain that Eli was entirely innocent. He would never have harmed anyone, let alone the boy he seemed to have developed a great affection for. But was I being too naive? A further terrifying thought crashed into my head: why would Eli have done something so drastic if he was completely innocent and knew nothing? Did this mean that he had actually harmed Jimmy, or was somehow responsible for his disappearance? Or were there darker forces at play here, adult things I had no experience of? Now that Eli had done what he had done, would the police – and everyone else – simply assume that he was guilty?

It was all too much to take in. 'Why, why, why, why?' I found myself banging the table with my fist, till Pa reached over and held it. 'It's okay, darling. We'll get to the bottom of this, don't you worry.'

'Did he leave any sign? A note?' I asked.

Her face darkened. 'There was something, yes. Hubby gave it to the police.'

'Did he read it? What did it say?'

'You shouldn't be asking, Molly,' Pa said, taking my arm.

'I want to know. Was it anything to do with my brother?'

Mrs D shook her head vehemently. 'Good heavens, no. Not about the little laddie. Some garbled stuff about the hut and the land, I think. Nothing we need to worry ourselves with.' She shrugged. 'It's all in the hands of the police now, my dear. As if you didn't have enough to worry about, you poor dears.'

The scene played itself in my head, over and over. How

Eli had returned to gather up some of his possessions and discovered that his beloved hut had burned to the ground. How would he have reacted? Did he light one last pipe and smoke it? Did he say anything? Did he cry? And where was Sarge? I felt sure Eli could not, even in his most distressed state, have been able to kill the dog, too.

He would have had to throw the rope over a branch, knot a loop, climb the ladder, put the loop over his head and then . . . Once he'd jumped, did he struggle, try to get back to the ladder and regain his footing? How did you die when you hanged yourself? Do you break your neck or slowly suffocate from the pressure on your windpipe? It was all so unthinkable, and yet my mind could not stop itself thinking.

And all the while the terrible dread: that we might never see my brother again.

It was that day they brought in the divers. We didn't see them ourselves, but Mr Blackman reported on every step of the police search, so we had little choice but to hear about 'black-clad men with breathing apparatus' rowing around the lake and then jumping in at various points to search underwater. I found myself imagining how one of the divers might later report about coming face-to-face with an angry crocodile or dragon. My distracted brain was threatening to lose its grip on reality.

The hours dragged by. I had never known time move so slowly. The police came to give an update: they had conducted a thorough search of the lake, the islands and the woodland around, but had found no sign of Jimmy. This was good news, they suggested, although I could hardly see why.

Pa pressed them about what they would do next. They had two theories. The first, and most likely, they seemed to think, was that Eli Chadwick had something to do with it. I protested that I felt sure he would never have lifted a finger to harm Jimmy, but they looked at me as though I was a fool.

The second theory they were working on was that Jimmy had taken *Robin*, 'that red canvas craft' as they called her, to retrieve the toy parrot. To me, it seemed completely implausible that Jimmy would have gone out in a boat on his own at night, however anxious he was to get the parrot back. But I refrained from saying so.

'We have to explore every possibility. But that doesn't mean we have given up hope of finding your boy safe and well,' Weasel Face told us. His intention was to reassure, of course, but each time he said that, it felt like another blow. What if Jimmy wasn't 'safe and well'? The alternative was too horrific to contemplate.

By mid-afternoon that second day Pa and I seemed unable even to summon the strength to comfort each other. Our optimism was fading fast. Nearly thirty hours had passed since we'd found Jimmy gone, and he had never been away from us for more than an hour at a time, apart from attending school. The police returned to the vicarage, questioning us again and again. In the absence of any sign of Jimmy at the lake, they seemed to be more and more certain that Eli's suicide was linked to Jimmy's disappearance, although their theories were vague.

According to Mrs D, this was also the main topic of gossip in the village. 'They're saying he topped himself out of guilt,' she hinted darkly.

I knew all too well the kind of assumptions people were making. Jimmy liked Eli and was often seen in his company. Soon after Jimmy disappeared, Eli had hanged himself. The conclusion was obvious, except that I was still convinced Eli would never have hurt a single hair on Jimmy's head.

'But there was nothing about that in his note, you said,' I snapped back.

'There wouldn't be, would there?'

At dusk the police told us they were calling off the search until the morning. Again Mrs D cooked, but we couldn't eat a thing.

Dr Mortimer came from Bures in his old Austin Seven. It seemed that he'd been summoned by Mrs D. Pa appeared to be fading more and more, both physically and mentally, with every passing hour. He was increasingly distracted, and the things he said sometimes didn't make any sense. He seemed glued to the chair in his study, but when he did leave it, he was as unsteady on his legs as a man twice his age. His hands trembled so much that he could barely lift a teacup.

The doctor offered pills. 'To help you sleep, so you can stay strong,' he said. He had such a kindly face that I felt like asking for a hug instead. Pa said we should take the pills, but I wasn't so certain. What if they left us so comatose that we couldn't wake up when Jimmy arrived back, or we received news that he needed our help? I pretended to agree to take them, just to reassure Pa and Mrs D.

Pa retired early and his bedroom door remained shut

– he must have taken the pills. But I stayed awake, slipping silently downstairs from time to time making more cups of tea or, sometimes, cocoa, and eating nearly a whole tin of biscuits. I wandered listlessly around the house and even went out into the garden. Wading through the cold, wet grass in bare feet offered a temporary distraction.

A fox screeched somewhere in the woods beyond, sounding so much like a child in distress that it was all I could do to stop myself calling out Jimmy's name. An owl flew past me at the height of my face, just a few yards away: a silent, ghostly white shape that disappeared into the darkness as fast as it had appeared.

After that I went back to bed, my mind churning, ranging through every eventuality, from the perfectly probable through to the completely unimaginable. If Jimmy had been hiding somewhere, he would have come home when he got hungry. He was always hungry. Or perhaps he'd been locked in a shed by mistake? But they'd searched all the sheds in the village. Twice. Perhaps he was hurt and unable to move? But they'd searched the woods and fields in a three-mile radius, they told us.

What if he had, as the police thought, gone out in the boat? It was very unlikely, but still a possibility. He couldn't swim, so if he capsized and panicked, he might have drowned. I couldn't help thinking about Melissa Blackman's crocodile and those disappearing legs. But in my saner moments I reminded myself that dragons are only found in fairy stories, and crocodiles exist only in zoos and in Africa.

Thinking about the river terrified me. I'd seen what the storm had done, turning a placid, friendly stream into a hungry, raging torrent that crashed through the meadows, bursting its banks and uprooting ancient trees. But Jimmy and I had never visited the river. It was a good quarter of a mile beyond the lake, or over the grassy hill. I couldn't imagine why he might have gone there on his own, on such a fiercely stormy night. If he'd fallen in, he would have been washed away in an instant.

The more I tried to reason, the muddier everything became. There was only one remaining possibility. Perhaps he had got into someone's car? He was a sociable soul, after all, and assumed everyone was a friend. But he'd never done that before. So why now? And what would that someone want, with a boy who could barely speak? Or perhaps someone had taken him against his will.

The notion of him being held captive, being frightened, confused and alone, was too painful to imagine.

***

I must have slept eventually, for I became aware of light streaming through the curtains. Outside the weather was bright and sunny once more, with little white clouds scudding across a perfectly blue sky. The terrible, oppressive heat of the summer had given way to autumn, all in the space of a few days. Nature's heartless beauty seemed to mock the nightmare that we had found ourselves locked into. It was Day Three, and still no sign of Jimmy.

There was activity in the kitchen, so I went down in my pyjamas. Mrs D was cooking bacon and scrambled egg, but the smells that would normally make my mouth water just made me feel nauseous.

'Morning,' she said. 'I hope those pills helped you get a little sleep, my darling.'

I nodded, to save lying.

'Thought we'd have a proper cooked breakfast today – build up your strength. Why don't you see if your pa's ready to eat something?'

I doubted it, but went upstairs to please her and knocked on Pa's bedroom door. There was no answer. Those pills were strong; he was probably still sound asleep. I knocked again, louder this time. There was still no answer; his bed was empty.

I ran downstairs to his study. He was not there, either, but the piles of books on his desk and the side tables had been dashed about, as though a hurricane had blown through the room; some lay on the floor, their spines broken, and papers had flown everywhere. A sudden ray of hope slipped into my head: had Jimmy returned in the night and, for some inexplicable reason, been hunting for something among Pa's papers?

Mrs D was behind me, in the doorway.

'Great heavens above,' she exclaimed. 'Whatever's been going on in here? Have we been burgled?'

I shrugged. 'The windows are locked. There's no sign . . .'

'He must have gone out for a walk, poor man,' she said. 'He'll be back soon, no doubt. I'll put his breakfast in the warming oven. Now, why don't you come and eat yours while it's still fresh.'

And then I saw it, lying on the study floor. It was a copy of the local newspaper, always delivered early on a Friday morning. On the front page was this headline and story:

MISSING CHURCH FUNDS DENIAL

A vicar has denied any knowledge of nearly £5,000 missing from church funds in Wormley, near Colchester.

Rev. John Goddard, who took over in the parish of All Saints nine months ago, said: 'We are aware that the money is missing and are working with the bank to try to discover what has happened to it.'

Villagers claim that when they enquired about the money, they were 'fobbed off'.

'We feel very angry about this,' said a parishioner who did not wish to be named. 'It is a substantial amount of money badly needed for church repairs, and nothing seems to have been done to find out what has happened to it.'

We understand that the matter has been referred for investigation by the diocese, but no one at the diocesan office was prepared to comment.

I sat down heavily on a chair. Mrs D took the paper from me, muttering, 'The poor, poor man. Whoever would accuse him of something like this?'

A sharp knock on the door made us both jump.

'Miss Calver, what . . . ?'

She was panting and looking more dishevelled than usual, and she glanced at the newspaper in my hand. 'Oh, Molly. You've seen it already. I'm so sorry.'

'It was *you* who spoke to the newspaper?'

'Of course not, silly. Can I come in?' She closed the door behind her and lowered her voice, although I felt sure Mrs D, who had disappeared into the kitchen, would hear every word. 'I know who it was, Molly. Who leaked the story.'

It was just her tone of voice. My heart fell into my boots. I knew what she was going to say.

'The Blackness?' She nodded. 'But why . . . ?'

'Think about it. He's the only other person whose name is in the frame. It's a pre-emptive strike, so to speak. A friend of mine, a reporter who knows I live in the village, rang me to ask if I could throw any more light on the story. He didn't name his informant – a reporter always protects his sources – but from what he said, I knew immediately. No one else would have had access to the information.'

'Except Mr Abbott. He pressed pretty hard at the last committee meeting – the one you missed.'

'Ah. Well, I suppose it could have been him. But he's not an educated man, and the language the informant used was absolutely the sort of thing Blackman might say: divesting assets, illegal encampment, serious financial difficulties. You know the sort of thing.'

'Did you tell them anything?' I asked.

She scoffed. 'Of course not. I'm on your side, Molly, for goodness' sake. I didn't say a word.'

My head was spinning. Blackman might be evil, but was he seriously capable of doing such a terrible thing to another human being? 'What do you mean, a pre-emptive strike?' I asked.

'He must have thought someone would go to the newspapers. So he was trying to silence them by getting his side of the story in quick.'

And then I remembered my parting threat to Blackman

the day the diocesan men came to the house: *The news-papers are going to hear about this.*

'Now, where is your father?' Miss Calver asked. 'I realise this is a terrible time, but we do need to make some kind of response.'

A sudden terrible fear gripped my heart. Pa was in such a fragile state of mind that if he'd seen this article, it could easily have tipped him over the edge. 'We have to find him,' I said, rushing to pull on my boots and throwing a jacket over my pyjamas. As we opened the door, George Diamond was crossing the road towards us. 'Come quickly, Miss Goddard. Over to the church.'

In the churchyard stood a group of villagers, their faces tilted upwards, arms pointed to the sky. I followed their gaze. High up in the tower a small figure was just visible, yet unmistakeable: it was my father.

'What's happening?' I shouted.

'He won't come down,' someone said. 'He's gone and locked the door at the top of the stairs, so we can't get to him.'

In a brief flare of optimism I thought Pa might have gone up there to find Jimmy. Or to scan the countryside, using the advantage of height? I remembered how, when we'd first arrived in the village, he'd taken us both up the narrow winding staircase to the top of the tower. And what he'd said: 'Makes you feel closer to God, being up here.'

Around me, people were talking all at once. 'Get her to try calling him down,' someone suggested, and it was a moment before I realised they were talking about me.

'Perhaps if you could call to him, Miss Goddard? Ask him to come down. Tell him we're concerned for his welfare.'

'It's all right,' I said, feeling strangely calm. 'He's just gone up there to be closer to God.'

The villagers went silent. Some of them looked at me as though I was mad. Pa disappeared for a few moments, but then reappeared again. He was climbing the spire now, using the metal ladder fixed there for inspecting the lead roofing and the weathervane, a single arrow set on a swivel above a fixed horizontal cast-iron cross with the letters N, E, S and W. He looked like an ant, dwarfed by the height of the tower and the scale of the spire above him. There was a collective holding of breath. Someone swore: 'What the . . . ?'

'We have to stop him.'

'Miss Molly, please. Call up to him. Tell him to come down.'

I took a few steps forward. 'Be careful, Pa. Please.' My voice was carried away by the wind. I tried again, louder this time. 'Pa, it's me, Molly. You must come down. It's not safe up there.'

This time he must have heard me, because he peered down and waved. I could see his face clearly now, and it filled me with fear. It didn't look like Pa at all, but like someone possessed: grinning wildly, the features distorted into a grotesque mask. His mouth opened wide and he emitted a terrible, blood-curdling howl.

I burst into tears. Arms were around me, holding me, passing handkerchiefs. Someone put a jacket over my shoulders; another was laid onto a gravestone, on which I was urged to sit. When we looked up again, Pa was no longer climbing the spire, but had climbed back to the roof of the tower and was now peering down at us from the parapet wall.

'Is that you, my dearest?' he shouted, sounding almost sane.

I sprang to my feet. 'Yes, it's me, Molly. Whatever are you doing up there? Come down, please. You're scaring me.'

To my horror, he began to climb onto the narrow section between two corners of the wall, grasping the spindly flagpole with one hand, the other waving freely. Around me, people gasped.

'Look at me, Molly. I can fly,' my father shouted. 'Take me, God, I'm coming.'

'No, stop. Get down!'

'Don't you worry about me. I'm going to find Jimmy, my darling. And Sarah. We can all be together again.'

My blood ran cold. Sarah – my mother.

'You have to stop him,' I pleaded, desperate now. 'He's going to kill himself.'

At that moment there was a mighty crash and George Diamond's face appeared at the top of the tower. He lunged towards Pa and then both of them disappeared below the parapet.

'He's got him,' someone said.

'Good old George. Must've broken down the door.'

'Someone call an ambulance.'

The world went dark and that was the last thing I heard.

PART THREE:

SPRING 2019

24

Molly is exhausted but feels curiously elated, energised even, by her journey back into the past, and presses Bella to stay for a cup of tea before she leaves.

Bella hesitates. Lewis and his dad will be sitting in front of the television eating pizza by now, the house will be in chaos, and her work blouse is still waiting to be ironed. But after such a momentous day it's too soon to rush away.

'I'll put the kettle on then,' she says. 'Are you okay, Mum?'

'Fine, dear. Just fine, thank you.'

Bella returns from the kitchen and sits down again. 'I can't help thinking about it. What terrible things you had to deal with, as a young girl.'

Molly shrugs. 'You just have to get on with it, I suppose. Face each day as it comes.'

When Pa was sent off to hospital Mrs D took charge, looking after everything until Aunt Mary arrived. The police continued their search for Jimmy, but they seemed convinced Eli was the most likely suspect, and after his suicide all they would say was that they were 'pursuing a specific line of enquiry'. Whether they'd told her aunt, or anyone else, what that line of enquiry consisted of, Molly never discovered, but they didn't interview her again, or consult her. And they never found Jimmy.

When she tries to remember what she felt, those following days and weeks, her mind goes into a blur. Dr Mortimer prescribed more pills and made Aunt Mary promise to make sure that Molly took them. She'd slept like the dead, and one day followed another in a haze, as though the feelings of utter misery and despair belonged to someone else, not her. Looking back, she recalls it as a dark tunnel, knowing that you have no choice but to move forward, even though there is no reassuring light in the distance to draw you on.

She remembers being told that Sarge had been found, and being ridiculously pleased at this small piece of good news. The dog was half-starved and dehydrated, refusing to leave the woodland glade and growling at anyone who came near, and they'd had to call in a vet to tranquillise him before he could be retrieved. George Diamond told them that Eli's friends 'down Bures way' had taken Sarge in.

Each week she and her aunt would take the bus to visit Pa in a vast, gloomy Victorian mental hospital on the outskirts of Colchester. The first time was a ghastly shock: he looked about a hundred years old and barely recognised them. But as the weeks went by, he regained something of his old personality and at last, after about two months, he was discharged. They took the train to Buckinghamshire and stayed with Aunt Mary for the rest of the year. Mrs

D had cried, her husband by her side, when they left. What good people they were. They'd exchanged letters at first, but it tailed off after a while.

'Those first few months were very hard,' Molly admits to Bella. Auntie Mary had reminded her so much of Mum, like her sister both in looks and gestures, which served as a constant reminder: a phrase, a tone of voice, a tilt of the head. Molly went to the local school for the autumn term and hated having to be the new girl all over again.

'Poor you. Such a lot of tragedy in your short life.'

'At least Pa recovered. Some don't, you know?' Although he'd never been strong enough to take on another parish, the church was always kind; after Christmas they'd found him a curacy back at St Martin's, where he could be supported by a big team. They were given a new flat and Molly went back to her old school, which made everything feel a little more normal, although, of course, it was like her old life but without Jimmy or Mum.

'Whatever happened about that missing money from the church funds?'

Molly smiles. 'That was the one bit of good that came out of our time at Wormley. Blackman got his just deserts.'

'How? Oh, do tell.' Bella sits forward.

❈

It was some months later, when they were already back in London, that Miss Calver's letter arrived, having been forwarded by Aunt Mary from Buckinghamshire. It was long, two full pages of close typescript, and it enclosed a newspaper cutting:

VICAR AND CHURCH TREASURER CHARGED

The Reverend Michael Morton, former vicar of Wormley near Colchester, and church treasurer Henry Blackman have been jointly charged with the theft of nearly £5,000 from church funds.

Both deny the charges, and the case will be heard at Chelmsford Crown Court in June. A church spokesman said: 'This is a significant amount of money and we have been aware of its loss for some time, so we are pleased that at last it is being properly investigated.'

If found guilty, the men could face prison sentences.

Miss Calver wrote:

You may be interested to hear what's been happening here in Wormley since you left. It's been quite the scandal. It turns out that before he killed himself, Eli Chadwick sent a letter to the newspaper with all kinds of accusations against Mr Blackman. The paper passed it to the police. Of course, none of us knew about this, and it took the police a long time to get round to dealing with it, but it transpires that Eli had evidence that Blackman had already been blackmailing Morton, the former incumbent, threatening to expose the fact that he'd been siphoning off church funds to cover his gambling debts, and trying to get his hands on that piece of woodland. Yes, even back then.

The police forced the bank to give them access to their records. Guess what? It turns out that not only was the vicar siphoning off funds, but some of them were also

being diverted to Blackman's account. No wonder
Blackman was trying to blame your poor father. Both he
and Morton have been charged with theft, and neither
Blackman nor the sainted Melissa have been seen since.
Too ashamed, I suppose. I hope they stay away forever.
The village already feels like a happier place. The trial is
in a few months' time. I'll keep you posted.

'So Mr Evil got his come-uppance. Did he go to gaol
in the end?' Bella asks now.

'Yes. They were both found guilty of theft and attempted
fraud and sentenced to six months. Not long enough, of
course, but the real punishment for Blackman was the
disgrace. He sold his cottage in Wormley and they were
never seen again.'

Bella raises a triumphant fist. 'You must have been pleased.'

'Not pleased, no. Saddened that what could have been
a new start for Pa turned into such a nightmare. Saddened
that we never found Jimmy,' Molly says, swallowing down
the lump in her throat. 'Saddened that an individual could
bring such terrible evil to a small community – all down
to one man and his desperate need to prove himself as Mr
Wormley.'

'You did the best you could, Mum,' Bella says. After a
while she starts to gather her things. 'I'd better be off. See
you on Friday, for the DNA result?'

'You'll be here?'

'Of course. It's really important. I'll take the day off, and
Lewis can go to a friend's house after school.'

'Can't you bring him with you?'

'It's a school day, Mum.'

'I never see enough of my grandson these days.'

'I'll bring him at half-term. That's only a few weeks away.' Bella pauses. 'Will you be all right, Mum?'

'All right? Of course I'm all right.'

'I mean, discovering whether they've found Jimmy.'

Molly takes a deep breath and thinks for a moment. 'To be honest, I'd be relieved. At least we'll know for certain what we always expected, after all these years. I'm only sorry my poor old pa isn't here. It ate him up for the rest of his life, not knowing, always wondering whether it was something he had done, or left undone. He suffered terrible guilt and would spend hours on his knees, asking for forgiveness, so in a strange kind of way it brought him closer to his God, which he was grateful for – so he told me at the end.'

'Well, that's some kind of blessing, I suppose,' Bella says. 'Now, can I make you a sandwich or something before I leave?'

'No, I'm fine, love, thank you. That pub lunch will keep me going for days.'

'Well, I hope you get a good night, and that you can relax a bit this week.'

She kisses her mother on the forehead, pats her gently on the shoulder. Lately, each time she leaves, Bella finds herself wondering whether this could be the last time. Now she knows it is not: her mother won't allow herself to die before finding out about Jimmy. Not after all these years.

A few days later Bella is back again, arriving at the same time as the police car, with the same socially awkward man and smiley woman emerging from it. They exchange welcomes and walk up the path to Molly's bungalow. Once again the little room seems overfilled until they all sit down.

'So, have you got the results?' Bella asks.

'We have,' the man says. 'And I'm not sure whether you will be pleased or disappointed.'

'Tell us then,' Molly snaps. 'Don't keep us in suspense any longer.'

'I'm afraid your DNA shows no match with the bones that were found at the lake, Ms Goddard. This makes it very unlikely they are your brother's. They *are* human bones, though, but it is possible they could be very much older, perhaps dating back a century or so.'

No match. The news is dizzying and for a few seconds Molly finds it hard to breathe. She was so sure it would be him. If it wasn't Jimmy in the lake, then all of the imaginings that have been running through her head, keeping her awake throughout the night, were for nothing. Perhaps, after all, he did not take out *Robin* and capsize her, or try to swim back from the island after getting marooned when the little dinghy was blown away by the rising winds. He did not drown, nor was he attacked by a vengeful dragon.

'Mum?'

She drags herself back to the present. 'What does this mean, Officer? If the bones are not his, then where is he?'

Beard-man shakes his head, slowly. 'I'm sorry . . .'

If there is no body, then perhaps Jimmy did not die, Molly thinks to herself. She has always cherished this slight glimmer of hope, although she knows it is absurd. The doctors predicted that, with his heart condition, her brother might not even make it to twenty, let alone nearly eighty, as he would be now.

'And the piece of red fabric?' she asks. 'Did they analyse that?'

'Yes, it is just a piece of ordinary plastic. Probably a fertiliser bag, they said.'

'Just what I suggested, if you remember,' she says, enjoying a crumb of comfort from this little victory. Nothing to do with *Robin*, then. Or even Jimmy's raincoat.

'Are there any grounds for reopening the case?' Bella has been silent up until now.

'We've checked back in the files and we are satisfied the police at the time carried out every possible line of enquiry. They found no evidence of foul play, nor did they find a body. There are no grounds to reopen the case, unless we find new evidence. Unfortunately, these DNA test results mean there is no further evidence. We will be in touch, of course, if anything else comes up,' he says, and they gather up their things.

'We understand you will have been hoping for some kind of closure about your brother, Miss Goddard,' the police-woman says. 'And I'm sorry we couldn't bring you more positive news.' She stands up, and her colleague stands with her. The room feels strangely empty and hollow, once they have left.

'What the hell is "closure" when it's at home?' Molly grumbles.

'They mean an answer. So you can grieve properly and move on with your life,' Bella tells her. 'They use it all the time these days.'

'Well, I don't have *closure*, or anything like it,' Molly mutters. 'In fact, they've made it worse, now.' She feels deflated, like a birthday balloon left forgotten in a corner.

Bella knows that she cannot let it rest there. This business of the bones has started something, opened Pandora's box. She cannot let her mother go to her grave without knowing what happened that terrible evening in Wormley.

That night she searches the internet for Kit Waddington and finds nothing helpful, until she remembers that at one point in her mother's story someone referred to him as Christopher. She searches again, and finds someone with that name who founded an apparently successful vineyard in Dorset, producing wines called, she notices with a jolt, 'Dragon Valley'.

The website has a photo of the managing director, a Mr Chris Marshall. He is good-looking, dark-haired, with high colour to his cheeks, just as Molly described Kit. Apart from apparently having the same first name, what relationship – if any – does he have to Kit Waddington? The old man must be in his late eighties by now, if he's even still alive. But there is no harm in trying, and no time to waste.

She emails the vineyard, marked 'for the attention of Mr Christopher Waddington':

Dear Mr Waddington,
I am the daughter of Miss Molly Goddard, whom I believe you may have known when you were both youngsters, living in Wormley, Suffolk. She and I recently revisited the village and she spoke about the wonderful times you had on the lake at Wormley

Hall, as well as the sudden tragedy of her brother's
disappearance. If you feel able to reply to this email,
she would love to make contact again.
    With best wishes,
    Bella Browning, née Goddard

A standard acknowledgement from Dragon Valley
Wines arrives almost by return – 'Thank you for your enquiry, which has been passed on to the relevant team' –
but then nothing. She calls and speaks to a pleasant woman
who says she will chase it up, but then hears no more.
A week passes, then ten days, and Bella begins to give up
hope.

But who else is there to try? All the others who might
have known anything – the Waddington parents, Mr and
Mrs Diamond, the Blackmans and Aunt Mary – will all
be long gone. In an idle moment she googles Jane and
Juliet Timpson, but the search reveals no likely leads.

Then, quite out of the blue:

Dear Ms Browning,
    Thank you for your email addressed to my uncle, Kit
Waddington. He is an elderly man now, but his mind
is still strong and he is thrilled to hear that your
mother, Molly, is alive and well. He has many happy
memories of the family's time in Wormley and would be
pleased to be in contact again.
    Shall we speak on the phone? This is my number.
    Best wishes,
    Chris Marshall
    CEO, Dragon Valley Wines

With a thudding heart Bella picks up the phone and dials.

'Ms Browning? Hello there.'

'Bella, please. Thank you for agreeing to speak to me.'

'It's a pleasure, Bella. Please call me Chris. My uncle is delighted to hear that your mother is alive and well.'

'Very much so,' Bella says. 'Did you know that she was rather in love with him, once upon a time? I think he broke her heart.'

He laughs. 'He was quite a charmer in his youth, I'm told. I owe him everything, you know. I was named after him, and he was there all through my childhood and mentored me, so I was ready to take on his wine business. These days he lives in a bungalow on the vineyard, and I see him several times a week.'

The ice is fully broken now and they natter away like old friends, to the point that Bella feels able to risk mentioning the discovery of the bones in the lake, and her mother's renewed desire to find out what happened to her brother. Chris says he's got a trip to East Anglia planned for the following month – to visit a fellow wine-maker – and promises to ask Kit whether he feels up to the journey. Perhaps she and Molly could meet them there?

'We'd be thrilled to,' she says. 'Just name the day.'

25

Molly is all of a flutter. The hairdresser visited the previous day, but she isn't satisfied.

'My usual girl was on holiday, and this one cut it far too short,' she complains, yanking at the grey curls as though trying to force them to grow.

'I think it looks rather chic,' Bella says. 'Here, let me just brush it back, off your forehead.'

'I don't need chic, whatever that means, at eighty-four,' her mother grumbles, but then insists that her daughter retrieves from her dressing-table drawer the ancient lipstick, blusher and powder compact that have lain there, unused, for years.

'Honestly, anyone would think you were getting ready for a first date,' Bella says.

Molly frowns disapprovingly, saying nothing. She's too nervous to enjoy being teased.

The journey is straightforward. Molly stares out of the window as the landscape broadens and opens up into Cambridgeshire. Further towards the city itself, she recalls, the landscape flattens into fenland, but here in the east of the county are rolling hills and she squints her eyes against the bright sunshine, enjoying the wide vistas, the kind you never really get in Suffolk. A sign to the Gog and Magog Hills reminds her how ancient legends persist; they were twin giants rather than dragons, but the same applies and she is glad for it.

She has been trying not to think about Kit. Ever since Bella told her she'd made contact, a small tender spot has reopened in her heart. He was her first love, after all, but he never reciprocated romantically – not even with a touch or a glance, not even for an instant. It left her with the sense that she must somehow be unattractive to boys, a belief that it took many years to overcome. If any boys should happen to show an interest, she would shun them, for fear of being rejected. Which was partly why she made such a disastrous choice of husband, Molly reflects now; he was the only one desperate enough to persevere.

But, of course, that brief union brought a very happy outcome. She glances at Bella. 'You're the best thing that ever happened to me, you know.'

'Blimey, Mum, where did that come from?' Bella smiles back, keeping her eyes on the road.

'I don't know. I was just thinking about your dad.'

'Odd, since we're on our way to meet your childhood sweetheart,' Bella says. 'Are you excited, Mum?'

'Nervous, more like,' Molly says.

'Well, not long to wait. We're nearly there.'

As they pass a sign for the vineyard her heart seems to flutter in her chest and she hopes it's not the sign of an impending heart attack. It would be a shame to conk out before they've even had a chance to meet, after all these years. At last the car slows and they turn onto a long cement driveway.

It's been arranged that they will meet in the cafe that is part of the visitor centre. Whoever thought a vineyard would have such things, Molly wonders? The car park is surprisingly busy, presumably with people taking the Vineyard Tour that is advertised all along the approach. Thank heavens it also has disabled parking, which means she will not have to use the wheelchair to cross a long distance. She refuses to greet her old flame at waist level.

It turns out that they are the first to arrive. Chris and Kit are held up in traffic – so Bella informs her, after a series of pings on her mobile phone – and Molly and Bella are well into their second round of coffees and buttered teacakes when, through the glass window, Molly spies a tall, handsome man helping an older man, his back bent but still walking well, out of the car and into the building. And then there they are, approaching the table with beaming smiles.

For a moment she is struck speechless: even after nearly seventy years she'd have recognised him anywhere. His almost-white hair is still thick and the blue eyes astonishingly bright. Bella and Chris – his dark hair and high cheekbones remind her so much of the young Kit – are shaking hands and greeting each other. For a long second Molly and Kit say nothing, just staring silently into each other's faces.

'Hello, Molly. We must stop meeting like this,' he says at last. The voice is so familiar, still strong and unwavering, and as he smiles, his teeth are still straight and white.

'Is it really you? I can hardly believe it.' She hears an

unfamiliar giggle and realises that it's hers. Everyone is sitting down now and getting through the tiresome business of ordering. But Molly cannot take her eyes off Kit. All she wants to do is reach across the table and take his hand. 'I never thought I'd see you again,' she says.

'I remember you as clear as though it was yesterday. You're still a beautiful woman, Molly Goddard.'

She feels herself blushing beneath the blusher. 'And you always were a charmer, Kit Waddington.'

'All these years,' he says with a small sigh. 'Getting to know you that summer was one of the best things that had ever happened to me – such a golden time, in my memory. Well, up until that terrible business when Jimmy disappeared. And your father, poor man. Did he ever recover?'

'He came back home after a couple of months, but he was never really the same,' Molly says. 'None of us were.'

'It must have been horrendous for you, losing Jimmy like that. Such a lovely little boy. I suppose they never found him?'

Molly shakes her head. 'They stopped searching after a while. Closed the case.'

'Dreadful, dreadful,' Kit says. 'You know they actually held me as a suspect?'

'What? You? They held *you*?' Molly is astonished. 'Whatever for?'

'Someone told them they'd seen Jimmy alone in the boat with me.'

'So what? You taught him how to row. No crime in that, surely? You were just being kind.'

'That same someone also helpfully told the police that

I was gay. It was illegal back then, of course. And being seen with what they called a "vulnerable young boy"' – Kit makes speech marks with his fingers – 'raised suspicions, apparently. The police put two and two together and came up with five.'

Something clicks in Molly's head. 'Hold on a minute. You were . . . you are . . . ?' She cannot quite bring herself to say the word.

'Gay? Yes, that's me,' Kit says cheerfully.

'Wait. You'll have to explain. When did you find out?'

'Oh, I've known forever. I meant to tell you, that day when I said I had to go away, remember? But I chickened out. Thought you'd never understand.'

'How could I forget?' she murmurs. 'They were sending you to a crammer.'

'That, too. But the main reason was that I'd been expelled by my school after being found in bed with a boy. My parents hit the roof, of course. Thought there was something wrong with me – something a doctor could cure. They packed me off to see a psychiatrist in London, who said it was probably a passing phase and I'd grow out of it. What a joke!'

As their food arrives, the conversation pauses, allowing Molly a moment to process this information. If Kit was gay – always gay, even then – no wonder he seemed so reluctant to kiss her. He preferred boys. The revelation is so astonishing that she finds herself chuckling.

'Mum?' Bella nudges her.

'What?'

'What're you laughing at?'

'At my girlish self,' she says. 'For wasting all that time

longing for Kit to fall in love with me. Little did I suspect
that I was onto a loser from the very start.'

Everyone laughs then, along with her.

'But I *was* in love with you,' Kit protests. 'Just not in a
romantic way. I thought you were the most exciting girl I'd
ever met. Your energy, your appreciation of nature, the way
you cared for your brother, your passion for getting justice
for Eli. You were wonderful.'

'Well, thank you. But poor Eli. We failed him, didn't
we?' she says, suddenly saddened.

'You did everything you possibly could,' he says.

Bella chimes in. 'Did you say the police suspected you
because you were gay, Kit?' she asks.

'They must have thought I was some kind of child abuser.'

'Oh, for heaven's sake,' Molly says. 'I've never heard of
anything so ridiculous. You were just about the only other
person in the village who was nice to my brother. You and
Eli. If they'd only asked me, I'd have told them.'

'But that was after your father threatened to jump off
the church tower, remember? And got carried away in a
straitjacket? The search for your brother carried on, but I
suppose they didn't want to bother you too much after that.
You must have been in pieces.'

'It's hard to remember now. Mrs Diamond moved in, and
she probably tried to keep everyone away. But I'm so sorry
about you coming under suspicion, Kit. Was it horrible?'

'Horrible enough,' he says. 'I never really believed they
could pin anything on me, but it wasn't nice being inter-
rogated. They held me in a cell, overnight.'

'You'd only just turned seventeen.'

'A very immature, troubled seventeen at that. The worst

thing was they wouldn't reveal who'd told them about seeing me with Jimmy.'

'Did you ever discover?'

He shakes his head. 'I always assumed it was Blackman. He was always sneaking around Eli's hut, and would have been able to see the lake from there. He could easily have seen me rowing *Robin* with Jimmy, that day we played pirates.'

'And I was back on shore, waiting to come and find you.' Molly remembers so well; it is etched into her mind. It was only the day before they discovered the hut deserted and the horrible, official notice. The day Eli disappeared. She shivers, recalling her growing understanding that it was Blackman behind so many of the terrible things happening in the village.

Kit sighs again. 'Oh, Molly. I was such an idiot. My head was in a complete mess, I didn't know which way was up and which was down. I had no idea how Blackman could have known why I'd been expelled, but then my mother admitted that she'd confided in Melissa. They were best buddies, remember?'

'And it was the Blackmans who told the police you were gay?'

'We never found out for certain. It doesn't matter now.'

'It's all so long in the past,' Molly agrees. 'None of it really matters any more. But what happened to you after that?'

'I got sent off to a crammer in London, but it didn't work. When I failed all my exams, my father sent me out to Australia to turn me into a "real man".' Kit scoffs. 'Would you credit it? He actually used those words. Mum had a cattle-farming cousin out there, and they reckoned I couldn't get into any more trouble in the middle of the outback. How wrong they were. The place was full of gorgeous men.' His eyes twinkle and both of them chuckle. It feels almost like old times. 'Anyway, that's where I learned about the wine trade and got the crazy idea that it might work in the UK.'

'Bella told me about your vineyard. You look as though you've prospered.'

'It's been a good life. And I had this wonderful nephew, Christopher. What about you?'

'I've had a good life, too. My husband was hopeless and disappeared early on, but I have a lovely daughter and grandson.'

'Chris says you're a famous writer.'

'Only children's books,' Molly says, blushing.

'Best-selling, award-winning children's books,' Bella adds. 'You're too modest, Mum.'

'You told me you were going to be a writer, that day on The Retreat. I was impressed that you were so clear about what you wanted to do, even at that young age, Molly.'

'It's been a way of keeping Jimmy alive in my mind, imagining him as my reader.'

The smile fades from Kit's face. 'I've just remembered. Those bones in the lake. Were they his?'

'No, they weren't. We're still none the wiser, I'm afraid.'

'Did they never tell you what I told them about Jimmy's plan?'

'No,' Molly says, more cautiously. 'Go on.'

'Do you remember how we talked about occupying Eli's hut to save it from demolition?'

'Like the suffragettes occupying buildings and chaining themselves to railings?'

'Just that. Jimmy must have overheard us, because he told me he was going to save the hut. He made me promise not to tell you, cos you'd stop him . . .'

No. No, no, no, her head screams.

Kit is still talking, '. . . or something like that. I just wondered . . .'

Molly finishes his sentence. 'And then he couldn't get out?' She gasps as she pictures the scene: Jimmy letting himself into the hut with the key he knew was always kept under the wheel arch. She drops her head into her hands, overcome with the sudden, terrifying memory. That day Eli showed them how to set the fire, how to use the matches – Jimmy loved that. Had he tried to keep himself warm, brew tea? Perhaps gone to lie down on the bed and then somehow the fire caught and he couldn't get out. And no one ever knew.

'I did tell the police about that,' Kit was saying. 'But who knows whether they took any notice of me. After Eli killed himself, I think they became convinced that Jimmy's disappearance was all to do with him. It was a lazy conclusion, an easy way out.'

Molly's head is full of flames and her ears ring with the screams of a terrified little boy. She is too horrified to weep.

'Did anyone find out who torched the hut?' Bella asks.

'Most people thought it was lightning,' Kit says. 'Or Eli himself.'

Although she hasn't the heart, or the voice, to say so right now, Molly has never believed the lightning theory; and Eli would never have burned his beloved hut. She'd always believed it was Blackman. But now she is beginning to think it might just have been a tragic accident.

'I'm so sorry,' she hears Kit saying. 'I thought you already knew.'

Bella says, 'Seems not, Kit. But we'll definitely follow that up with the police, won't we, Mum?'

'I didn't mean to upset your mother.'

Although her head is spinning with this new information, Molly takes a deep breath and looks up, summoning a smile. 'I'm fine, really.'

Chris and Bella begin to chat and, as the conversation buzzes around them, Kit gives a wicked grin and pushes his hand forward. It is veined and wrinkly much like her own, and covered in liver spots, but the fingers are still long and elegant. Molly takes it in hers, feeling its warmth, and they both give a gentle squeeze. She looks up into eyes that speak of their sympathy and their sorrow, and her heart is warmed by his humanity. How she has missed him, all these years. There is no one else left in the world who knows what she went through, that summer. And here they are together again, in their own little bubble, trying to shield out the rest of the world for a few precious seconds.

'We must stay in touch,' she hears him whispering. 'I can't let you go, now that I've found you again.'

She's wants the moment to go on forever; never to relinquish the warmth of his hands. But all too soon they are saying their goodbyes and wrapping each other in fond, regretful embraces, and promising to meet again before they both get too much older.

❄❄❄

All the way home Molly has been hugging herself, as though to hold the memory of Kit tightly against her.

'That was a bit of a shock, wasn't it?' Bella says, once they are back in the bungalow. 'Do you really think Jimmy could have done such a thing? Locked himself inside the hut to stop it being demolished?'

Molly shakes her head. 'I'm not sure he'd have known how to, to be honest. But the stove was by the door, so if it caught fire, it would have blocked the exit. And he had such a dodgy heart, the doctors always warned us that he might go at any time. Perhaps that is what happened?' But he was only ten. And disabled. And stubborn, fearless and loyal.

Her brother's face appears before her, as clearly as though Jimmy were really here. He is smiling, of course – that cheeky smile. He always seemed so innocent, so guileless, she thinks, but because his speech was so limited you couldn't ever be certain what was going on behind the smile. She recalls Mrs D saying, 'That boy understands more than he ever lets on.' And she was right, of course, as she was in so many things.

Jimmy had considered Eli a true friend, his only friend. He loved that hut, instinctively understanding that it was a safe place, and he returned again and again. He must have felt desperate to help, and hearing her and Kit talking about how they could save the hut could have inspired him to do the same. Did he really have the courage to go into the woods in that storm?

But he was a very strong-minded boy. He'd spent his life battling his disabilities and, once he'd decided on something, very little could be done to dissuade him. She can imagine Jimmy fighting his way through the wind and the rain, his eyes fixed, his jaw set, doggedly determined to help his friend, and her heart overflows with pride. He was a remarkable individual – something she'd completely failed to appreciate when he was alive.

Why hadn't he told her about his plan?

The shame floods back: how she'd resented him, dismissing his ideas as silly or childish. She can hear herself shouting at him: *Go away and stop bothering me* and *Do it your way, if you think you're so clever.* Siblings say such things to each other every day, but Jimmy couldn't answer back because he didn't have the words. The cruelty was all one-way. No wonder he'd decided not to tell her.

Molly grips the arms of her chair, trying to anchor herself in the present, and the reassuring sight of Bella returning with a tea tray helps.

'Oh, Mum! Look, here's a tissue. Dry your eyes and have a cuppa. We can talk about it.'

Suddenly Molly knows what she has to do. 'I need to go back, Bella. To Eli's hut.'

'You said it'd all gone, Mum. Burned to the ground seventy years ago. There won't be anything left. Perhaps we ought to tell the police? Let them investigate.'

'No!' Molly almost shouts. 'I don't want them involved. But I need to go back to the glade. To ask him.'

'Ask who?'

'Jimmy.'

She's being illogical, of course; it's ridiculous. But Bella calmly pours the tea and says, 'If that's what you want, Mum, we'll try to make it happen.'

Molly knows it is impossible. How is she to get down

a woodland path when she can only shuffle twenty steps with a walking frame? As Bella leaves, she promises to make what she calls a 'recce'.

A few days later she telephones to say that the route is reasonably wheelchair-friendly, but only up to a certain point. After that, the track is narrow and full of tree roots. Besides which, she says, she could find no trace of any hut anywhere.

But Molly has set her heart on going.

Bella promises to try and get her there. 'By hook or by crook, Mum.'

'You never say that. It's one of my phrases.'

'Then you won't mind me stealing it?'

'Just so long as you get us there somehow, my darling.'

26

The following Sunday, Bella arrives with Lewis, a strapping lad of sixteen who suffers from terrible acne but is an ace sportsman.

'No football this weekend?' Molly says.

'Nah,' he grunts. 'Training pitch is being dug up. Going to make it all-weather.'

'Lewis has got an idea,' Bella says, nudging him. 'Go on, tell your gran.'

'You know those firemen's-chair thingies,' he says, fingering a spot on his chin, 'they use for evacuation?'

Molly nods, although she hasn't really got a clue.

'Dad says we can borrow one from the fire station.'

A chair? How's that going to work, she wonders? But he's still talking.

'He's going to come too. Reckons we can manage it, easy, between us. Over the bits where the wheelchair won't go.'

She glances at Bella. Her daughter's divorce was acrimonious – *he's married to the ruddy fire service*, she used to complain – but as the years have gone by, they have stayed civil for Lewis's sake. 'Andy's going to help us? That's kind.'

'He's always been fond of you,' her daughter says quietly.

'Well, thank you, Lewis. If you really think it's going to work, we'll give it a go, shall we?'

✿

Two weeks later, Molly finds herself being bumped along that familiar path and down the slope. The bluebells are nearly over now, but they seem to have been even more widespread than she remembers.

Halfway down, Bella shouts, 'There it is,' and the little procession draws to a halt. She leans down to her mother's level and points. 'Look – between the trees, Mum.'

Molly peers. At first she can't see beyond the greenery but then, between their trunks, she can just catch a glimpse of something white in the far distance. She tilts her head and waits for her eyes to adjust. Slowly a shape comes into focus.

'Good Lord. I see it now. Look at that. It's the outline of a giant dragon. Carved into the hillside. Whoever put that there, do you think?'

'Apparently it was a millennium project, organised by the landowner.'

'Now that's what I call a real dragon,' Molly says.

It has a fine set of wings and a long, curly tail and is apparently breathing fire. Perhaps this is how the crocodile ended up, proudly taking her place as a proper grown-up dragon. One day she might write the final chapter for Jimmy's book. But she will never offer it to her publisher – it's too personal. It is her brother's special story.

'I think that's just marvellous,' she says, as they resume their slow procession down the path. They reach the place where the stile used to be, but there is now a gate, which is easier to negotiate, although after that the path narrows and the wheelchair can go no further.

'You're light as a feather, Molly,' Andy exclaims, hardly breaking breath as they lift her in the fireman's chair. It is surprisingly comfortable. She is reclined backwards at about forty-five degrees and feels positively regal, like a queen in her sedan, or an Indian maharajah in his howdah – but perhaps that was only for elephants? Andy's carrying the front of the chair with his back to her, and she can see the muscles rippling reassuringly beneath his T-shirt. Keeping fit is a religion for her former son-in-law, and essential for his job as a fireman. Lewis, who is behind her, seems to be doing fine, too.

After a few minutes they reach the junction – at least that's what Bella seems to think, although what used to be the path to Eli's hut is now almost completely overgrown. Andy takes from his backpack a fireman's axe and a lethal-looking machete and they start hacking at the brambles and saplings, following the trail of small rocks that Eli laid there all those years ago to mark his way at night-time. All the whitewash has gone now, of course, but the rocks lead up the slope to a grove of shrubby trees that are slightly smaller than those around them. This must have been Eli's glade.

They set Molly down and she stays in the fireman's chair while Andy and Lewis begin to clear away the bracken and brambles. Bella takes out a flask of tea and some biscuits from her backpack, and Molly remembers the flapjacks Eli used to cook on his little pot-bellied stove, and the sweet tea he served in enamel mugs that burned your lips.

Resuming work after tea, Lewis stubs his toe and lets

out a curse that no sixteen-year-old boy should know, in Molly's opinion. He continues hacking until he's cleared the undergrowth to reveal the curve of something solid stuck in the ground, heavy and immovable. Something metal . . .

'It's the wheel,' she exclaims. 'Of the shepherd's hut.'

'Then we're in the right place, Gran?'

'Definitely,' she says. 'Keep going.'

After a few moments half of the wheel has been revealed, lying at forty-five degrees into the ground. As Lewis digs some more, she hears something rattling.

'Whatever's that?'

'Some kind of chain . . .' Kit's chain. In the rucksack. What if Jimmy took it?

The world goes pale and the sound of birdsong seems to fade, and then blackness.

When she opens her eyes Molly finds herself in the back of an ambulance.

'You gave us such a fright,' Bella says. 'They say it probably isn't anything too serious, but when you passed out, it took you such a long time to come round and you were so confused. We thought it better to be safe than sorry.'

The paramedic looms over her, fiddling with wires and other bits of apparatus they have attached to her.

'Hello, Miss Goddard,' he says. 'You had us a little worried there for a while. How are you feeling?'

'Perfectly fine,' she says, struggling to pronounce the words clearly because her tongue seems to be stuck to the roof of her mouth and her lips don't move very well. 'Can I have some water?'

They take her to hospital anyway and, after a very long wait and loads of tests, she's declared fit to go home.

Next morning Bella is there in her bungalow, sleepy and tousled, bringing her a cup of tea in bed.

'You stayed the night?'

'I couldn't leave you alone, could I? Not after that. The sofa is surprisingly comfortable.' Bella sits down on the bed. 'That was quite a day yesterday, wasn't it? I'm sorry it all got a bit too much for you.'

'Don't be sorry. It was what I wanted, remember. You got me there, my darling, and I'm very grateful. But what happened?'

'Lewis found the chain.'

Ah, yes, of course. That terrible clinking sound.

'Do you suppose Jimmy really . . . ?' Bella asks.

Molly shakes her head. 'I don't think it's likely, my darling. It was probably the chain Eli used for Sarge.' She sighs. 'It's all so long ago.'

'Lewis also found this.' Bella reaches into her pocket and brings out a small piece of white porcelain tube. Molly weighs it in her hand, remembering the long, curved stem it was once part of, the small round bowl that was constantly refilled and relit, and the clouds of smoke that really did deter gnats.

'It's a piece of clay pipe. Thank you, my darling. And please thank Lewis. I shall treasure it. It'll help me remember Eli and the good times we had, bless his poor, kind soul.'

A month passes and Molly receives a letter from Kit, in spidery old-man's writing, saying how much he enjoyed meeting her again after all these years and enclosing a photograph of Chris's two children, whom he considers his 'grandkids'. They are lanky teenage boys, both in sports kit, with dark floppy hair and high colour to their cheekbones: miniature versions of their great-uncle at the same age.

She writes back, sending a photograph of Lewis, who is nothing like her, of course, but of whom she is immensely proud, she says. And she tells Kit something of their visit to Eli's glade, and finding the wheel and the piece of clay pipe.

It is while she is writing about Eli that the idea comes to her. He killed himself out of desperation and shame, and she has no idea where he was buried. But Eli was a true countryman and loved that woodland; he taught her and Jimmy to love it too. And he fought a lonely battle, over several years, to save the land from being sold and developed. The woodland is still there, a testament to his success. Thanks to him, local people can still walk in those woods, enjoying the snowdrops and bluebells, the birdsong and the peace. She would love to see Eli's contribution recognised, his name remembered.

So she starts another letter: *Dear Vicar*. She asks him who looks after the woodland these days, and how the work is funded. Would she be able to make a contribution, she asks? After all, international publishing success has brought greater riches than she could ever have imagined and, even after generous gifts to Bella and her grandson, and a large annual donation to the Down's Syndrome Association, Molly has more money in the bank than she will ever be able to spend in her lifetime.

Within a week she is visited by the new vicar – a charming middle-aged woman with curly grey hair, who strongly reminds her of Aunt Mary – accompanied by the parish clerk of Wormley, an older man who walks with two sticks.

Over tea and biscuits, they probe her gently about what she has in mind. She tells them about Eli – although she skips over the details of her own tragedy, and how Eli died. 'He was an eccentric old boy who lived in a shepherd's hut in the woods for at least a decade,' she says. 'And he taught me and my brother how to love nature.'

By the time they leave, it has been agreed that they will take the proposal to the parish council: a proper path through the woodland, which might – if they agree – be waymarked as 'Eli Chadwick Way', with benches placed at appropriate points, signboards with information about flora and fauna and, most important of all, a fund to maintain the woodland, which will be known as the Jimmy Goddard Bequest.

After they have gone, Molly finds herself smiling. She takes her walking frame and goes to the chest of drawers in the bedroom, leaning down with difficulty to retrieve, behind a pile of unworn and probably now moth-eaten woollen jumpers, the small box in which her old papers are stored. The sticky tape has long since lost its stick, the box is falling apart, but she manages to carry it back to the kitchen table where she sits and, with heart pumping, opens the lid.

Here are long-forgotten letters; the first commission of a story; a particularly poignant letter from a young fan with Down's syndrome; a photograph of herself with Jimmy and Pa, taken by Miss Calver when they first arrived in the village, and one of Pa and Mum on their wedding day. Also a handkerchief with the initials CMW from that stormy night, which she must have failed to return. Molly still doesn't know what the M stands for – she will ask Kit next time she writes. She expects to cry, but strangely enough she finds these small items comforting.

And there, at the bottom, is *The Ugly Dragon*: pages torn from a lined notebook and stitched together with string between cardboard covers. She remembers how tough it was, pushing the thick needle through so many pages, how she pricked her finger and, yes, here it still is, the stain of her blood.

Outside the daylight is fading; she has to switch on the light to read, although it doesn't take long. She sits back and folds her arms. They aren't that bad, these stories, for the first attempts of a fifteen-year-old. She can read clearly between the words the love she had for her brother, as well as the frustration she felt at having to look after him. She can sense the longing of a young woman in love, believing herself to be on the brink of adulthood. And she can feel, almost palpably, how the writer was trying to make sense of the anxiety and confusion around her, of a village riven with mistrust and hidden, malign forces.

The stories could do with some serious editing, of course. An introduction, and maybe a final chapter. She's always sworn she would never offer it to her publisher, but perhaps now is the right moment, after all this time? It will, of course, be dedicated, as are all her books, simply 'To Jimmy'.

A month later something entirely unexpected happens. The police return. It seems Bella has ignored Molly's instruction and written to them anyway, saying she has new evidence to suggest that a line of enquiry into Jimmy's disappearance was never properly pursued. Knowing Bella, Molly suspects that it was probably a rather forceful letter, leaving them no option but to act, for fear of a future complaint. And act they did, with surprising speed. A couple of coppers were despatched to do a search of the area around the hut, and they've found something they want to show Molly.

'Something that might . . . ?' she asks, scarcely able to catch her breath.

As the policewoman holds out the transparent plastic bag, Molly gasps. Inside it is a small rectangle of flat metal, barely an inch long, so rusted that it is impossible to tell whether anything had ever been inscribed on it. But from the size and shape, and the position of the hole in one end, Molly knows at once what it is.

She holds it to her heart, and tries to suck in a breath. The colours in the room around her have blanched, all sounds are muffled, the air is heavy as though a fog has somehow descended, and everyone else seems far away, a series of insubstantial shapes.

'Mum, are you all right?' She feels Bella's arm around her, pulling her back to the present. 'What is it? Do you recognise it?'

Her throat is tight, she cannot speak. Someone offers a glass of water, which helps.

'It's Jimmy's,' she croaks. 'The identity tag with his name and address on it. In case he got lost.'

'Oh my Lord,' Bella says. 'Does this mean he died in the fire?'

They both look at the police, who look at each other. After some hesitation, the man starts, 'It might indicate that scenario, Miss Browning. But it could have been lost there at some other time, previous to his disappearance.'

He turns to Molly and says, quite gently, 'It's a long time ago, Ms Goddard, but do you recall your brother losing this, erm, identity tag at any point beforehand?'

She shakes her head, unsure whether to be horrified or somehow, in the strangest way, relieved.

'But we understand that you and your brother were frequent visitors to this hut, before it burned down?'

She nods.

'Then I suppose we may never have absolute proof,' he says, measuring his words carefully.

'Did you find anything else, like . . .' Bella hesitates.

'No, madam. If you are referring to human remains, no. Nothing else. And we did take a very good look, let me assure you.'

Molly suddenly knows. 'I don't want you to go digging around any more, thank you very much,' she says, loudly and firmly. 'What good would it do? We'll never find out who was responsible, and whoever it was will be long dead by now. Let my brother rest in peace.'

She takes out the piece of metal from its plastic envelope and cups it in her folded hands. A little sob escapes from her throat. They will never be certain, of course, and somehow she doesn't really feel the need for certainty any more. It is enough to know that she is holding something of Jimmy; something that will always stay with her.

'Will you bury this with me when I go, sweetheart? And Eli's clay pipe?'

'We will, Mum. We most certainly will.'

Something is different, now. A weight has been lifted, but it takes Molly a few moments to identify it. The knot in her stomach has finally disappeared.

THE UGLY DRAGON
by Molly Goddard

Chapter 7: Jimmy takes a ride

*The next time Jimmy went to the lake the crocodile was nowhere
to be seen. As usual, he called, and rustled the paper bag – he'd
brought fruitcake, this time. Then he waited, watching a family
of ducks trailing across the water in an unruly line and listening
to the pigeons cooing in the woods behind him. It was a perfect
day, with little clouds scudding across a deep-blue sky, reflected
on the still surface of the water below.*

    *At last she appeared, or at least he thought it was her. To be
honest he wasn't sure at first, because she looked so different. In
the few days since he'd last seen her, her legs seemed to have
grown, her tail was long and curly and on her back, either side
of the lumpy ridge, were two new humps.*

    *'Whatever's happened to you . . . ?' he began to ask, but he was
stopped mid-sentence by the most astonishing sight. She grunted
once or twice, and the humps on her back started to unfurl into
wide, ribbed sheets of tough, green hide. With a powerful movement of her shoulder blades she began to flap them, up and down,
and as she did so they grew higher and wider still.*

'Oh . . . my . . . goodness,' he managed to gasp. 'You've got wings.'

'Like a proper dragon,' she said, grinning widely, and flapping so enthusiastically he feared she might blow him off his feet. 'And there's something else, Jimmy. Better move away, just in case.'

He scuttled backwards until there were five or six yards between them.

'That'll do.' She sucked in an enormous breath and then let it out with a loud whoosh that turned into a bright red-and-orange flame, smelling of wood fires and toffee caramel.

Jimmy burst into astonished laughter and she laughed along with him, with a deep fearsome roar. Each time he tried to stop she flapped her wings again, whipping up dead leaves and bits of grass into a great whirlwind, which made him laugh all the more. At last he got so out of breath that he had to sit down, and she noticed the brown paper bag.

'Have you brought buns?' she asked, folding away her wings. 'All that flapping is hungry work.'

'Fruitcake, with marzipan and icing. You'll like it,' he said, passing her a slice.

'Yum, this is delicious. I'll miss you, you know,' she said, through a mouthful.

'Miss me? Why? Where are you going?'

'Now I've turned into a proper dragon I'm in too much danger, living near human beings. They'd shoot me down like one of those poor pheasants. I have to go and live in Dragon Land, where I will be with others like me, and they will keep me safe.'

'You can't,' he said, close to tears. 'You mustn't leave me.'

'I have to, Jimmy.'

'Can't I come with you?'

'You would have to live with dragons for the rest of your life.'

'I wouldn't mind. Just so long as I can be with you.'

'Are you really certain?'

Jimmy nodded. 'But how will we get there?'

'I'll carry you.'

'You mean fly, with me on your back?'

'I don't know for certain, but we can try, can't we?'

And so, when they had finished all of the cake, he climbed onto her back and clung tightly to one of the large scaly lumps at the back of her head. She unfurled her wings and began to flap them, slowly at first and then faster and faster and faster, till they seemed to be leaving the ground. As they lifted upwards, she gave another huge roar, sending a brilliant burst of flame spurting from her mouth.

The lake was now far below them, and Jimmy could see the big Hall, and Eli's hut in the woods, and then the street and the houses and the church tower, growing smaller and smaller until, finally, they disappeared into the distance and all he could hear was the whoosh of air as the dragon's wings carried them higher and higher into the sky.

AUTHOR'S NOTE

Although this novel is in no respect autobiographical, its setting is very personal to me.

I was fortunate enough to spend my childhood years living in a house beside a flooded quarry that had become a small lake, with islands and inlets and huge willow trees, just like my fictitious Wormley Mere. It was my playground, my swimming pool, my boating pond, the home for my pet ducks and the rabbits that lived on the islands. It taught me to be curious about flora and fauna, and gave me a love of all living things. It was obvious that one day I would feel compelled to write about it.

Just a few miles away from there is a village with its own lake where, it was said, a fearsome dragon lived. Even the name of the village, Wormingford, suggests the connection with a dragon, which was often referred to, in early English, as a 'worme'. In the church there is a wonderful stained-glass window showing a 'dragon' – which is obviously a crocodile really – with a pair of white legs waving from its mouth, being threatened by a knight on a white charger.

The creature was said to have escaped from the menagerie of an early king and found its way to the River Stour, stealing sheep and eventually demanding to be fed virgins until the supply began to run out. Desperate, the villagers turned to a local knight, Sir George of Layer de la Haye, who efficiently despatched the beast, as though his mother had named him for the task. Neighbouring villages, including Bures, also lay claim to the dragon myth.

After seeing this, I became fascinated by dragons. One of my very earliest forays into fiction, at the age of eight, was a story about the Wormingford Dragon.

That said, the rest of *The Secrets of the Lake* – all of the plot and all of the characters, as well as the layout of the village and the vicarage – are entirely my own invention. The stained glass was installed in 1950, through the generosity of a local woman in gratitude for the safe return of those who came back from the Second World War. It is a charming design.

My thanks to the people of Wormingford and the present church community there, for the inspiration your window gave to a young aspiring author all those years ago. And to the landowner who in the year 2000, as a millennium project, was inspired to cut out a huge dragon into the hillside just a few miles away. I visit as often as I can, delighted to see the legend still being celebrated in this way.

ACKNOWLEDGEMENTS

Massive thanks to my lovely editor Caroline Hogg and all the team at Pan Macmillan, as well as my brilliant agent Caroline Hardman of Hardman & Swainson, for their clear-eyed advice and support in helping *The Secrets of the Lake* make its way into the world.

As ever my family, David, Becky and Polly Trenow, have been amazingly supportive, as have other relatives and wonderful friends, without whom life would be infinitely less fun.

Under a Wartime Sky

Bawdsey Manor holds a secret.

1936: the threat of war hangs over Europe. Churchill gathers the brightest minds in Britain at a grand house in Suffolk. Bound to complete secrecy, they work together on an invention that could mean victory for the Allies. Among them is Vic, a gifted but shy physicist who, for the first time, feels like he belongs.

Local girl Kathleen wants to do more than serving tea and biscuits to 'do her bit'. So when the Bawdsey team begin to recruit women to operate their top secret system, she dedicates herself to this life-or-death work. Kath and Vic form an unlikely friendship as the skies over Britain fill with German bombers. Little does Kath know just whose life she will change forever, one fateful night . . .

In Love and War

Three women once enemies. Their secrets will unite them.

July, 1919. At the Hotel de la Paix in the small village of Hoppestadt, three women arrive at the end of the war, searching for traces of the men they have loved and lost to the battlefields of Ypres in Belgium.

Ruby is just twenty-one, a shy Englishwoman looking for the grave of her husband. Alice is only a little older but brimming with confidence; she has travelled all the way from America, convinced her brother is in fact still alive. Then there's Martha, and her son Otto, who are not all they seem to be . . .

The three women in Liz Trenow's *In Love and War* may have very different backgrounds, but they are united in their search for reconciliation: to resolve themselves to what the war took from them, but also to what life might still promise for the future . . .

The Silk Weaver

1760, Spitalfields.

Anna Butterfield's life is about to change forever, as she moves from her idyllic Suffolk home to be introduced into London society. A chance encounter with a French silk weaver, Henri, draws her into the volatile world of the city's burgeoning silk trade. Henri is working on his 'master piece', to become a master weaver and freeman; Anna longs to become an artist while struggling against pressure from her uncle's family to marry a wealthy young lawyer.

As their lives become ever more intertwined, Henri realises that Anna's designs could give them both an opportunity for freedom. But his world becomes more dangerous by the day, as riots threaten to tear them apart forever . . .

Inspired by real historical events and characters, *The Silk Weaver* is a captivating, unforgettable story of illicit romance in a time of enlightenment and social upheaval.

The Dressmaker of Draper's Lane

The richest silk hides the deepest secrets . . .

1768, London.

As a foundling who rose from poverty and now runs her own successful dressmaking business in the heart of society London, Miss Charlotte is a remarkable woman, admired by many. She has no need, or desire, to marry. The people she values most are her friend Anna, her recently found sister Louisa and her nephew Peter.

She considers herself fortunate, and feels she should be content with what she has. But something is missing.

A small piece of rare silk discovered in a bundle of scraps at auction triggers a curious sense of familiarity, and prompts her to unpick a past filled with extraordinary secrets and revelations . . .

'Trenow's exquisite novel puts a real focus
on the characters' journeys'
Woman